# Renaissance

## Part Three of

## Changels Genesis

## by Peter King

Peter King Publishing
Wellington, New Zealand

Renaissance
Part Three of Changels Genesis
Copyright Peter King 2015

Cover Image:"Silhouette of Person in Hoodie on Boardwalk at Night" by Image Catalog (Flickr) Public Domain. Cover Design: Peter King

Interior design by Peter King.
Interior maps are derived from Google Maps and are under Google copyright.
Typeset in 12 point Georgia. The cover and chapter headings use Exocet Heavy licensed from Emigre Foundaries. Type design optimised for remedial and ESOL readers.

Edition 3
First Published 2013
ISBN-13: 978-1-927264-39-3
Fiction
Publisher and Distributor: Peter King Publishing
Wellington, New Zealand

For more information visit http://www.changels.info

## SPECIAL NOTE TO READERS

Renaissance is the third part of Changels Genesis. It is not a stand-alone story. Changels Genesis is a six part story.

Changels Genesis is not suitable for children under 13. As fact-based fiction it contains details about real war violence and crime not suitable for younger readers. Profanity has been included but with omitted letters.

Changes of scene due to teleportation (termed "bending") are marked with a [+] on a new line.

Dialogue that originates telepathically is rendered in *italics*.

The transition back and forth from Sam's recalled story (in the past tense) to his present (in the present tense) is marked with an initial ellipses "…"

Non-English words have been hyphenated on their first use to expose the syllabic structure and ease pronunciation. The exception is Karearea (falcon) which is always hyphenated e.g.Ka-rea-rea. Maori words ending in the 'e' have been given a non-standard accent acute (e.g. Tané) for the same reason.

Translations the narrator understands are parenthesised e.g kara-kia (prayer).

Facts have been indicated with a superscripted dagger symbol[+] There is a detailed fact and fiction section at the end of this part of the story.

The action in part three oscillates between Auckland and fictional Aotea Island. While Aotea Island is based on Great Barrier Island's shape the location of the island is significantly closer to Auckland.

# AOTEA ISLAND

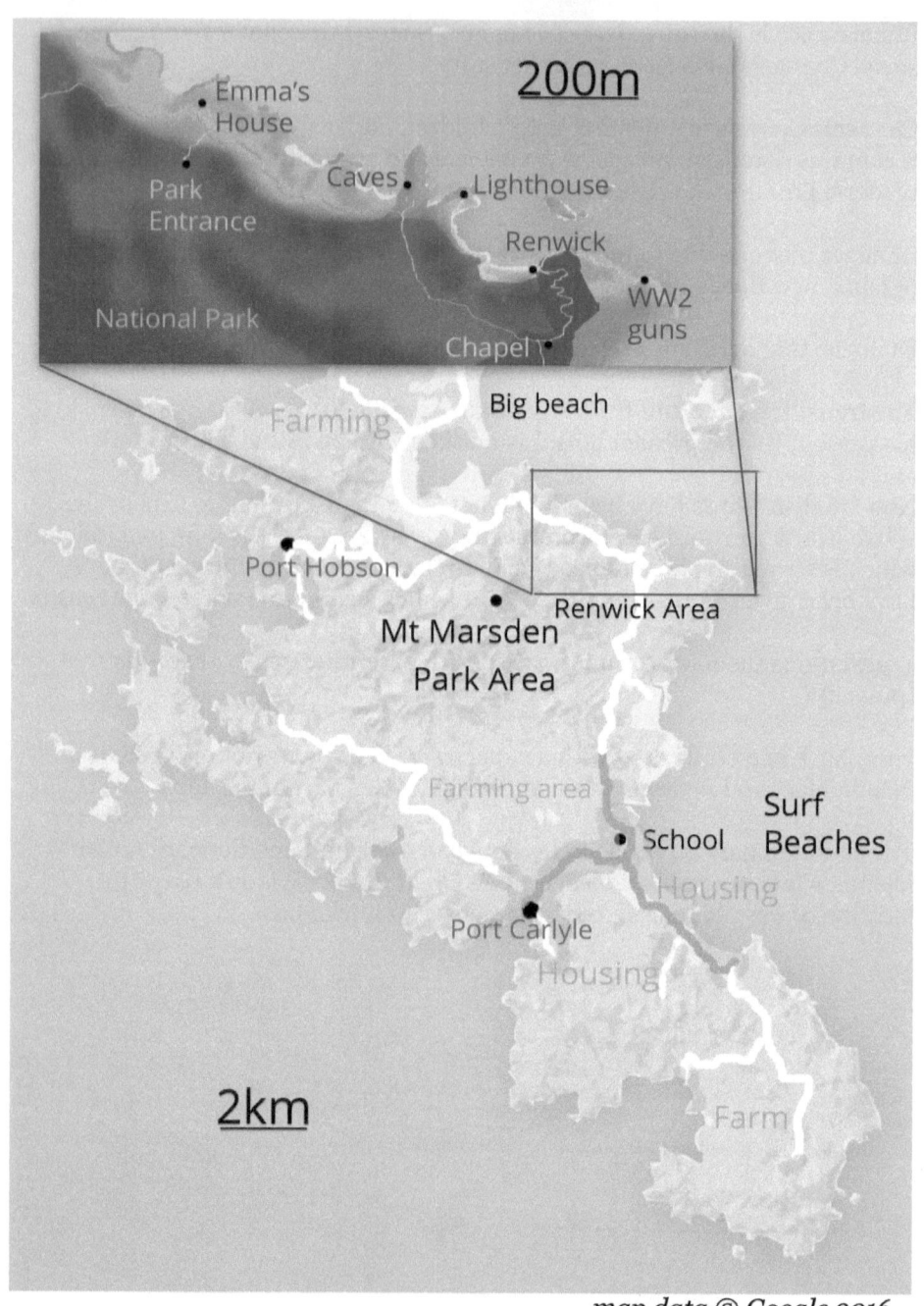

200m

Emma's House

Caves

Lighthouse

Park Entrance

Renwick

National Park

WW2 guns

Chapel

Big beach

Farming

Port Hobson

Renwick Area

Mt Marsden

Park Area

Farming area

Surf Beaches

School

Housing

Port Carlyle

Housing

2km

Farm

map data © Google 2016

*Nothing of him that doth fade, But doth suffer a sea-change Into something rich and strange.*

— **The Tempest, Act 1, scene 2**

## CHAPTER THIRTY: MISSING

"You were right," Sue says from beneath her sunnies, as the sounds of the city on a Sunday afternoon slouched around the back garden.

"What?" I ask, sitting up.

It may be March, and heading for autumn, but Auckland, New Zealand's largest city, is pretty warm – almost hot. Sue's soaking it up like a lizard planning a cold swim.

"You're story is weird. Way too weird."

I smile at her as she lies there.

"So what's so weird about it?"

She snorts.

"What isn't so weird about it? I could cope with the fairies. Just … No, to be honest, I can't cope with the fairies. They're ridiculous. But I can cope with the fairies better than the eight hundred year-old Welsh witch. And the idea that alien fairies … Fae or whatever … could be drawn in to recover their teleported daughter and suddenly meet up with a bunch of their old mates on Earth – that's just silly."

"What about Lucky, Dr Prosperov's spirit guide?" I check, smiling.

"Off the scale. Ludicrous. Not even worth talking about."

She's still lying there, looking very relaxed. I'm not sure I get it.

"So ... what? Do you believe me?" I ask getting up.

"Ummm ... well," she sits up and looks at me. I couldn't see her eyes behind the shades but I can tell she's sizing me up.

"Well, the last time I thought you were crazy you proved me so wrong I'm still ..." she gulps.

"... Being chased down a cave by a flying saucer is a pretty heavy way to expand someone's horizons. So let's say I'm suspending my extreme disbelief – for the moment."

It was funny thinking she's a cop. On one level she is. Why else would she be listening to me tell her about Renwick House before the fire? But on another level we are becoming friends. Trust had a lot to do with that. I'm trusting her with the most important facts about Renwick; its people and its mission. She had trusted me to save her from a flying saucer and fly her, in her car, around Auckland at night suspended from my roof capsule-like speeder.

I get up. I need to walk around.

"Yeah, even two years later there's still a lot about Lucky I don't get either. Or Mrs Jones. It's what Tabika called 'weaving'. Weaving was also exactly how Mrs Jones described 'magic'. The creation of coincidence. Coincidences can get spooky."

"Yeah ... I get that. We get weird coincidences in police work all the time. Car crashes where both drivers have more in common than you'd expect if it was just random. Witnesses who just happen to be in the right place, or victims in the wrong place, by mistake. They're spooky sometimes. But creating coincidences? That's a bit of a stretch."

"Yeah, of course it is. They used to argue about it at Renwick. It all went over my head though. The only thing that mattered to me was whether it worked. Problem was you could never tell.

Stuff happens. I just take it as it comes."

"Yeah, OK, but an eight hundred year-old witch? Come on!" Sue checks, looking over the top of her sunglasses.

I shrug.

"It's what happens when you have total control of genes. Extra-long life, strange body shapes. If you get to meet any Fae you'll see it makes sense. I mean think about it. What would you do if you could change your body to exactly what you wanted?"

"Hmmm," Sue wonders.

"Ultimate nose job? Any colour hair, eyes, skin? Longer legs, or shorter? What would you do if you could change your body rather than have to get it all from your parents?"

"I dunno, what would you do?" Sue looks at me.

I'm a bit surprised by that question. I've never thought about it before. As I think about it I realise it's bigger than I had thought it was. It makes me think about my dead parents differently.

"I s'pose I'd like to look a lot less like Ax, and a lot more like a movie star or something."

Sue sits up a bit, taking her sunnies off.

"Was that really such a shock for you? Realising you look like your father?" she asks.

I sigh.

"Yeah, it was actually," I admit.

"Why?" she wants to know, changing her position so she can see me better.

"Because ... well, because you can't help wondering if you're more alike than you want to admit eh? ... I mean I'd spent years imagining Ax like this zombie that was out to get me ... and it turned out ... well, he wasn't a zombie at all. He was just like me. I really look like him eh? It made me wonder if underneath it all, maybe I was like him. That maybe I could be the kind of man who could throw a little kid against a wall and beat his wife to death."

I realise I'm talking too loud. I look around to see if anyone has heard me. I feel weird. I sit down again and try to get my head straight.

"I don't think you're the kind that would do that, Sam. I really don't," Sue says evenly.

I had to take a deep breath.

"Thanks."

"It really bothers you, doesn't it?"

"He was just such a bastard, Sue."

Sue doesn't even tell me off for swearing.

"Do you know why?"

"Why? Why what?"

"Why he was such a bastard?"

It makes me feel better she says it too. I feel less like I'm in school.

"I know a bit about him," I admit. "A bit about him and mum. But I dunno what made him bad. His dad was as bad as he was. His mother is still a drunk, mean-as old cow. Even Rebecca, his sister, doesn't talk to her. His older cousin was real bad news. Maybe he never got a chance to be straight. I dunno."

I think for a moment, then go on.

"Grandpop says he was just lazy. Always trying to cut corners. Go the easy way. But that's not true either. He worked hard for the respect he got from his gang. He had to be mean to ... well, I dunno. Like it was the only thing he could be. It was his only hope. Does that make sense?"

Sue comes up beside me and puts her arm along my shoulders.

4

It feels nice.

"You aren't responsible for him Sam. He did what he did. You do what you do. You don't have to live up to him. You don't have to prove you're better either. You just have to be you."

"I just don't always know who 'me' is Sue," I tell my shoes.

She chuckles. I look up.

"Make it up Sam. It's what the rest of us have to do. It's what I do and what he did."

She gives me a sideways hug. I give her one back.

We sit for a moment and then wonder what we're doing. Sue stands up and goes back to her chair.

"Did you know you get a Russian accent when you remember what Prosperov told you?"

"No," I have to admit. "To be honest it all comes pouring out as I recall it. That's the problem with total recall. It's completely accurate but it's not the same as memories you think about. It's just blaaaaaaah. Half the time I'm surprised by what I remember too."

"Well, that's the best kind of evidence us detectives can hope for. Untarnished recall. Tell me more Sam. Maybe I'll find it easier to believe the more you tell me about it."

"Well, it stays a bit weird."

"Why?"

"Well, remember how Dr Prosperov walked into the Fae Ring?"

"Of course."

"Well, they took him away."

"What?"

"They kidnapped him."

"For how long?"

"Let me tell you how it was for me. By the way, what's the time?"

5

She glances at her wrist.

"A bit before two."

"When do you think Julia and Caz will be back?"

"I don't know, an hour? Why?"

"I don't know how long my voice will last."

"Oh, shouldn't be too much longer."

Sue flops back into her chair, gets comfortable, lets a small smile creep under her nose which I suspect is because she's finding this very relaxing. I get the impression she finds the idea of fairies much less scary than UFOs and this part of my story is like some sort of fantasy which makes the UFO seem like a distant dream. She doesn't really believe what I'm saying but she does believe I believe it, so she is using this time to understand me. She thinks if she can get that right she'll start to understand what happened to her on the island better as well.

"Please continue," she says.

•••

The exciting start to the Fae council meeting gave way to a long and boring gabfest. It might have been more interesting if we had known what was being said but it was silent. The only sign anything was happening at all was the swivelling of heads around the circle. It was like watching the longest tennis match on TV where you only got to see the crowd's reaction but not the players or any idea of the score.

And it went on for hours. After half an hour Rewa and Asal were asleep. After an hour we were all struggling and before two hours had passed and they were still hard at it most of us decided we'd rather sleep. We left Khenbish and Dr Morozov to watch out for Dr Prosperov.

I slept late that morning and just for once had a fantastic sleep.

When I woke up I discovered nobody was in our apartment. I looked out the window at a gray, still day with the sea washing half-heartedly at the beach. There was no sign that anything had happened the night before.

I went downstairs and walked in on a scene of terrible grief. Everyone was looking shocked and distracted. There was a huddle around Dr Morozov who was weeping quietly. Khenbish was looking stunned and Mrs Jones was talking quietly to Dr Morozov.

I found Aunty Liz had kept a place for me and even put some toast in front of it. I sidled up to her and when she had stopped talking to Patricia on the other side of the table, with Ashley who looked very alert and worried I finally asked what was happening.

"Dose creatures took Dr Prosperov," she whispered.

It was my turn to be shocked. I hadn't missed Dr Prosperov because he usually had his breakfast in his rooms but the idea that he was gone rocked my world. Surely this wasn't part of his plan? Something had gone horribly wrong.

Aunty Liz started talking to Patricia again about money so Ashley filled me in.

"Apparently just before dawn they stopped, stood up and the whole circle just vanished in a big twister."

I couldn't think of anything to say.

Neither could anyone else. Everything relied on Dr Prosperov. Without him the whole place had no purpose and would eventually run out of money. Dr Morozov could keep things running for a while but Dr Prosperov was the finance expert and she wasn't even sure how everything worked. She was worried sick and in no position to make decisions about anything.

I couldn't help wondering if Morganne had organised to abduct Dr Prosperov as a punishment for his taking Tabika. It certainly made us all realise how worried Morganne must have been when her daughter had simply vanished from her home world without a trace for two whole months.

Everyone lost their appetite. Even Mariko's Easter Egg hunt was forgotten. It felt like we spent the whole of Saturday moping. The weather was wet and cold, the cloud very low overhead. We felt trapped inside and the house seemed stuck in depression. To get over it we kids put on our jackets and went out into the pine forest.

The pine needles were wet and slippery and the rain still fell between the trees. But at the same time the pine smelt fresh and free, and even if we slipped on it, it was better than the stifling sadness which held Renwick House in its grip. We found our way to one of the larger cave entrances up behind the house. We crouched there watching the rain drip from the rocks and trees.

"So whatchoo two reckon then?" Tarik asked Tahira and me," What will vey do wiv 'im? 'Old 'im prisoner? Kill him? Torture 'im to make him talk? What?"

"Zey will not 'urt 'im," Tahira replied at once.

"They might bore him to death with all the yakking they do," I suggested sarcastically.

"Me dad said wiv usual physics there could be time problems. They fink they only go away a short time but time passes 'ere faster. Somefing to do with the speed of light init? So Dr P finks e's only been away a day or so, but in our time years have gone," Tarik said.

"I don't think it works that way for them. Tabika counted the days she was away as days not as anything else," I said.

There was silence as we thought some more.

"Will they listen to that ... Lucky ... whatever it was?" Scotty asked.

"I dunno. Sure creeped me out though," I replied.

"Shure was seriously freaky when he took over Dr Prosperov like dat," Ashley agreed. Her glasses were getting wet and she kept trying to dry them.

The others agreed.

"But 'e let 'im," Tarik pointed out," E's known all about that thing an et's plan inhe?"

"But is it Dr Prosperov's plan or Lucky's?" Ashley asked.

"Is there any difference?" I wondered.

"I don't think so, "Scotty agreed.

"Zey are joined," Tahira nodded.

"But Oo are these 'future leaders' 'e's on about? Is it us?" Tarik asked.

Everyone had a quick think about that.

"He don' need no aliens to help find us," Ashley reasoned. "We already here."

"Yuh think, like Lucky wants their help to make us future leaders?" Ashley suggested.

"That could work!" Scotty agreed.

"Whatchoo think we'd be leaders of, then ?" Tarik asked doubtfully.

We all looked at each other.

"Ashley is president?" Cam suggested.

Ashley shook her head, making a face.

"Mebbe you start Kurdistan?" Ashley responded.

Tarik shook his head.

"Nah mate, can't see that 'appening."

"I can't see me leading anything," I said.

"Me either," Scotty added.

"Or me," said Cam.

"Perhaps we are leaderz in uzzer ways," Tahira said. "Like religion or art, per'aps."

"So you'd be like a Baha'i leader?" said Tarik.

"And you also an Alevi?" Tahira said.

"Might work for you but us three aren't 'specially religious," I said indicating Cam and Scotty.

"OK, but maybe Scotty's an environmentalist and Cam is ..." Ashley looked at her critically " ... an inventor and Sam is ... a marine biologist ... or something?"

"I don't think it's us," I disagreed.

"Me neither," said Scotty.

"Or me," added Cam.

"The main fing is we's all psychics, init?" Tarik pointed out, "That means we're like, the tool, not what it works on, yeah?"

"So are aliens," pointed out Cam.

"And we are link wiz zem," Tahira agreed.

"For the plan to work Lucky needed someone capable of working with the Patu-paia-rehe," I said.

"Whatchoo call them?" Tarik asked.

"Patupaiarehe."

"Anyone got an easier word to say than that?" Tarik asked.

"Peri?" suggested Tahira.

"Yeah, I like that," Tarik agreed.

"Fairies?" Ashley suggested.

"Same fing, init," Tarik said.

"Except 'fairies' sounds pretty lame and I don't think those guys are," I said.

"No, they look tough enough to me," Scotty agreed

"Maybe we call them Fae," said Cam, "after place they come from?"

"Sounds good to me, coz it's their name not ours, right?" Tarik said.

"Better dan 'fairies', anyways," agreed Ashley.

"OK," said Tahira.

And from then on we called them "Fae".

Not that it made Dr Prosperov come back any faster. Saturday limped into night. The ghosts seemed almost as lost and uncertain as we did. One rarer one, we didn't know even walked into our lounge looking confused when we were still in it. It looked a bit hunted when it noticed all us psychics were staring at it and it fled through a wall.

Easter Sunday dawned misty, still and cold. You couldn't even see the lighthouse. Renwick seemed alone, not just in space but in time as well. In the echoing sound of a lost seabird it was possible to feel that all links to the rest of the world were gone. Renwick House had become an island in space waiting on visitors from another world.

Mariko's Easter egg hunt was still fun though, and Mr Trân made these crusty hot cross buns and hot chocolate for lunch after the hunt that warmed not just our tummies but our spirits as well.

The cold stillness of the weather seemed to have snapped Dr Morozov out of her grief. While she hadn't liked the summer sun the cold brought her to life. She was busy organising the house and the company with a steely determination that showed she was not to be underestimated. The effect on our parents and caregivers was to give them a renewed sense of hope. Despite the cold and the loneliness Dr Morozov was determined we would show her husband that things didn't fall apart simply because he was abducted by aliens.

The night of Easter Monday there was another storm. Lightning flashed on the mountain and out along the horizon. In the blackness, with the sea roaring and the sky crashing great window pane rattling drum rolls overhead, we sat in the lounge lit only by the fires expecting something to happen. Even the ghosts were in the gallery keeping watch. But nothing happened and we all crawled off to bed one after another.

Easter Monday was windy but clear. The sun seemed pale and the day uncertain. We hung around the house playing games and doing homework. At about two in the afternoon Dr Morozov and Dr Gursoy set off for the lighthouse to do some sort of check. Ten minutes later they were back and everyone was crowding around them in the downstairs lounge. They had found Dr Prosperov's walking stick outside the lighthouse and the door was open.

"He had walking stick when entered circle. So not dropped near lighthouse then," Dr Morozov said.

"Children," Mrs Jones said in one of her commanding voices. "I think your talents would be most useful now."

We all climbed aboard 'Betty' which Mariko drove over the rough road to the lighthouse. It was windy and cold but dry and the sea was rough but not especially bad. For some reason as we approached it the lighthouse seemed especially symbolic. A symbol of both warning and comfort. Dependable and strong despite the anger of the elements. That the stick, a symbol of both frailty and authority, was found there seemed meaningful somehow – but of what exactly, I didn't know.

We got out of the bus and came to the place where the stick had been left outside the lighthouse. We were each passed the stick in turn.

When it came to me I knew at once that if it had ever had any power in the past it had gone now. Dr Prosperov had discarded it because he found it unneeded. I felt an impression of blue light and a gleeful sense of lightness. I passed it on.

"Vell?" Dr Morozov asked when we had all handled it and passed it back.

Mrs Jones looked at us all carefully as if to signal, "watch how I do this."

"My impression is your husband will return to us tonight by rather more conventional means than he left," she began.

Dr Morozov looked at her, unimpressed.

"That is intuitively obvious Mrs Jones," she said.

There was a rather thick silence as the two women eyed each other.

"The Fae gave him a short term energy feed like Tabika did with us and I guess he flew around the island. I get the feeling his connection with Lucky has been changed and he is more in control now," I blurted out.

Dr Morozov looked from me to the others to Mrs Jones.

"Is correct?" she asked.

"Yeah," the others nodded and shrugged.

"Essentially," said Mrs Jones.

"Then say so. I need information Mrs Jones, not management," she said dryly.

"Now is any point to search party?"

"He could be anywhere on the island Dr Morozov," Mrs Jones told her.

"Then he will find us. We must wait," Dr M said simply. I caught a flash of the number of times she had done this when Dr P had been in Siberia, or sent to war. Her faith in him was as strong and stubborn as she was, and that was a lot.

"We could have a welcome back party," Mariko suggested, grinning.

"He won't want that," Mrs Jones said. "Not at first anyway."

So we all got back into Betty and went back to Renwick. We were just getting out of the bus when a Department of Conservation pickup came down the gravel road. Dr Prosperov, his suit tattered and dirty, jumped out, waved farewell to Tama Reeves as the truck circled around and drove back up the hill.

We all formed a semicircle drawing close to Dr Prosperov. Somehow he seemed younger. Younger, straighter and more full of energy. He smiled and walked straight up to his wife, who had melted completely, and kissed her passionately, sweeping her off her feet. I was surprised at the energy these two older people were showing. Then he whispered something in her ear. She gasped and questioned him in rapid Russian. Then kissed him with renewed enthusiasm. After holding her for a long time with his eyes closed and tears in his eyes Dr Prosperov drew back.

"Council of Free agreed to indirect support mission to secure Earth future," he began. He seemed out of breath. "They to provide technology and training but not to intervene directly. Providing technicians to build new secret technical facility to be ready by middle of year."

We all stared at him as he grinned at his wife. It was funny to see Dr Morozov who was usually so icy look so gooey. But it was Patricia Robinson who broke the spell.

"Dr Prosperov?"

14

"Da," he said, still looking at Dr Morozov.

"I'm not sure we know what you are talking about."

He seemed to take the longest time to understand what she had just said.

"Is not obvious?" he asked.

Everyone looked confused. He looked around at our faces. Even Dr Morozov looked uncertain. Dr Prosperov seemed surprised and even a bit defensive.

"Dozen leaders of critical period aged four to fourteen!" Dr Prosperov said as if this explained everything.

"Who are these leaders?" Patricia persisted.

"Exact identity unknown. First task is to find."

That didn't exactly explain anything either.

"How?" she asked simply.

"Process of elimination," he replied, still distracted by his wife.

That didn't wash with anyone.

"Gennady there must be hundreds of millions of children in that age group," Ken interrupted.

"Is 1,220 million children aged five to 15 on Earth at present time," Dr Prosperov nodded looking up.

I was blown away. All those millions and millions of kids.

"How are we to find a handful of future leaders among that number?" Ken asked.

"Is problematic," Dr Prosperov nodded letting his wife stand and straightening his tattered clothes.

"If not impossible," Gunter muttered darkly.

Dr Prosperov started laughing like a crazy man. It took him a while to stop. We all watched, mystified by what was so funny.

"Friends, colleagues," he chuckled, wiping his eyes and shaking his head. "Contacting alien civilisation and securing their help in quest to save our world. That was impossible! Finding handful of children among a billion? That is merely difficult."

There were a few smiles in agreement with that. He began to draw everyone inside. We followed.

"But Dr Prosperov how can we find dese children?" Patricia asked. "We ain't gonna all travel da world interviewing kids are we?"

"Is job of facility," he replied waving his arm at Renwick. "Here we to host psychics and experts – therefore staff. Task is make short list of candidates."

This was an enormous "Ooohh" moment and the news made everyone relax. It was obvious that the adults had been wondering how they fitted in to Lucky's plan too. The idea that they would simply be hosting people squared with what we had been told at the beginning, far more than his experiments at the lighthouse.

"But even assumin' you are successful and do make a short list then what will you do?" Bernard asked. "Simply knowin' who these children are won't change anythin' for them," he pointed out.

"Assessment is correct but incomplete. Further problem is identifying correct interventions. Is trivial given identities of children to spend money but such intervention may contradict needed outcome. For example effect of spending possibly makes them not future leader. Is possible future leaders must not even know of interventions if they to become future leaders. So analysis suggests three problems. Identify children; assess need for intervention; execute interventions."

"But you've already done that – with us," Tarik blurted out excitedly.

Prosperov's eyes flashed and he grinned wolfishly.

"Only partially true insightful young friend. First Lucky identified you easily, second intervention in all cases clear. This stage too complex and physically beyond human resource hence need for assistance from outside. Also added complexity other alien civilisation may also be involved with target children."

This was a new and creepy bit of news for those who hadn't talked to Tabika about it.

"What other alien civilisation?" Ken asked for us.

"Civilisation which drove off our new friends. Our world is protectorate of their larger galactic civilisation. They seek to control us." Dr Prosperov shrugged.

"Dr Prosperov, are you involving us in a war?" Dr Gursoy asked alarmed.

"Is possible interpretation but not goal. Goal is long-term safety of our planet. If this makes war with other aliens why must we not defend ourselves?"

Everyone looked at each other. They were nervous and wanted to object, but Dr P's logic had them. If there were aliens that were opposed to Earth's long-term survival one way or another we would end up in conflict with them. Back then we just didn't realise what that might mean.

## CHAPTER THIRTY ONE: THE ENGINEERS

The weather after Easter was bad. Rain, rain, and more freezing rain, driven by an endless series of thick lines on the weather map marching north from the South Pole.
Dr Prosperov and Dr Gursoy had retreated to the lighthouse again armed with new plans. Dr Prosperov said now that the Fae were helping him he could see there were plenty of improvements to turn the lighthouse into a reliable teleportation gateway.

He also explained that once the gateway was ready, building a secret base under the hill behind Renwick could begin. The Fae preferred building underground and had already noticed the area was full of caves. Naturally we could not tell anyone outside Renwick about this – not that anyone would have believed us anyway.

We already lived on an island that felt like the edge of nowhere, but now we seemed over the horizon of the world, lost in our own private reality. It created a strange mood around the house. There was no doubt that Dr Prosperov was not mad and that we had certainly made contact with a strange and so far – well "friendly" might be pushing it, but at least *patient* – alien civilisation. But it was still hard to make sense of it all.

Of course it was the only thing anyone talked about at home

and it was intense. I think we all wanted reassurance we weren't going mad together. Even Mrs Jones, who had known the Fae in her youth, would sometimes stop to think about the strange new world we were entering.

In Betty the Bus on the way to school things were quiet. That was partly the rain, because we knew we were headed to another boring day at school, and partly because Mariko had changed the music from her usual bouncy 80's dances to the strange twisting twangs and gentle rhythms of Indian ragas. We tended to sit looking out the window at the rain, not quite sure what we were thinking, as music settled over the roaring and grumbling of Betty's engine and gearbox.

At school Mr Wakefield's new enthusiasm was for water. So we studied water: different uses for water; pollution; and water in society. But he couldn't possibly admit that Ashley, Scotty and Tarik had interesting experiences with water, or that Maori have a few thoughts on the subject either. No, everything came from the faded posters and textbooks he already had. The date on one was 1974.

Marshall's table decided it was going to do a project on hydraulics using plastic pipes, straws, sponges, waterwheels etc. Table B was doing water quality by collecting samples from around the island and testing them for things. Emma was getting a lot of help from her Dad on this. And we were doing a project on water around the world, which was a great idea to begin with, but which we soon realised meant we had to do a lot of writing which none of us enjoyed.

And during the breaks there was no end of water. Water flooded the play areas and gutters. It streamed down the windows and hammered on the roof. It made you want to just go to sleep.

The others played games or read. But I just daydreamed, mostly about Tabika.

I was in a corner with my eyes closed, dreaming about flying around in warm rain, when someone nudged me. It was Tahira.

"Do you zink she will come back?" she asked quietly.

"Who?" I asked, pretending innocence.

Tahira gave me a scornful look one psychic gives another when they try to pretend they can't be read.

"Dunno," I admitted, giving in.

"I 'op she will,"Tahira said wistfully, slumping down next to me.

"Me too," I agreed.

"Why?" she asked, challenging me.

"I miss her."

"Why?" she asked darkly.

She thought I was being sleazy.

"She means freedom ... escape," I sighed, looking around at the classroom and the rain.

"Daghighan," Tahira sighed to herself.

She turned to look out the window. She was thinking about everything at Renwick.

"Djou ziink doc-tor Prosperov will want *uz* to do anysing?" she asked.

A lot of thoughts went through my mind. The first one was not hopeful. When did adults ever let kids do anything important? But then he *had* dropped hints here and there.

"I dunno. I sure hope so."

"Me also," Tahira sighed, "me also."

I noticed Emma watching us together and made my excuses to leave.

But for ages nothing happened. April went and May continued

the rain but even colder. There were thunderstorms, which Dr Prosperov used to test the portal. And the first thing the Fae sent was a new power source. It looked like nothing. Just a perfectly black cube not quite half a meter in size. Dr Prosperov went to pick it up and it instantly transferred all the knowledge about how to use it to him. He and Dr Gursoy then installed it and announced that night we had enough power to run the whole country.

The Fae began sending all sorts of strange stuff. Seeds, a dozen winged ants suspended in an amber ball, purple and green jewels, a smooth silver thing about the size of a pen and a grub-like creature the size of a rat in a bowl full of dirt. Dr Prosperov took them – apart from the grub that Dr Morozov wrinkled her nose up at.

Dr Prosperov was extremely pleased that his machine was working so well. But there were a lot of jokes about what the Fae were sending us. Gunter told a good one about Dr Prosperov receiving a pile of dirty clothes and instructions for washing Fae socks. He told it with such a straight face with his deep German accent it took us a moment to realise it was a joke. Of course we realised later that nobody else would get it. Most people would be gobsmacked that we were receiving things from an alien civilisation *at all*.

Still, for us kids real life was not about communication with other worlds but surviving school. Dr Prosperov did do one little thing which helped lift the boredom a little. He'd bought us all a very detailed pocket atlas and told us that each week there would be a contest to find a place in it. The first won fifty dollars, second thirty, and third twenty. There was ten dollars off if we agreed to ask for a country hint and we lost ten dollars from each prize for every five minutes we took. All of us were saving for things so a bit extra got our attention.

The result was we had a simple game where one person would find an obscure place in the atlas and the others would try and find it. It was a lot of fun. You soon learned to tell Asian places from European ones and Indian from African. But the real competition was because we were all psychic. It taught us how to obscure our thoughts by naming the target and then focusing on somewhere else.

When we went up against Dr Prosperov we found we couldn't read him at all. He was an expert at not being read. His mind was so full of complicated stuff that came and went in an instant that he was impossible to make sense of.

Tahira won the first contest, with Tarik second and Cam third. It was obvious ability with languages helped. Still Scotty, Ashley and me were not going give up without a fight, so we practiced together and next time I came second after Ashley with Tahira third.

The second week of May was the full moon. We had expected the Fae would reappear and reappear they did. Tahira and me were hoping Tabika would come back. She didn't. Instead after dinner at moonrise a bright light flared before Renwick House as we sat close to Mrs Jones in the gallery on a rare cloudless night. Ashley went up to get Dr Prosperov to let him know the expected guests had arrived.

Filled with curiosity we all trooped down to see these Fae. There were two. The male was neither old nor young. He had short horns, a handsome face with a closely trimmed beard, quick brown eyes and real hardarse body – all golden with lean muscles. His lower half was all brown and white fur with the split hooves that were not like an animals, but not human either. The female was a cat crossed with a very curvy woman. Her face was still human except for the green catlike eyes, but she was covered in black fur with a tail. She also had the black leathery wings.

The two of them were smiling – the female showing her fangs – with a kind of amused curiosity as we gathered in a huddle. We realised we looked like cute Earth natives to them. Dr Prosperov was not slow in coming down to greet them, while Dr Morozov stood back by the stairs watching with Ken.

To our surprise as Dr Prosperov approached the male stepped forward and embraced him, followed, in turn, by the female. Then the male spoke to us in words accompanied by thoughts so that his meaning seemed more natural than the odd English he sometimes used. It was kind of hard to remember them both and I can really only remember the meaning.

What he said was:

"Hi, everyone my name is Hekator. I am here to help you with your new equipment."

The female too spoke.

"Hi, I'm Hekati. I'm here to build the base."

They were very relaxed. As if coming to other planets to build bases was no big deal. It made everyone feel a lot calmer about something which could have freaked us all out if we'd thought about it too much. Again I got the impression that everything about our home was sorta primitive. Like we lived in a grass hut or something.

"My friends it is good to see you again," Dr Prosperov told them. "Our house is open to you," he gestured towards it.

"Thank you, Gennady," Hekati replied, "but iron surroundings

23

are dangerous to us. We shall find a cave and live there. We are quite able to make ourselves comfortable."

"Any suggestions would be helpful," Hekator put in.

"*We* know a good cave," I blurted out. "We can show you if you like."

The Fae smiled at me.

"*This must be Tabika's friend, Sam,*" Hekator 'said' silently to Hekati, but so I could psychically 'hear'. I nodded. They smiled, as Tabika had, at my nodding and thinking "yes".

"Thank you Sam, that would be most helpful," Hekati said aloud. "We will stay for a month. During this time you will not see us during your day, nor will you hear anything," Hekati told us. "However, you will see our workers in large numbers. Please do not interrupt their columns as they are programmed to defend themselves. We will need depots for building materials and food. These include wood or wood products or waste in any form, sand, limestone and a lot of sugar. If you wish to limit their foraging please let us know before cloning begins."

"Ah ... Hekati ... If I may? How many workers do you expect to have on this project?" Dr Gursoy asked. He was thinking of the Gap scheme back in Turkey.

"Roughly four trillion," Hekati smiled.

We all goggled at each other. Where would four trillion Fae fit?

"Gennady, do you have the amber ball?" she asked.

"Ahh ... yes. Is upstairs! You want?"

"No thanks. Our workers will look to you like very large columns of ants. They are a kind of ant, of course, but we have adapted them. They will supply the constructor polyps which will grow the structure. When the fuseworm matures it will achieve the necessary temperatures to form service tunnels out of all this

**24**

lovely sand you have here," Hekati explained.

"What happens to all these ants and things when the job is finished?" Patricia asked.

"Most will die and be recycled. A small maintenance colony will persist. The fuseworm will form a chrysalis and we will remove it and return it to its normal world. You wouldn't want an adult Worm flying around here burning everything. They soon become a pest without the broodbane parasite to control them," Hekati added.

The picture in her mind gobsmacked us.

"Does she mean dragons?" Rewa asked me quietly. I shrugged. Hekati, however, had heard her.

"Draca. They're a very large insect which inspired the idea of dragons but are nothing like as clever. Dragons like Pegasi and Unicorns we created for watching over our little boys and girls. Tabika's favourite is a unicorn named Sky," she smiled at her.

Rewa's eyes were bigger than ever. Unicorns! Real unicorns! It was pretty crazy.

"Tonight our task is simply to set up camp and introduce ourselves," Hekator said. "Things will seem slow at first but they will get very fast by the end. That's how bioconstruction always goes. In the meantime I'll be working on the operatives' equipment."

Dr Prosperov coughed suddenly.

"Yes. Good. Is excellent. We shall arrange supplies tomorrow. Sam and … yes Tahira please to show guests cave. Is plenty of time for further discussion. Perhaps Ken we shall have barbecue tomorrow?"

"Depends a bit on the weather…" Ken frowned. But Dr Prosperov was already hurrying off.

**25**

"Mrs Jones please to organise meeting of all residents in upstairs lounge. Is number of important matters I am needing help."

And he scurried back to Dr Morozov and upstairs. Surprisingly he seemed almost embarrassed. I couldn't get him on that either. His mind was a blur of calculations.

I led the Fae up the hill to our cave hangout. We had sometimes thought about staying there overnight, but the dark inside had always creeped us out and we hadn't ever done it.

Tahira followed us up the hill and then to my surprise asked a question.

"Ah Hekator?"

"Yes Tahira?" Hekator said kindly. At first I was surprised he knew her name but then I realised he had known mine and would know Tahira's from Tabika as well.

"Who are 'agents'?" she asked.

I was so shocked by her daring I stopped and turned to look. We had all stopped in the gloom of the pines.

"Tahira, you are," Hekator told her. He looked at me as well. "You both are. Dr Prosperov's plan relies on it."

"So *we* find children with our powers psychic?" Tahira asked.

"If it were possible using mind alone our master weavers would find them. The cyberminds of the Center would identify them soon enough as well. But that isn't possible. To do this sort of weaving one must enter the frame, one must be part of the situation."

"It's the only way the strands of destiny can be woven. To act and be acted upon. Living is choosing, choosing is acting. The future is a choice by both you and those who would be chosen. Without the act of choosing it is impossible to find those whose choices will make them future leaders of your world.

I think he could tell we were less interested in abstract ideas and more in the main points affecting us.

"So the only way you can find these children is to go to the places where they are sensed to be and move among them. Your senses will guide you to the children you seek. This is why *you* children are so important. No adult can move among children. But children of all civilisations relate to one another – this is after all how it was with you and Tabika."

"But how will we go to where these kids are?" I objected, "will we be on private jets or something," I asked thinking of Sir Michael. Hekator and Hekati smiled. I couldn't see what was so funny.

"Sam," Hekati cut in, "we are to provide you your equipment. Your private jets are to us as you would find ..."

"Canoes?" Hekator suggested.

"Exactly," Hekati agreed, "the tools we will give you will be closer to what we are used to. We need you to be both successful and safe. Don't worry, we will be with you in this mission, but ultimately only children can do this. Dr Prosperov has found the six most capable children in this world but he is relying completely on you to be successful. We all are."

I was stunned. They totally meant it too. I looked at Tahira in the darkness, and although she was a smudge in the dark, I could see the shocked look on her face too. Our faces must have surprised the two Fae.

"Were you not aware of this?" Hekati asked.

"No," I gasped.

"*That could be a problem*," Hekator muttered to Hekati.

"Let's find this cave," Hekati said with a forced smile.

It was now so dark I couldn't see anything in the deep dark

shadows of the trees.

"Here," said Hekator behind me.

Light flooded from behind me lighting up the bank as if someone was spot hunting from a truck. I turned and looked back at Hekator. His chest was too bright to see. We climbed up to the cave in silence.

When we got there the shadows from Hekator's light were sharper and darker than ever. The blackness of the cave's interior was total, not just as if it wasn't lit, but as if it was part of the world God had forgotten to fill in. I couldn't help wondering why it was these superior beings wanted to live like cavemen. But they seemed well pleased with the cave and Hekati lit up too. Then they moved inside casting an orange red glow. Hekator held out his hand and a ball of bright electric light, buzzing and sparking, formed in it.

"Follow the ball down the hill," he said. "It will light the way down. We will see you again tomorrow night."

He dropped the ball and it began to roll slowly, sparking and buzzing, and briefly setting the damp pine needles on fire. It moved as if it was sticking to the ground somehow, so it didn't roll down as fast as a ball would normally have. It was quite easy to keep up with, but we noticed as it rolled it was getting smaller and smaller. By the time we got to the bottom of the hill it had shrunk from a softball to a marble, and then it just disappeared altogether in a puff of smoke.

We ran around the house, up the stairs through the main doors, and ran past the presences in the gallery to the upstairs lounge where everyone was in a semi-circle around Dr Prosperov.

"... therefore is impossible to conduct search by psychic means alone. Agents must become integrated into multidimensional equation through active participation."

He paused and sucked his teeth.

"Is now moment of supreme delicacy. From outset is apparent crucial leaders are at this time themselves children. Is also apparent that as general principle societies protect children from potential external threat. Exogenous adult-child interchange is subject to potentially mission critical social constraints. But is also apparent child-child relations not so constrained. Exogenous adults are potential threat. Children, indigenous or exogenous not classed as such. Universal assumption is all child-child relations resolve within local customary pedagogical framework."

I had *no* idea what he was talking about and I don't think I was the only one. You could tell that he was nervous because he used big words and very short sentences which made him really hard to understand, but he went on.

"This specifies operatives to some degree of accuracy. Is necessary operatives have strong psychic abilities, are resilient and adaptable, and *are* children. In fact there are no more than a dozen such children on Earth capable of this and the six most likely to succeed are in this room."

"Therefore all turns on two choices. Parents whether you will allow children to act as operatives, and children whether you wish to carry out this mission. I have no moral, legal or physical means to compel you. For all the investment I have made in this venture in money, years, and effort at this crucial juncture I am reduced to begging. I beg you to consider your options carefully. You have my assurance that everything within the power of myself, and the Fae, will be done to keep your children safe, but we cannot guarantee anything. The fate of many worlds hangs on what you decide."

Then he sat down exhausted by the stress of the situation. Dr Morozov closed behind him and put her hands on his shoulders. He took them in his. It was hard to describe her attitude. She believed fervently in her husband but she was sympathetic to the parents. She had obviously searched her feelings and was unsure how she would react.

Patricia had already made up *her* mind.

"No!" she said firmly, standing up. "No *way*! Dr Prosperov dis is too much. Mah contract is for supplying mah services not dose of *mah child*. I lost my husband to some dumb sense of duty and adventure I will not risk my daughter. Come on Ashley."

"But muuum," Ashley began.

"No! I will *not* allow it. Dere ain't nothing to discuss."

"But can't I..." she wheedled.

"No. Come now!"

And, obviously upset, Patricia followed by an embarrassed Ashley, walked down the corridor to their apartment.

Dr Gursoy was next.

"Dr Prosperov you are the greatest scientist of this and possibly any other century. It has been an honour and a privilege to work with you on this project. But my enthusiasms cost my wife and daughter their lives. I cannot risk Tarik. The price is too high. I am afraid we too must withdraw from your project."

And he too left with Tarik trailing after him, not as sure of himself as he usually was.

Mr Trân was next.

"I like work here very much. But I scared for Cam. She only daughter. She my only girl. Cannot do this Mr Prosperov. Is not right."

And they left. I sneaked a peak at Aunty Liz. She had the same unimpressed look as Mitra and Soraya. Then Bernard stood and spoke in his rich voice.

"Dr Prosperov I must express my distaste for the manner in which you have brought this question to us. It is underhand and manipulative and my wife and I believe you have brought the rejections you have just experienced on yourself."

"However we do *not* reject your proposals out of hand. Scotty has proven himself and earned the right to choose the risks he is willing to face. But we stress he is not *your* agent he is a *free* agent. And we demand too that we know what he is asked to do and can exercise our judgement as adults, where his is captured by excitement of the moment and youthful inexperience. If we are unhappy at any time we will withdraw our consent. But if you agree to these demands you have our consent to put your case to *Scotty* who will make his own decision."

Dr Prosperov who had looked very gloomy now simply looked tired.

"Mr Khumalo your conditions were tacitly assumed anyway. I cannot ask more. Scotty what do you think?"

Now everyone was looking at Scott. He looked so small, his cheeks were all pink and he looked a bit nervous. But there was something about him. Something of a lion. He thought for a moment and then started to speak so quietly it was hard to hear him.

"Ahh well, I was just wondering. We're *paid* to clean the house. Will we be paid for this too?"

Dr Prosperov softly began to laugh and laugh until he coughed.

"Very astute Scotty. Very good. You have my attention. What sort of money do you want?"

"Well, I suppose I'm not a grown-up, but on the other hand you did say there were only a dozen people on Earth who could do this. I don't want to be greedy but I do know my father was paid $500 a day as a mercenary. That sounds fair."

I couldn't *believe* Scotty's cheek. But there he was, red-faced but looking Dr Prosperov in the eye and not blinking at *all*. I held my breath. Dr Prosperov rubbed his chin.

"Scotty, you raise interesting problem not previously considered. Is true you deserve payment," he nodded.

"Is also true I cannot ask you to take risks just to save world. Is nebulous idea which dresses many stupid adventures. You are right to take mercenary view. You may not see benefits in lifetime. The sum you mention is approximately $200,000 a year. If all six paid the same is one point two million. Is not impossible, but not small either. Also occurs there is no particular reason why *I* should pay you to save civilisation. Is debt civilisation will owe all of us. So perhaps is justified to find means for civilisation to pay us. By this I mean using Fae technology to make our mission financially as well as morally sound. So yes, I agree to pay $500 a day."

"U.S," Scotty interrupted. Dr Prosperov winced, but smiled at his opponent.

"U.S," Dr Prosperov acknowledged, nodding, "but we should also come to an arrangement on shares of treasures or other actions designed simply to keep our mission afloat financially. My proposal would be operatives collectively keep half and I take other half."

"Sounds fine to me," Scotty agreed.

"Of course you still have to do cleaning though. We can't hire locals now," he added with sudden sharpness.

"Oh, OK," Scotty shrugged. After winning such a big sum for himself he wasn't going to worry about the small stuff.

I looked at Aunty Liz. This was *huge* money! I was really excited! I couldn't imagine anyone making that much and now *I* could. Even Aunty Liz also had a different look on her face. She stood.

"Dr Prosperov I fully support Mr Khumalo. You have not been straight with us."

Dr Prosperov looked uncomfortable.

"But so long as Sam is free to make his own calls on risk, and I am kept informed and able to withdraw consent at any time too, I too am willing to listen and let you sort out something with Sam."

She sat down and I was so happy I kissed her. I quickly agreed to the same terms as Scotty who was my new hero. Meanwhile the Khadem family were having a whispered discussion in Farsi. It went on for a long while. Soraya seemed to have a few things to say. Finally she was finished and Mitra stood.

"We agree with Mr Khumalo but have a few more points. First health insurance. If Tahira faces any risk of disease she must have the best healthcare."

Dr Prosperov frowned.

"Mrs Khadem health insurance will only buy you best health care on *Earth*. Fae offer best health care in *galaxy*."

Mitra looked a bit put-out by that. Then she added something about Tahira should not face any disadvantage because she is a girl and it might not be proper for her to go to some places or do some things at some times of the month. I didn't understand it then.

Dr Prosperov looked at Dr Morozov and shrugged.

"We will look after your daughter as much as is possible. As

**33**

for femininity I have seen no evidence female is weaker sex. Opposite in fact. I doubt any concessions needed but if so we will make them. Tahira what you think?"

"I will try, so long as I can stop," she said looking at us.

Mitra nudged her.

"On same terms as uzzers of course," she added going red.

Dr Prosperov smiled.

"Naturally."

He paused for a moment looking around.

"Well, is perhaps not so bad. Yes, must confess Mr Khumalo I have made mistake in presuming too much of parents. Have been too distracted by almost impossible technical issues to consider simple but equally critical emotional ones. For this I apologise. Failure is mine. I hope it is not too late to repair damage with others. I understand fears but cannot share them. I ask you who have conditionally agreed to reassure others they need not take risks they don't want to. And now I am very tired and little sad so unless any more questions I will go to bed," he said wearily.

Nobody had any questions or indeed anything to say when he left, and we left the room to the ghosts. That night I dreamed I was in a garden full of roses and tall hedges with Rewa and Aunty Liz and Grandpop and a bunch of people from home. It was sunny and happy. And then it was as if I was looking down on us and I was getting higher and higher. And as I got higher I saw that the garden was part of a carpet flying high over the countryside and I realised we had left the others behind and I wanted to go back and get them but the garden-carpet was flying ever faster and higher. I woke in the night and lay awake.

"What in hell are you getting yourself into?" I wondered.

I fretted for a while and then fell asleep.

The atmosphere at breakfast the next morning was so tense I thought someone would explode. Mr Trân's baking had suffered and he himself looked worried and scared. We kids were bundled on to the bus. Mariko must have been upset too because she didn't even notice she hadn't put any music on.

As soon as we got going Ashley wanted to know what had happened. When Scotty told her about the money her mouth fell open and stayed open for almost five minutes. Tarik seemed frozen and Cam just nervous.

"Braa, what made you tink to ask him *dat*!" Ashley asked Scotty when she could finally speak again.

"I don't know. It just occurred to me he wanted to employ me for another job, and all I could remember was my dad boasting when he was drunk about the money he made."

Ashley shook her head in wonder at him. Tarik however just looked sick.

"It won't matter to me dad," he said gloomily. "he feels to'ally guilty about mum and completely paranoid about me."

"My dad is the same. He was in the war at my age. He knows how dangerous it was and he says I am all he has," Cam said quietly.

"I ahm so mad wid my mom," Ashley said. "What Bernard said is right. If we know da risks we's facing we can cope wid them, right? I mean, I ran risks everyday jus' goin' to school in da Easy. Dere was gangs, Dere was knives, dere was guns and ah didn't see her gitting all twisted up about it den. Den *she* swipes millions and ends up in a car chase wid gangsters wid machineguns like dat *didn't* put me in danger? I say her problem

**35**

isn't me in danger. It's her not bein' in control o' me dat has her pissed. Ah mean what she goin' to do when ah git older? Follow me around protectin' me?"

I could see Ashley and her mum were as headstrong as each other and this was going to end with a fight between them. I hoped Ashley would win.

Tarik and Cam had opposite problems. Tarik's dad probably had the best understanding of all the parents of what was going on, while Mr Trân had the least. Cam felt sure that her dad would be reassured if everyone felt what we would be doing was safe. But Tarik was not sure what would sway *his* father.

"We came here cos he thought I was in danger. He's not going to want to send me into it, now."

Ashley was in an argumentative mood.

"But yo daddy's a *standout*. His bosses is always gonna want to advertise his big degrees 'n shit wherever he goes. Unless he wants to drive cabs he's always goin' to be easy to find, ain't he? You are *far* safer wid us dan anywhere else."

"Yeah, but dad will argue Dr P can't make us kids work for him. It's probably not even legal for us to work like that anyway."

"If we still go to school it's OK," I said. "They used to have some kids working at my Aunt's hospital making tea in the café who weren't much older than me. Aunt Liz wanted to get me a job there when one came free."

"Well, OK," Tarik admitted. "But nobody can make an employee's kid work for 'em. It's not on."

"No," we all agreed.

"But he could fire your dad," Ashley said darkly.

"He won't do that, will he? He needs my dad more 'an anyone."

That was true too. Dr Prosperov had said as much, too.

"But your father is clever man," Cam said gently, "he will see reason in Bernard Khumalo's idea."

"Yeah maybe. But Ee's not always reasonable is he? Ee gets all moody and stubborn like. When he's like that he won't listen to anyone. You know what I mean?" Tarik complained.

"Maybe we just have to show them," Scotty said quietly. We all looked at him.

"Well if me and Sam and Tahira are OK, maybe they will change their minds," he shrugged.

"So long as we stick around," said Ashley. "My mom's got enough stolen money to retire. We only here cos it's a good place to hide. But we could go anywheres. Dhey'll have stopped lookin' for us by now. If my mom don't feel OK, she'll go – and drag me wid her."

She was looking rather intensely at Scotty who wasn't quite sure what to say. Tarik and Cam looked at each other. They knew they would be staying. Both their fathers felt safe at Renwick. Mr Trân wouldn't leave unless he was thrown out, and Dr Gursoy was confident enough of his value as an engineer to remain. Still, they obviously didn't want to be left out of the action and felt they might be left behind.

Mr Wakefield must have noticed we were distracted that day because he gave us extra homework. We had to mix water with a long list of other things and list the properties of the result and whether the water had dissolved them in any way. Meanwhile outside our house two aliens from another planet were going to start building a secret base. I mean honestly!

Mariko came back for us in a happier mood than she had left. She was playing Japanese pop songs which made no sense to us but at least sounded a bit more hopeful. Mariko said Patricia had been talked out of leaving by Ken, and agreed there was no harm in at least seeing how things turned out, but she was still dead set against Ashley travelling anywhere without her.

Dr Gursoy and Mr Trân were swayed a bit by Bernard's argument but they were still closer to Patricia Robinson's view than Bernard and Zoe Khumalo's. Dr Prosperov had talked to them all and reassured them he respected their views which had helped a lot, but his rep' had taken a hit, and they still thought he was sus'.

To break the tension Mariko announced she was thinking of having a Mata-ri-ki party. Matariki is the Maori New Year which is in mid June, in midwinter. Matariki refers to a constellation of stars which drops below the horizon and reappears just before dawn at midwinter. For Maori it was an important reminder of when to start the sweet potato planting for the new year. Celebrating Matariki is pretty low key. Typically we just have a bonfire on a beach before dawn and eat sweet potato and stuff. Though some people prefer a barbecue.

Having a beach party in the middle of winter is pretty hard-out. So long as it's not raining, and you wrap up, it can be OK up North where it's warm. But the problem with Aotea is the weather changes every five minutes so you could easily end up with no bonfire and a whole lot of wet, cold, tired, grumpy people in no mood to celebrate anything. I thought it could quite easily backfire.

That night everyone was trying to act like everything was normal, but underneath, you could still feel the tension. Ken, Gunter and Mariko were talking to everyone keeping everything relaxed. Mrs Jones was still on our cases to do our cleaning and we still had Mr Wakefield's homework to do. We couldn't

even split it up among us and copy one another. We'd tried that
before and he marked us all zero and then gave us a long boring
lecture about all doing our own work.

Being winter it was dark by seven so it wasn't long before
Hekator and Hekati were back to see Gunter and Dr Prosperov.
They gave them a long list of materials they needed and talked to
them about where they should be placed. We kids followed them
around as they talked and pointed.

Then Hekati started drawing her plans in coloured lights
in mid-air showing both the ground level, the underground
cave network that already existed, and the plans to reshape
the interior, as well as redirect the groundwater, provide air
circulation, and channel the power supplies. I lost track of all the
coloured lines after the first three colours but there were at least
a dozen. The detail lost me and Gunter just kept saying "Mein
Gott!" over and over as Hekati zoomed in, zoomed out, and
turned the image around and over with casual ease as if she did
this sort of thing all the time. Then she just waved her arm and it
all disappeared.

The adults talked and agreed to go to the lighthouse. We were
about to go back inside when Hekator came up to us.

"Kids, I wonder if I could ask you to help me," he began.

We shrugged uncertainly.

"If you would just run up to uh ... here," he traced a line with his
hoof, "and jump as far as you can."

It seemed a pretty weird thing to ask. But we did it.

Then he wanted us to do standing jumps, and finally he got us to
climb a small tree. He just watched. Finally Tarik had to ask.

"What is this for?"

"I'm measuring you. I need to have a general idea of your sizes

**39**

when you move and stretch. Without it the equipment I make won't feel right."

"But djou av no tape," Tahira objected.

"I measure by eye. You for example Tahira are 1,374 millimeters from fingertip to fingertip and 1381 millimeters tall. Look!"

And just as Hekati cast a light plan so Hekator drew a Tahira in the air, and made her do a little dance. Then he waved it away.

"Of course for the final detailing I'll need to capture you out of all those clothes you people wear."

Although Hekator was a very good looking goat-man the girls looked outraged. Us boys just felt a bit exposed. He smiled gently.

"But don't worry I know how vulnerable that makes you genetic inheritors feel so we'll work out a way to do it without upsetting you. We may be able to do it without you even knowing it so you don't have to feel self-conscious."

We went inside feeling very self-conscious.

## CHAPTER THIRTY TWO: BIOCONSTRUCTION

The winter weekends were short, dark and wet. We spent them either playing this computer role-playing game Gunter and Mariko had made, or hanging in the lounge playing pool or watching TV. We were watching these documentaries about places connected to the people at Renwick. It was interesting to see a film about Vietnamese boat-people, or Katrina, or the Kurds, or even my home in the Hokianga, with people who had been there. It made our worlds more understandable to each other.

The game was a sword and sorcery one where you saw what your character saw. They had done a great job with it, but the horses were still a bit chunky-looking. I was a hero with a magic sword, Tarik was a wizard. Scotty, Ashley and Cam were our elven bowmen and Tahira was an Amazon warrior. We mostly relied on Tarik and the elves to shoot dangerous things while me and Tahira held them off. It worked pretty well. Of course when it came to puzzles we were left with just our brains.

The deliveries over the next few weeks had the truck drivers scratching their heads. First we got barrels and barrels of sugar. Then we got a huge pile of sawdust. Then we got several truckloads of crushed cars. Finally we got loads of limestone. Apparently the beach would provide both shells and sand. And then nothing happened.

We just got sick. We all felt bad. On the worst days we got runny noses and fever and had to stay in bed, but that went away and was replaced by a weird feeling that our heads were changing. We felt lightheaded and vague. Aunty Liz and Mrs Robinson thought we had caught some sort of virus. The funny thing was nobody but the six of us ever got it. Mostly it made us feel tired and grumpy, but sometimes we got terrible headaches with bright flashing lights. Other times we tripped over our tongues and said things which sounded like what we meant, but used the wrong words all the time.

The girls decided they had migraines and kept escaping to the sick bay. For some reason they got away with it, but if us boys said we had a headache Marshall's mates would jeer that we were soft. Or if we had garbled speech or saw flashing lights, it was because we were on drugs. It was just so unfair.

For two weeks we didn't even see Hekator or Hekati. Emma asked difficult questions when she came by and saw these piles of sawdust, stone and crushed cars, but we just acted like Dr Prosperov was up to some weird stuff which he'd probably get over. Emma never really bought these excuses but she didn't have any reason not to believe us. Dr Prosperov was always being weird around her so she wasn't sure what to believe.

School plodded on in its dull way. We had some storms which blew some of the stuff around and just as we began to feel better June arrived and everything became dead calm. Mariko announced that Aunty Nea was coming to help with Matariki which we would celebrate that weekend. I wondered if Aunty Nea would get to see anything of Hekator and Hekati.

Mariko seemed to have found the Fae very inspiring from

a design sense. She found all this interesting driftwood and started polishing it. She sent us out looking for sheep skulls and bones and Tarik actually found one although it was pretty stinky. Then she got to work with Gunter and Ken and built these things she called "beacons".

So on Saturday morning we got up at four to find a constellation of burning driftwood logs laid out in the same pattern as the Matariki stars on the drive outside the gallery. The fire smelt of kerosene but it had rocks in it that burned pretty blues or greens or oranges. In the middle was a big barbecue.

It was real cold so we all dressed warmly. Tama arrived with Fiona, Emma and Andrew. He pressed noses with Aunty Nea and Aunty Liz and shook hands with everyone else.

Aunty Nea, leaning on her stick, led the Maori prayers.

Maybe I'm biased but her clear, old voice calling out over the sea and the mountain, the quavering she added to the words and the dying fall as she let each breath go made my hair stand up. She was calling to the land and the sky, to the gods of sea and man, to bless our lands and make them fertile. She called on the dead to watch over the living and the living to watch over the dead. And she called on us to honour our ancestors and think of them. The power in her little frame was so strong it was hard to believe it.

Then we ate sweet potato and sausages – which were delicious but slightly out of place because they were one of Gunter's recipes made by Mr Trân.

The presences had been drawn by Aunty Nea's prayer. There were quite a few of them – a small crowd of a dozen or so soldiers hanging around outside the tall flaming beacons. Sergeant Aroha, the Maori ghost soldier and his men were

**43**

there too. They didn't do anything – they just seemed like they were waiting for something. Of course Emma and Andrew, like Rewa and Asal, couldn't see them but Mrs Jones, Aunty Nea and the rest of us kids, could. But as the eastern sky paled, and pinkened, the ghostly crowd began to melt away.

It was Mrs Jones who noticed it. Many of the ghosts were descending stairs outside the house into the ground! But there was no staircase there. I noticed Mrs Jones looking at them and I watched too, as did Ashley and Scotty. Then Emma joined in.

"What are we looking at?" she wanted to know.

"The light," Scotty lied.

And as the last of the presences descended the first gold broke over the bay and lit Renwick House. It didn't look amazingly special but it was a good enough excuse to keep Emma happy. The discovery was more interesting to Gunter. Long ago he had found what he'd assumed was a bricked-up well in the cellar. Now he wondered if it hid something else. So that day he, Ken and Bernard set to work digging out the sealed-in well.

I spent the day with Emma, Cam and Tarik exploring the caves. We had the whole thing pretty sorted now. We all had bike helmets with lights, walkie-talkies and loads of cheap reflectors to mark the way. We were also using ropes and poles to secure ourselves so we were getting pretty good at underground exploring.

But when we got back that evening we discovered the most interesting caving had been happening in our own home. The men had smashed their way through the well to discover what looked like an old sewer underneath. The tunnel was round and made of bricks tall enough for them to stand up in.

The tunnel to the east went down to the sea and was flooded

with seawater. It obviously served as a bit of a drain because there was a rusted old pipe in the middle of it. To the south they said the tunnel climbed and twisted upwards in wide staircases until it arrived at some fairly large underground storerooms. These too had tunnels which turned west. They'd followed one until they had arrived at a steel barrier set in concrete.

Dr Prosperov was very pleased, and as soon as darkness had fallen climbed the hill with Gunter to go tell Hekati. Tarik, Cam and me followed to see if we would be allowed to go in.

We stood outside the cave and called for Hekati. Quite soon a bright white-blue light appeared in the depths of the dark cave and bobbed its way toward us. The light dimmed as the black furred woman-shape got closer. Gunter told Hekati about the tunnels. Hekati smiled but said she had already discovered them and the cave she and Hekator shared were now linked to them.

"Come in and see if you like," she smiled. Dr Prosperov looked at Gunter, who shrugged, and followed after her.

"Can *we* come?" Tarik asked.

The two men looked at each other.

"Of course," Dr Prosperov's voice said from the darkness.

Hekati put out a lot more light going in than she did going out. The cave was narrow and twisty and there were some unexpected, and apparently, bottomless holes to get past. But slowly the cave became bigger, and less and less natural. The walls seemed to be covered in a coating that emitted a soft green light. The floor too became smoother and climbed until we came to a big door.

The door was simply a black and glassy rock that blocked the cave. As Hekati approached it her light dimmed to nothing, leaving us in total darkness for a second. Suddenly the door slid up into the roof and we were blinded by the warm, wet light that poured through the opening.

It took a while for our eyes to adjust. It was as bright as daylight! Then we went through the door that was as thick as I could reach.

The chamber inside was about as big as the Renwick ballroom. In the roof was a brilliant marble-sized "sun" set into a black mount which you could barely see because it seared your eyes. The air inside was warm and moist and the whole place was full of plants.

The floor and walls of the cavern were covered in a soft moss except where the tiny "sun" was. The plants included small palm trees, flowering bushes, and soft springy bushes that were like beds, sofas and chairs. Fantastic butterflies fluttered about and small metallic coloured green and purple flies whizzed around the flowers. It was like a very small paradise.

Hekati smiled at us.

"Do you like our room? It's taken a while to grow but it's finished now."

"It beautiful," Cam gasped. And she was right.

"Fantastic," Gunter added.

We were so fascinated we couldn't help staring.

"This is how we normally make our homes. It means all we need bring is a few seeds and a fusion reactor. Don't worry about the reactor by the way. It only emits radiation in the safer ranges of the spectrum and of course you are more resistant to radiation than we are anyway. Would you like to see the site?" she asked.

Dr Prosperov certainly did.

Hekati led us to another door which slid open as the previous one had. The tunnel was different to the cave. Its walls were black and shiny with luminous green moss on them. We walked for a short while until we came to a new door.

"Now I have to remind you this is a construction site. Keep inside the blue lines at all times or you will be recycled into the project."

I noticed she glanced at Dr Prosperov and Gunter. They moved so Gunter was behind Tarik, Dr Prosperov was behind me and Hekati ushered Cam before her. The door slid open.

The blue lines led into a dimly lit hall. We followed it in. The green light was coming from brightly lit moss. Then we noticed the black lines. Hekati lit up and we could see column after column of ants marching to the walls of the chamber. There was no noise except us our echoing footsteps and talking. It was kind of eerie. The walls were white but with lines of black ants climbing them.

"The ants are feeding the polyps which build the structural parts of the chamber."

"Vat is the material zhey are making?" Gunter wanted to know.

"It's a woven micromesh of carbon nanotubing. It's very strong and reliable. Nothing fancy but it works well in this situation where there's plenty of spare oxygen. Building in space is much more difficult."

"And zese creatures build all zis...?" Gunter began,

"By instinct," Hekati finished for him.

"It's fantastic."

"It's a lot easier than trying to build it yourself, that's for sure! Tarik watch your feet! Over that line and the ants will attack you."

Tarik had been fascinated but now jumped back. I noticed I was close to the edge myself.

"Let's go down and see the hatcheries and the fireworm. Follow me."

We followed Hekati into some more tunnels which would later become like a home to me and then came to the cathedral.

It was the same as the chamber but much larger and had its own tiny sun. You could see the structure built by ants in the corner. It was large for ants and there were streams of black lines coming and going from it like a heart pumping.

"The hatchery is the temporary nest with five clone queens all laying nonstop. The population is still low. Later on it will peak. The maintenance nest hasn't started yet but we'll probaby put it closer to the top of the hill so the population forages from nature not your home."

"Where do the polyps reproduce?" asked Gunter.

"Where they are. They're like coral but much faster and produce stronger material. They live and die in the structure. Let's go see the fireworm."

We went down further. The tunnel was bending around. The walls were shiny black without the green glowing moss on them. Only the bright blue lines underfoot gave us any light and not much to see with. Then we could see a yellow glow. Hekati led us forward. A weird tiny voice in my head said, "this is it. She's a devil. She's taking you to hell," but I knew that was stupid.

As we came to the corner the light got brighter. It wasn't the light like from the tiny sun, it was redder and much hotter. It took up the whole tunnel. We got to within thirty or forty meters of it where the blue line stopped and we could get no closer. The heat was fierce.

Ahead we could see the grub's tail. It was the size of the whole tunnel. It was bright red and covered in sticky goo that was cherry red.

"It's chewing its way toward the service tunnel you found. Then it will backtrack and tunnel to the lighthouse. It excretes glass to make the tunnel walls."

There was a jet of flame about five meters long from the rear. The already hot air got hotter.

"It vents gas from time to time. Just like us all," Hekati added.

There was a strong smell like hot pools and burning.

"But it smells worse," Hekati admitted, leading us back the way we came.

I was impressed – a creature that farted like a flamethrower. Hekati led us back the way we came until we got to the garden. Although there had been no noise in the whole construction site I found myself relieved to be away from it. Hekati bounced onto a couch bush and indicated we should do the same. The leaves were soft but the whole bush was springy and comfortable.

"So that's your base. Of course once the main structure is finished we can fit it out, but I think you should do that Gunter. It will make your people feel more relaxed if the furniture is familiar."

"Where's Hekator?" I asked.

"He's taken Sister Lana back to Fae. It's her first trip since her conversion. She's helping us with your equipment. We want to disguise everything so our involvement isn't too obvious."

The equipment was still a sore point because Dr Gursoy and Mr Trân hadn't given their permissions yet, so in theory Tarik and Cam wouldn't be using it. Dr Prosperov looked a bit uncomfortable.

"Is material in optimal position?" he asked.

"The sugar could be closer. If you opened a few barrels on the route that would increase the amount reaching the Polyps and that would increase production by about five percent per unit mass. Otherwise there is nothing much else that needs attention."

Hekati saw us to the door. Then she waved and a swarm of large insects with brightly lit bodies came and flew around us. The insects lit the way through the cave with their shimmering blue light dancing on the ground before us. They were very pretty. Like flying glow worms. I wished Emma could see them.

The insects followed us all the way down the hill and then abruptly turned and sped back to the cave. Dr Prosperov told everyone in the lounge what we'd seen. Everyone wanted to go and see but Dr Prosperov said we should take Hekati's warnings seriously and limit contact to avoid suspicion.

Nor was it long before the black columns appeared and began swarming all over the materials. Day and night, rain or shine they were there. They could even cut through the metal of the crushed car parts. To avoid suspicion we had to get Hekati to halt operations while we covered everything with big tarpaulins. Even then there were quite a few bites from the thousands of stragglers who were obviously confused. There were casualties too.

Tarik spotted the skeleton of a baby possum among a column. Even that vanished within an hour. Other animals, especially birds made the mistake of trying to eat the ants. The bright ones gave up real quick. The not so bright ones were eaten themselves. We couldn't help being fascinated by their unstoppability. Tarik even put some in a jar to take to school. But away from Renwick the ants were confused and when he let them escape near Mr Wakefield's desk they just wandered about randomly until they either got squashed under Mr Wakefield's shoes as he walked in front of the board or slipped away. Tarik's evil plan to send Mr Wakefield leaping and slapping himself from the room came to nothing.

It was amazing how fast the tarpaulins flattened. In less than three weeks the huge mounds of junk had vanished and the armies of ants with them. But now Hekator was back and the question marks hanging over Tarik, Ashley and Cam were becoming impossible to ignore.

The first parent to give in was Dr Gursoy. The pressure on him came not from Dr Prosperov or Dr Morozov but Tarik. He simply pointed out that all his father's work was part of a larger project and no matter how clever he had been, the project would not progress if Tarik's part didn't happen.

"You can't play half a game of chess," Tarik told his father. The Russians said nothing, but Tarik's quiet logic ate away at the foundations of Dr Gursoy's self assurance. He talked to Bernard and Soraya and finally agreed to the deal on the same terms as the others. He shook Tarik's hand and there was a solemn moment in the lounge one evening. Tarik translated what his father had said to him for Cam to see if it would help her.

"He said,'God alone knows what is in store for us. I would protect you from Satan himself were there a need but I cannot prevent you from growing up. There comes a time when I must trust you to use the judgement you have shown in arguing your case. Thus I consent but only if you make this promise:"

"Promise me this on the memory of your mother: that you will be open and honest with God from whom you can hide nothing; you will be open and honest with me from whom you can hide everything and, most important of all, that you will be open and honest with yourself from whom you can hide only by failing these first two duties."

Tarik promised.

The change of mind by Dr Gursoy brought new pressure on Mrs Robinson and Mr Trân. But where Tarik's success was quiet and methodical Ashley's was a battle of enormous emotions.

The fight had been brewing for two weeks and when it erupted it was like a bomb going off. Mrs Robinson roared, Ashley screamed. They would return to the States. Ashley would run away. They shouted arguments. They snarled insults. They called each other hard-out names. They dragged out history nobody wanted to hear. They slapped each other. It went on all over the house upstairs and down.

When anyone tried to say anything or offer a perspective they were angrily told to "butt out" or worse.

Finally after it looked like every accusation, every insult, and every threat that *could* have been made *had* been made, they collapsed into each others arms crying their eyes out. That took about an hour. Finally they started coming to an agreement and by the time everyone else had gone to bed they had decided to give it a try on the same basis as everyone else.

Mr Trân was a mixture of the two. He gave in to the inevitable quietly but instead of shaking Cam's hand he burst into tears and cried for two hours.

I think for one hour he cried with the grief he still felt for his lost wife and his fear of losing Cam. It was a voiceless cry that shook his whole body. I don't think he had ever done it before because he didn't seem able to stop.

But the next hour he cried in joy not pain. For everyone in the whole place rushed to hug him and promise to keep Cam safe. Even Dr Morozov. Even the men. He was a thin man so used to living on scraps of love and the leftovers of other's good fortune this show of affection from people he had mostly 'spoken' to only through his food completely overwhelmed him.

"My father says he has never had so many good friends," Cam translated one of his sobs.

Mr Trân wasn't the only one with wet eyes by the time it was clear Cam too would be allowed to join us. We were all so emotional it seemed we'd become a house full of cry-babies.

Not long after Hekati announced the completion of the base. That weekend she was ready to show us through. Mariko decided to turn it into a special event and Aunty Nea returned to say a blessing. Her only difficulty was the entry through the cellar but the men rigged up a seat to lower her with.

The base was very impressive. We walked up the shiny black tunnel lit by green glowing moss and blue lines on the floor following the old service tunnels. Then we came to the doors. They were recessed into rock so that the roof could be collapsed over the entry way if the base had to be sealed. The doors were huge black shiny slabs as thick as I could hold my arms wide but they slid silently open to reveal a dimly lit room big enough to take all of us quite easily. The light came from what looked like holes in the roof except they weren't. In the middle of the room was a podium on which stood a transparent image of Morganne. Morganne gave a little welcome speech on behalf of the Fae: "People of Earth today we break a three thousand year convention against giving advanced technology to other worlds with this small but we believe sufficient operations centre. With it and the other tools we provide you, you will be able to carry out interventions affecting the future of your world which some believe will have repercussions for the entire Galaxy."

**53**

I think we all realised then, from what Morganne had said, this meant that Lucky had convinced some Fae, but not everyone, and a small centre was as much as even Morganne could get from her government.

"It will be up to you to ensure that your actions are not detected by the Center. If they are, we cannot predict how they will react and we cannot protect you or your species from them if they believe there is a conspiracy between Earth and Fae."

"We are and have ever been good friends of Earth and we will monitor your progress closely. Where we can provide assistance that helps your mission and reduces your risks we will do our best to help. But all of this assistance is predicated on your loyalty to us. What we give we can also take back. Never forget this."

"Your task is, by any standards, a difficult one. There are more paths before your world now than any can truly know. The outcome of your mission may not be known for fifty or even a hundred years. Certainty will be elusive, you will never be truly sure that what you are doing is leading you on the path that will secure your world. But let me offer this advice."

"The right path is only visible to those who act selflessly in the defence or assistance of others. The right path is often the one least travelled. And the right path is more often than not the most difficult. Only by setting aside your self will you find the way and the fellow travellers you seek. I wish you well with the adventure before you."

Then she vanished.

We all looked at each other both a bit surprised and a bit worried by the distance in her words. We had not realised the Fae's support was not as strong as Dr Prosperov had suggested.

Then loudly and strongly Aunty Nea began to sing.

It was a short prayer blessing the meeting place but it lifted everyone's spirits and gave us a strong sense of unity and purpose. Even if the Fae were distant we were here, we were together, and we were determined. I realised how much I had come to know and rely on all these people, gathered from all over the world. We might not be the most powerful people in the galaxy but we knew who we were and we were determined for our world to survive and prosper.

After Aunty Nea, Hekati turned the platform Morganne had been standing on into a sculpture in light. She explained the structure of the main chamber was modelled on an upside-down sea snail's shell. The inside coiled down around a series of chambers at the centre of which was the fusion reactor, the dimensional vortex and the intelligence which ran it who she then introduced as 'Control'.

Control appeared on the platform. He was coffee coloured guy with deep brown eyes, black curly hair and stubble wearing a white puffy shirt, a long brown waistcoat, tight brown trousers and boots. All the girls and even the old women just loved *him*! Looking at their big eyes I don't think they heard a word he said. Even Rewa was doing it! But basically all he said to us was that he was there to look after us and make sure nobody came to harm.

The second set of doors opened. These were half the size of the previous doors. All that was in here was a passage leading left that had a bit of the old tarp we had used to cover the materials over it and a corridor that led around to a new room. The doors to this were even smaller and led into a picture theatre like room. Control reappeared and explained this was the briefing and supervision room where the parents would be able to see what we were doing. This was also linked to our network at Renwick house so they could watch us there too. The difference was the briefing room did 3D holograms.

The theatre lit up and the bay around Renwick at sunset appeared.

"I recorded this the other night so you could see how it looks," Hekati told us.

We were flying around over the bay with the image about six meters wide and three meters tall. I couldn't see that well but I noticed people shifting their weight on their feet as they 'flew'. It really was like being there.

Our next stop was the jumpstation. It was smaller still but brightly lit by what felt like daylight coming through the ceiling. Like the theatre it was on two levels. There was a consol desk and below it a jump chamber that looked like an empty swimming pool. The walls and floor showed a moving image of the surroundings outside Renwick so going down the steps into the jumpstation was like walking down the frontsteps outside Renwick.

The only controls on the consol were on two black glassy screens controlled by putting your hands on two black glass balls on either side of the screens. We weren't shown how they worked but we found we could move a blue line that bounced around the screens by putting our hands on the glass balls and concentrating on it.

"The jumpstation only works with the equipment Hekator is making the operatives. It folds them as four dimensional forms through a higher one dimensional carrier and back out again as four dimensional forms again. Your technology is about ten

centuries from achieving this but to us this is a bit like making
a sail on a boat. As you may have noticed Hekator and I can
do this without external machinery. We have it grown inside
ourselves. To give you some idea of how reliable and safe this
unit is, it was originally intended for one of our kindergartens,"
Hekati told us smiling.

We looked around but there was nothing to see.

"There is a one more thing, however," she said.

She led us out of the jumpstation back to the consol. She placed
her hands on the glass ball and after a moment a round section
of the ceiling began to protrude down. It was like a big short
bottle with a neck that remained above. It was six meters across
and fitted in the jumpstation perfectly. There was a door which
faced the stairs.

"This is a lifeboat. If you are discovered by the Center evacuate
to this lifeboat and Control will send it to Fae before firing
the self-destruction charges. Believe me you will not want the
Center to catch you. You can only use it once so make sure if you
have to use it you have everyone on it. We cannot rescue anyone
from the Center."

She put her hands back on the controls and the lifeboat raised
back into the ceiling again.

"Well my friends, my work here is finished," she said as she
walked down to the jumpstation. "It's been a month and now
I must return to my own world. But I must thank you for your
kindness. You have been much more welcoming than other
Earthlings I have met and I hope you find this little structure
helps you find what you are looking for. Hekator will be working
with you on the equipment and fit-out and he shall be returning
soon."

Dr Prosperov came forward.

"Thank you for your work, Hekati. Through it we hope that our children can join yours and others in a truly free and peaceful galactic civilisation."

Hekati gave a wave and then vanished into a small dark dot. There was a brief silence. We felt like children left without supervision in charge of a ship. There was a quiet pause as we all looked around. Then Mariko said.

"So do we party now or what?"

Everyone laughed and we walked back out to the ballroom where we'd left the food and drink. On the way I noticed Dr Prosperov draw Gunter aside and they chatted briefly.

That conversation led to the installation of the vault or panic room over the entrance to the tunnels. Gunter and Mariko cunningly camouflaged the entrance so that for the two weeks the security firm were building and installing the vault they had no idea there was another exit.

# CHAPTER THIRTY THREE: BIRTHDAYS

Unlike Christmas, Dr Prosperov showed no sign of making any special fuss about our birthdays. He seemed so distracted we weren't even sure if we were going to get a party. He was making a lot of phone calls and arranging flights both for himself and others. He was also putting pressure on Mrs Jones and Gunter to finish up the base and get the house ready for some new guests. They were going to arrive in mid-July after the school holidays.

The Fae had given us all some homework so we could understand them better. It was a set of beads on a string. If you held a bead long enough and just relaxed you began to have a strange kind of dream while you were awake. The beads were in a sequence like a story so you just went along the row of beads dreaming the story.

We learned that the Fae were one of ten civilisations that had grown up thousands of years before humans had got as far as making wheels. At this time they were called the Devi. They lived on a world similar to Earth and had a civilisation that was changing as they began to quickly adapt themselves. They were experts in bioengineering in particular. As they explored the Galaxy they met up with other civilisations.

The other civilisations included the small but clever Sverg who came from a larger, colder world than theirs and were smaller and heavier than humans. They were engineering geniuses who were experts in materials and robotics. The Sverg were already in contact with the Aesir and the Vanir, who were two civilisations that had met each other much earlier.

The Aesir and the Vanir were clever at politics and pointed to their own long peace as an example for the other civilisations to follow. They had already begun to work through such a process with the tall Jotnar who were looking for technological help in exchange for joining forces.

The Earth – which they called the Mid-world, because it was midway between the Devi and the Aesir and Venir – began as a project to speed up the civilisation of a primitive species. The project started with high hopes but it was not long before big attitude differences between the two civilisations began to appear.

The Devi were big on religious practices designed to improve mental ability and careful use of natural resources. The Aesir were heavily into competition. Both thought their own way would stimulate human development. The Aesir also put their own DNA into some humans to create a new hybrid race, the Watchers, the Iyrin, who would watch over primitive human civilisations and help humankind develop. At first the contest between the two civilisations were just to prove whose philosophy was better but slowly it became more and more bitter because the Aesir encouraged their humans tribes to conquer the Devis' humans. The war on Earth between primitive peoples with bows and arrows began to grow into a potential space war between the Devi and the Aesir-Venir.

The Sverg were disgusted with both sides and insisted that

they act like civilised people. The result was the Treaty on Undeveloped Civilisations which agreed to never to intervene in civilisations not capable of making their own contact with the space-capable civilisations. It allowed scientific research but not giving primitive civilisations technology for anything but medicine or education and then only if it was done secretly. No space civilisation was allowed to get involved in primitive politics or changing the DNA of primitive people. It did allow secret interventions to prevent primitive worlds from destroying themselves as had occurred before.

The Treaty on Undeveloped Civilisations led to the establishment of the Galactic Center on a new life-sustaining planet. The Sverg were early supporters of the Galactic Center and helped to build its systems. The Aesir-Venir, Jotnar and Devi all joined forces to create a galactic government at the Center.

But slowly over the centuries the Center changed. At first it was simply to make sure the worlds didn't fight. But slowly, it began to take more and more of a controlling role in the civilisations which had joined it. The idea of a global civilisation which was a mixture of all the civilisations started with the Aesir and Venir. At first there was support for a global civilisation but as the Center became more and more dominating and its use of synthetic beings increased more and more, people began to find the Center a bit sus'.

The Devi began to withhold technology and not meet deadlines for agreeing to Center demands. The Sverg became worried that the Aesir were putting too much emphasis on using synthetics at the Center as a way of increase their control of it. The Devi and the Sverg believed that the technology was beginning to take over on its own.

As the Devi ignored the Center, the Center's demands became louder. The result was another war. The Devi had expected a Synthetic attack but not its viciousness. They escaped to a new world called Fae they had settled in secret. The Sverg were split. Some sided with the Center, some with the Fae. The Center declared that those Sverg who did not move to the Center would be treated as enemies. Many did, but even more said it was their right to remain on their home world. A few joined the Devi on Fae but to the Sverg's shock the Center sent a fleet to destroy their planet. There was a huge fight and eventually the synthetics destroyed the people who created them.

Now the Center became dominated by the synthetics and their creed of enforced unity. The Aesir, Sverg, Jotnar and Venir were given places within the Administration of the Center but true power remained with the synthetics.

This also meant the Center was full of secret factions. All wanted to replace the synthetics but the synthetics cleverly used each challenger against the other. Many non-synthetics left the Center to settle on primitive worlds but they still remained under the control of Center Administrators.

On Earth the Center established a research post in terms of the original treaty. It monitored human development for centuries. The Fae also visited in secret, partly for their own entertainment, and partly for research, and to ensure that the terms of the original treaty had been kept. By and large they had.

I don't know if it was because I wasn't used to the way the beads worked or what, but I found it hard to take it in. Cam said if you really concentrated you got more and more detail. Tarik thought

there must be whole encyclopaedias inside the little beads.
But to be honest I didn't really care too much what a bunch of
old space guys had done thousands of years ago. It seemed like
just another dumb movie to me. I was more interested in things
that were a bit closer to home. Things like our birthdays that
were coming up soon.

In mid-June we had a meeting on the bus. The big questions
were whether we would buy presents for each other separately,
together, or not at all; and whether we going to have a party?
I wanted to have a party because I wanted to invite Emma. That
way she would know I wasn't interested in Tahira. The others
ranged in opinions. Ashley also wanted a party simply because
she liked parties. Tahira wanted to invite her girlfriends so
she was up for it too. Tarik could take it or leave it but thought
having a cool Mariko designed party would be a great way to get
one over Marshall. He also calculated you got more presents that
way. Scotty and Cam saw it as a lot of cleaning up and weren't so
keen.

So we finally agreed to have one and ask Mariko to help us with
it. Mariko loved any excuse for a party. But, to our surprise, she
said she would see what she could do but was a bit busy. She
said she'd heard there was a plan to take us to Auckland for a
party at Rainbow's End. That was OK but it seemed a bit of an
afterthought.

As for the presents we decided to pool our money again and
buy each other one big present rather than give each other five
smaller ones. It was cheaper and easier that way.

At school the bad weather meant we spent a lot of time inside
now. We could cope with that but Marshall, Paul Smith, Randall
Johns and Roland Soper got restless. They started games of

indoor baseball with screwed up paper for a ball and cardboard paper roll cores for bats. It was a small classroom and the "balls" were always whizzing through it followed by the players chasing the ball and barging around touching the bases. The balls seemed to have a special attraction for Tarik's chessmen.

Tarik and Harry Yee played some very intense chess games and were about as good as each other. I played the atlas game with Scotty, Ashley and Cam finding more and more obscure parts of the world to challenge each other with. We'd got to the point where we didn't even tell each other what page a place was on anymore. Some other kids tried to join in but they soon got discouraged. Playing a guessing game with psychics was never going to be exactly fair anyway. The spooky way we guessed what they were thinking just made them even more shy of us. Me and Emma were friendly but much more distant than we had been over summer. She, Charli and Melissa spent a lot of time with Stacey Graham chatting about horses and vampires in books.

Charli still liked Scotty but Ashley always made a point of showing up when they were together. Tarik on the other hand had bored Melissa and she avoided him. Cam was sarcastic about Tarik following her about and he gave up.

After the way Tabika had kept Tahira and me exhausted all the time I knew Emma suspected we had been up to something together. She seemed a bit disappointed with me. I sometimes caught her watching me but she'd always look away pointedly. Tahira herself, of course, showed no interest in me at all and never had. She had a clique going with Wendy Brown, Clare Yates and Jenny Fenton. They spent their time giving each other makeovers, rearranging their hair and talking about fashion.

In school we'd moved from water to pollution. We had to write about different kinds of pollution and find or draw pictures. None of us Kiwi kids had much idea about pollution. Scotty had never seen any either. Dried up waterholes didn't really count. But Tahira, Ashley and Tarik had no problems thinking of examples of pollution from the oil industry and could show off in front of the rest of the class.

Not that anyone really cared. The whole class was just staggering toward the end of term holidays that were to start a week after our birthdays, now just a week away. We all just wanted a break. The weekend meant we got to go into Auckland for another shopping trip. Ken took us in the Range Rover because everyone else was too busy.

After half a year's cleaning work, and nowhere to spend our wages on the island, we all had quite a lot of money now. We'd all put up a hundred bucks for each other's present so that gave us $600 each. It was more money than any of us had ever had, or spent on ourselves and we were going to go bananas.

Ken organised us to do our shopping in two waves. First we went through the whole place very fast checking out all the stuff we might want. Then we would go back in teams and buy it.

We looked at bikes and phones but Renwick had no cell coverage and the steep tracks and gravel roads weren't going to be much fun on a bike. We looked at snow boards but none of us had ever been on snowboards or skis and there was no chance of us getting to a mountain any time soon. Skakeboards and roller blades were hopeless for the same reason as the bikes. Tahira and Ashley were drawn to cosmetics and jewelry which there was heaps of. We all tried on some expensive shades.

Tarik was excited by the Nintendo Wii. But with the ballroom available for table tennis or volleyball, or whatever, I couldn't see the point. Cam liked the bookshop. There were some recipe books she liked and some big thick books with beautiful pictures. Scotty was more interested in getting some better shoes and clothes than anything else. In fact the more we looked the less we could find.

I remembered what Aunty Liz had said at Christmas when we'd had less to spend and now it seemed I was experiencing it myself. The only stuff I liked were some shoes, shades and some clothes that looked a bit cooler than my usual bargain bin look. About lunchtime we went to the food area and had to make some lists for the others. Then we made six stacks of gift cards, and divided into our teams with two names to buy for. I got Tarik and Tahira got Ashley. We split up with Ken telling us to meet back up in the same place again in two hours.

I got Tarik his Wii, and Tahira got Ashley some jewellery, perfume and some red boots to match her jacket. For some reason we all came home scratchy with each other and everyone went to their own apartments. I think we all felt a bit put out because nobody else seemed to be making a fuss of us.

There was something else gnawing at us too. This story about the shamans that Dr Prosperov had accidentally killed and us being their reincarnations. It made us feel like we were retreads. Like we were meant to be someone other than who we were. I had searched my feelings, I had talked to Ken and even Nergui, and I simply could not feel anything about being Mongolian anywhere in my heart or mind. Everything I knew, felt close to, or understood was Maori.

The next Sunday morning we were talking about it again in the Cafe. Cam was trying to explain how Buddhists view reincarnation but she was a bit vague and Tarik was asking annoying questions and being a prick. The whole idea just seemed irritating. Mrs Jones came in to order us off to work and overheard us.

"Children I think you've got this reincarnation thing terribly confused," she said sitting down with us in a bustly sort of way. We didn't really want to listen but Tarik winked and said "Why's that then Mrs Jones?"

So we looked at her with faked interest hoping to keep her talking and delay the cleaning work. She probably noticed Tarik being cheeky but she couldn't help herself.

"When we talk about reincarnation we don't mean your personality, my dears. Your personality comes with your body, your brain and your memories of the place and time you are born into. If your body or brain is damaged your personality changes too. It is part of this world and develops through your lifetime of experience. Your personality can't survive death," she said certainly.

There was something about that word death that kept our attention.

"What about the ghosts?" Tarik objected.

"Ghosts are unusual. They don't survive death. They avoid completing it. They hold back. They cling to memories of a persona but they gradually go mad because their capability for memory is poor. They are very unhappy souls and the kindest thing would be to release them, but of course they resist that."

"Couldn't you release them anyways?" Ashley asked.

"Yes, you could. But it's better if they do it. Ghosts fight back hard because they are often fighting for justice. And ghosts can do a lot of damage if they are forced to fight. You saw what

**67**

they did at Christmas. I have seen them kill. More important opposing justice isn't something we should do, when only we sensitive ones can hear what the last witnesses can say."

"But how do they ... exist?" asked Scotty.

"That, I do not know. Dr Prosperov has some theories but I don't pretend to understand them. All I know is what I feel, see and hear. They exist. Somehow their memory is engraved in a place. How, I don't know. But I do know they are rare. Most people go on. Most personalities are extinguished."

"So what's left to be reincarnated?" Tarik asked doubtfully.

"Logically nothing." he concluded.

"What gets reincarnated is what you don't know about yourself that is growing and developing over numerous lives. That's why the same soul switches from male to female and all around."

We looked at each other. She could tell from the blank looks on our faces we didn't understand.

"So what one doesn't know about oneself is who we are."

We must have looked a bit disbelieving about that. Tarik was grinning like he thought Mrs Jones was gaga.

"Tarik. Who are you?"

Tarik looked as if it was a stupid question.

"I'm me, ain't I? I'm Tarik Gursoy."

"Who is Tarik Gursoy?" she persisted.

"I am," he insisted.

"Who is this 'I'?" she asked.

I started to see what she was getting at.

"Take away your names, take away your memories, take away even the little chats you have with yourselves in your heads, who is it that experiences being alive? That is the unknowable self."

"Ain't that the subconscious?" asked Ashley doubtfully.

**68**

"No, the subconsciousness is the machinery of the brain we don't need to be conscious of. When we are small we have to think about walking, for example, but as we practice we no longer need to be conscious of walking, we just do it. What I am talking about is the fundamental perspective of being conscious at all. Not a clever robot made of flesh, but a being which understands its place in the world and can change it by choosing. That is not something a robot can do. I am talking about the window which looks at the Universe from its own perspective as we all do. The window is the self and is unknowable to itself."

"How do you know this self is unknowable as opposed to just plain unknown?" Tarik argued.

Mrs Jones shrugged. "It's a window trying to look at itself. It's simply impossible. We seek mirrors and only find other people, other windows. I have concluded the window of being feeds into a continuum of consciousness that has only a very slight overlap with this dimension. A point of light at the head of a long line of continuous experience as it were."

"So what does that mean for us Mrs Jones?" Ashley wanted to know, as ever getting down to the main point.

"It means who you were, or who others like Dr Prosperov or Nergui thought you were once, doesn't matter. You aren't those people in this world anymore. None of you are Mongolians like Ken or Negui. You may have experienced being Mongolians once, but you all might just as easily have experienced being Kurds, or Persians or Vietnamese before that. None of that matters to your essential unknowable selves."

"If these selves is so unknowable why they matter? They may as well not exist?" Tarik asked.

"Yes it's easy for people to think so but then you would be a robot. There would be no point to your existence except that given by orders. The unknowable self is that point where we give ourselves meaning and over many lifelines becomes a thread where dimensions of existing and meaning overlap. Changing the future by working with these threads of destiny is what the Fae call weaving. It is very subtle and very complex. But from a practical point of view it means the six of you are woven around each other and always end up together one way or another."

We looked at each other. We had always felt familiar with one another even when we first met. But Mrs Jones was still talking.

"You have a connection that is very strong and very deep. You may fall out, you may marry one another ..."

We looked at each other a bit embarrassed. I had already suspected Ashley and Scotty would get married and maybe Cam and Tarik but not me and Tahira. We were friends but there was nothing else there.

"... But the important thing is you are connected in a way that means you will always find each other again across lives even if you don't recognise each other. The six of you follow the same path."

It was a funny feeling. Like we were bound in some way. Almost like being family. Mrs Jones stood up.

"You should consider yourselves lucky. Many people never find their soul-mates from one lifetime to the next. Your connection is so deep it comes out even when you're spread all over the planet."

"But Lucky found us and brought us together didn't he?" Scotty objected.

"But why dear? Even Lucky was driven to that. This is what the

Fae mean by deep weaving. The shaping of convergences and coincidences. Even Lucky is part of something greater. Now, while this discussion is an important part of your education I'm afraid we still have work to do," Mrs Jones said firmly and we were packed off to do our cleaning.

Later we talked about what Mrs Jones had said. Tarik said as an Alevi and Muslim he couldn't believe in reincarnation.

"She doesn't know. Who is she anyway? What do the Fae know? I don't care what planet anyone comes from. Nobody alive can know about death. The only evidence we have is what God told us in the words of the Prophet."

Cam started to argue and they bickered away about Buddhism versus Islam. Personally I didn't think it was worth arguing about. I was in no rush to find out for sure, and it seemed to me that no matter what you had read or seen or how hard you believed what you believed there was always a chance you were wrong. Everyone was in the same boat and not many people were crazy enough to find out the hard way.

More important was the knowledge that Dr Prosperov didn't expect us to act like a bunch of Mongols we had no feelings for. Tarik was right. Such things might matter to old people like Mrs Jones and Dr P but as far as we were concerned they may as well not exist. Somehow that made us feel better. Freer somehow.

School that week was like it was in extra slow motion. The second hand on the clock seemed to take twice as long as normal to tick. We still felt a bit pissed off that nobody seemed interested in our birthdays which were spread over the middle of the week. Aunty Liz seemed vague and even Rewa was disappointed for me.

Mariko helped us wrap our presents to each other the night

before our birthdays began. But she seemed distracted and
rushed and we went to bed feeling thoroughly unwanted and
pissed off.

I'd secretly hoped there was going to be a surprise the morning
I turned thirteen but I awoke to disappointment. Aunty Liz said
we might have a birthday dinner but it was still a school day and
I was late. So me and Cam (who turned thirteen on the same
day) got nothing special for breakfast, although breakfast was a
pretty delicious omelette so I couldn't really complain.

I wanted to complain. Here I was turning thirteen and nobody
cared. I felt a bit grumpy about it all day. But when we got back
that night I had a huge surprise.

Grandpop was waiting for us with Aunty Liz outside! Rewa
screamed and ran off the bus leaping into his arms. Everyone
else looked on with surprised smiles as they went inside.

Grandpop gave Rewa an enormous cuddle as I came up.

"Grandpop I've missed you so much!" she cried.

I felt a bit shy as he doted on Rewa but then he stood up and
came up to me, offering his hand. I went to shake it but he
pulled me into a full hug which I returned.

"Happy birthday boy," he said.

But there was even better news.

"Dr Prosperov has hired Grandpop too!" Aunty Liz told me.
"He's moved in down the hall."

That was better than any birthday present I had ever expected.
Rewa and I whooped and yeehahed until Aunty Liz told us to
shut up. Grandpop just laughed.

It turned out they had been planning this for over two months.
Grandpop had been moving stuff out of his house quietly and
moving it to different places around Auckland. Then he had

followed and today both he and his stuff had rolled on to the
ferry in a rented truck and he had shifted in while we were at
school.

We went upstairs to his apartment. It was strange combination
of back home and Renwick house. He had his pictures of mum
and Nana, his old armchairs and some of his stuff from Vietnam
and home. It was kinda weird. I couldn't get used to it.

Aunt Liz left us with him for a moment when Mrs Jones came
by. In the quiet of his room I asked him the big question.

"Has Dr Prosperov told you about this place Grandpop?"

"What you mean Hekator and Hekati and the secret base?"
Grandpop asked.

"Yeah," I said, shocked that someone who hadn't seen their
arrival knew about a secret so huge I sometimes couldn't believe
I kept it in my head. He smiled at my surprised expression.

"Gennady called me two months ago and asked me to come
join the operation. But when he told me what it was all about I
thought the guy was completely cracked. I honestly started to
worry about you guys being here alone with him."

"Then he called again and asked me to meet some people on a
beach at midnight. I thought it would be Ken with the chopper
again. So I waited on the beach at the coordinates he gave me in
the full moon listening out for a chopper when flash! Hekator
and Hekati appear out of nowhere!" He stopped, remembering
then he chuckled.

"Man, I thought someone in Ax's gang had slipped me drugs eh?
I thought I was losing it," he said shaking his head.

"But they were good. They talked about you two. They acted
normal. And when they let me move again I ... I got over ... well,
I listened. They showed me what they had done and could do.

But they said they needed someone with my experience to help you."

"The next day Gennady called me again and offered me a consultancy job. I ... Well ... I wasn't making enough money, the pension's bloody hopeless ... I missed you guys ... and it sounded like they really needed me. So I agreed."

He shrugged.

"And here I am."

Rewa hugged Grandpop. "I'm glad you're here Grandpop."

"I am too, princess," he said hugging her.

"It's an amazing set up they have down there eh?" he said to me trying not to let his eyes water too much.

"Yeah," I smiled. I didn't care that my eyes were wet too.

Aunt Liz came in and told me to get started on my homework. So I went downstairs leaving Grandpop with Rewa. I just felt like a new person. I hadn't realised how much I'd missed him. Having him come and live with us just made me feel healed inside.

I went into the café to join the others with homework and snacks. Scotty couldn't help noticing my change of mood.

"Feels lekker, isn't it?" he smiled.

I remembered how he was when his mum arrived.

"Did you know?" I asked.

"Don't worry mate, nobody tells me a bloody thing either," he grinned.

## CHAPTER THIRTY FOUR: SUITS

Homework took half an hour and then we were packed off to clean at four. At five Mrs Jones came around and told us to meet Gunter and Mariko in the cellar. Tahira and I immediately knew this had something to do with the secret base.

Something had changed.

We went downstairs and found Gunter, Mariko and all the others waiting for us.

"OK, now zis iz an 'Istorical moment," Gunter told us in the dark of the empty vault.

"For zer first time in yuman history a bunch of kids have been given birthday gifts by the government of another planet," he smiled.

We looked at each other. It sounded crazy.

"No joke! Kom with us. You 'av to try zem on."

We went down the stairs and along the tunnels into the base. It still seemed new and a bit scary to us then. Then Mariko called out.

"Girls come with me. The boys have to change with Gunter."

The girls went off, a bit uncertainly, with Mariko.

We were led into a small room which looked like what it was: a changing room. Along the wall were three alcoves to hang clothes and below that a large drawer each.

"Okay guyz," Gunter began in his deep Germanic drone, "to vear zese suits you haf to strip off completely."

That explained why the girls had gone with Mariko – although to be completely honest I wasn't looking forward to stripping in front of Tarik and Scotty. I didn't need all that comparing. Tarik was already tugging at his top.

"But before we start," Gunter paused, so that Tarik stopped, "let me explain what you do next."

He opened what we had assumed were drawers. They were very large drawers. Big enough to get into. The inside was lined with something that looked disgustingly like liver.

"Ze idea is you lie in here, and pull ze drawer closed. If you don't close it completely, nuzzink happens. Zen lie flat. Ze biological machine vill dress you from za vaist down. During zis time you will be temporarily paralysed. Don't vorry it vears off instantly. I vas also reminded to varn you about somezing. Ze suit is designed to handle bodily vaste so obviously it vill attach itself to vere zat comes from, like your … vell … you get vat I mean. After it's dressed your lower half ze drawer slides through and stands you up on za ozzer side, zen it dresses your top half. Anozzer varning: because zis is your first time, it vill perform some minor surgery on you, even zough you von't feel it. Zis is for ze control interface and za air supply. Ven za whole process is complete you vill be dressed and enter za briefing room. Any questions?"

"How do we get out of it again?" I wanted to know, feeling claustrophobic already.

"Same in reverse."

I noticed the other two looked about as enthusiastic as I felt – which was not very much at all.

"OK guyz. I'll see you around the ozzer side. By ze vay, I bet

Mariko ze boys vould be faster zan ze girls and I don't vant to lose. So I vill double your veekly pay if you beat zem," he said going to the exit.

"Whatchoo bet, mate?" Tarik asked quickly.

Gunter paused and smiled, "don't ask," he said and left.

We looked at each other. That was a lot of money.

"Let's do it!" Tarik yelled.

We stripped and leapt into those drawers before there was time to even glance at each other.

Despite its squishy appearance the inside was more like a sponge. It was damp but not gooey. The drawer was warm so pulling it closed didn't seem so bad.

The drawer had barely clicked closed when a red light appeared right in front of my eyes. It was very close and seemed very bright. Then it began to blink slowly at first and then very fast and then slowly in time with a slow heartbeat. Meanwhile the surface I was lying on began to feel warm and a bit wet and slippery and suddenly I could feel it folding around my legs and closing around my waist. I realised at this point I couldn't move. It didn't freak me because the light seemed comforting somehow.

The closing around my feet would have felt great as it oozed between my toes and around my ankles if something hadn't goosed me at exactly the same time. That felt really gross, as it did when it attached itself to my penis. I couldn't help thinking the girls would have it worse. Still, as it slid me through the tunnel, I lost all sense of those parts of me and I just felt warm and comfortable from the waist down.

Then the drawer pivoted and I was standing up. I still couldn't move but the red light was still in my face. Something warm stuck itself to my spine and began to wrap itself around my stomach and chest. Then something took my limp arms and wrapped itself around them all the way to the wrist. My hands felt like they were dipped in warm water and then wrapped except for the fingers which just felt slightly numb.

It was at this point things got a bit hairy. First I felt a distinct shock to my throat, followed by something grabbing me around the neck and tilting back my head so I couldn't see the red light. Then something clamped around my head as well. It didn't hurt, but it didn't feel so great either. I was held in this position for quite some time with a slight smell of burning which I tried not to panic about.

"Not long guyz," Gunter's deep voice said quietly.

I tried to relax and think about something else. Then, finally, the wrapping started around my throat and neck and I felt something fold loosely over my head.

Suddenly the dark seemed to split open and I realised I was falling and stood to prevent myself hitting the floor. I felt like I was wrapped like an Egyptian mummy in a way I had never felt before. Usually you can feel clothes separate from your body. But whatever I was wearing now just felt like a thick but insensitive layer of skin or blubber about a fingerwidth thick. But the weirdest thing about it was that it felt almost part of me and almost alive, like it was wearing me almost as much as I was wearing it. I had to fight down the desire to claw it off me.

I stepped out of the booth and found myself in a dark room at exactly the same time as the others.

The room looked like the back of a small cinema except that we were standing in front of six black shower booths. Gunter and Mariko were in a small circular control desk wearing earpieces sitting on ordinary wheeled chairs looking at us.

I was on the end, so next to me was Scotty. I was totally astonished to find he looked normal. Completely normal.

He was wearing trainers, jeans, a blue hoody and a big school bag. The only unusual bit was the fingerless gloves. His hands looked just a little bigger than usual. He was looking at Tarik and turned to look at me. We were both as astonished as each other.

I looked at myself. The hoody I was wearing was green and I had jeans and trainers too. But it didn't feel anything like what it looked like.

"Dead heat," Gunter said dryly as Mariko burst into giggles.

We realised we'd been tricked. The system had worked at the same rate on all of us. The only possible result was a dead heat. The only way it wouldn't have worked out that way was if someone had freaked about getting into the drawer and the trick they'd pulled to get us in had worked. Mariko and Gunter high-fived each other smiling.

*"Sneaky shits."*

The surprise was that it was Cam who thought it, but we all 'heard' it.

*"Cam!"* more than one of us 'replied'.

She laughed.

We were moving from a line to a circle looking at each other. We were all dressed the same except our hoodies were different colours. Tarik's was red, Cam's was gray, Ashley's was yellow and Tahira's was pink.

*"I'll have to watch what I think now,"* Cam 'said'.

*"We all will,"* more than one of us responded.

"What are you doing?" Mariko asked suspiciously.

"*She can't hear us,*" Tahira 'said'.

"*They're behind you, Sam and Cam,*" Tarik added.

"*What we need is something to squirt them with,*" Scotty said. He was thinking of a water blaster. But the idea created a weird storm of ideas in my mind. Options I couldn't understand flicked through my consciousness. I put my hands to my head. We all did.

"Guys?" Gunter asked with a worried inflection, "are you OK?" The storm passed. I turned.

"Just finding all this a bit freaky," I told them.

"Well, you better come and meet the designers so they can tell you how to work it," Mariko told us.

We came forward and found there were a bunch of comfy sofas arranged in two levels just like a cinema. There were more places than we needed. We tried to take off our schoolbags but realised somehow they were a part of the suit and couldn't be taken off, so we had to sit forward on the sofas. The stage was not deep but it was dark. Suddenly Lana Vilenskaya appeared fading in from partial transparency.

"Hi guys," she greeted us.

She looked completely solid wearing a sleeveless summer dress. I knew she wasn't really there but I couldn't say how I knew. Then Hekator appeared in the same way. He was wearing a green metallic cloak and a big belt which divided his goat bottom half from his human top half.

"Children of Earth!" he greeted us happily, his orange eyes sparkling. He spoke English and the ideas entered our heads.

"I see the suits we've made you fit. I didn't think you would have any problems with them but there is nothing like the actuality to finally set one's mind finally at rest," he said.

**80**

"I am here to tell you a little about your suits before you go up and show them to your caregivers. Lana will then tell you a bit about her design and how it is intended to be worn among your peoples."

"So let's start with the most important thing," Hekator said. "These suits are what our children wear when they are outside their eggs."

As with Tabika, the concept of "egg" seemed to involve education and development.

"Your suits are not clothes as you are used to. They're living beings in their own right. When you aren't wearing them they are maintained in special nutrient tanks but they are currently adapting to your bodies and will become highly attuned to them. In time your suits will feel almost exactly like your own bodies and you will be able to wear them almost indefinitely."

"One of their main features is the way they digest and recycle your excretions. Hair, skin particles, sweat, urine, menstrual fluids and faeces are digested by the suit and fed into the energy and hydration systems. The suits will even dissolve parasites and treat skin abrasions or irritations."

"*Eeewwwwww*," Ashley thought. I couldn't help agreeing. It sounded gross. We thought he couldn't 'hear' us like Gunter and Mariko. We were wrong.

"Yes Ashley, at the moment you may think so but you will come to see the benefits when you have to use them."

"*Dude can listen in!*" Tarik warned us unnecessarily. Hekator glanced at him, but said nothing.

"This brings me to the interface. The suit has a nervous system and processing systems spread throughout it. It is connected directly to your central nervous system and in time you will find that things that take concentration to begin with become effortless as your nervous systems discover one another."

"Now what does the suit add to your body? Essentially strength and protection. The most important protection is its ability to blend into any surroundings. Maybe Lana you should explain, as you designed it."

Lana smiled.

"Well, I didn't design it. I just adapted it for Earth. So, I hope you like the initial colours we picked for you," she said," but you'll be pleased to know that if you don't, it doesn't matter. The suit's skin can change, not only colour and pattern, but also texture. We've preloaded a library of different styles for different kinds of clothing from around Earth. For example your suits can look like standard summer jeans and hoodie or they can puff up to look like winter-weight down. They can even change length slightly so that the outfit blends into tropical or desert environments."

"Of course the whole suit can also move into adaptive camouflage mode. This is where the suit blends into the environment to make you practically invisible at distances over fifty meters in the open or five meters or less against any background. Importantly you will not emit any thermal signature except around your face while it isn't covered. Any questions?"

"So we can change colours?" Ashley asked.

"Yes, in fact if you saw another outfit you liked which had a head covering all you would need to do is tell the suit what you want to copy and it will change for you. It will take a bit of practice though."

"Could it do fur?" asked Scotty

"Short fur or hair like horse or dog hair, yes."

"What about human hair?" asked Tahira.

"Yes, some styles. It does negroid hair well because it's frizzy and keeps its shape. It does short hair and a cap or turban for boys or a longish straight hair with a scarf that girls tend to wear in southern Asia. But many of the hairstyles will look odd to anyone standing close by – like on a train for any length of time. The surface is actually made of very thin fibres about two centimeters long which knit themselves and change colour. So no fibres can actually be very long although they might look it," she said.

There was a pause which Hekator stepped in to fill.

"The suit will increase your physical strength to that of a very strong adult. It will also protect you from both the sharp impact pressures and heavy pressure, such as underwater. Below the appearance layer the suit is a combination of diamond-mesh and carbon-polymer micro-assemblies that are both power and computing channels as well as providing strength to the structure. That said while the organic interface layer with your skin is slight padding, you will feel impacts and your suit won't stop you being hurt if you hit anything, or anything hits you hard enough."

Lana interrupted.

"Worst case, if you were hit by a pistol bullet there would be no penetration but a lot of bruising and broken bones. A car will still do you a lot of damage even at low speed and kill you at high speed. A rifle bullet will tear the diamond mesh and compromise the whole system. I should add, however, your back is much better protected than your front, so if you have any doubt, run away. But, as always, the best way to avoid injury is to not get

**83**

attacked in the first place."

Hekator nodded and took over again.

"Your legs and arms will be three hundred percent stronger wearing the suit and your weight is increased by only twenty percent so you should all be able to run, jump and climb faster and higher than before. Now if you hold up your hands like this…"

He held his hands up "… try and extend your climbing claws."

I looked at my hand and thought 'claws' and suddenly claws, like a cat's claws, extended from my hand at the base of each finger covered by what looked like fingerless gloves. They were short, hooked, and translucent like nails. I touched the point with my fingertip. It was strange, my finger was encased in a thick skin which looked exactly like my real skin, and while I could feel the sharpness of the claw tip, it felt like my fingers were slightly numb."

"And if you focus on retracting them," Hekator suggested.

I did, and they retracted.

"The claws are for climbing. You'll find you have more on your feet. The suit also re-forms to provide flippers on your feet and fingers for swimming. The exoskeleton provided by the skin and the back support will assist you to lift or hold heavier weights than you are used to. When swimming a whole body motion will be much more powerful than normal human styles and you should be as fast as a seal your size."

"Another trick with your hands is to retract them into the sleeves. Think 'retract'."

I held my hands up and thought, "retract". The sleeves lengthened over my hands and closed up.

"You will need that in high pressure or high temperature

environments. Your hands are insulated against very low temperatures but not against temperatures like inside an oven or under deep water. The suit will automatically retract them to protect itself and will not let you open them," he told us.

"You will also find that your hoods seal themselves so you can go underwater like this."

A head and shoulders of a hoody appeared in mid-air. Then a clear film like a bubble appeared from the top as if it was being zipped closed.

"Cool! A forcefield," said Tarik.

Hekator looked at Lana, confused.

"Sorry Tarik," Lana replied. "There are a lot of cool technologies in the galaxy but the idea of a forcefield is a bit like artificial gravity floors in spaceships. Nothing more than a TV invention to allow the staging of stories in space without having to worry about actual physics. 'Force fields' are the same. Real plasma fields aren't like glass they are brilliant like the sun. Your facescreen is made of a thick transparent biopolymer that goes rigid with a hormone. The seam is bonded at molecular levels through the release of another hormone. It unbinds again much faster. After two minutes the seal will withstand pressures down to 150 meters underwater which is about as deep as you would want to go when breathing air."

She looked at Hekator.

"So try it," Hekator suggested. "Think close up."

I hesitated thinking about the danger of putting your head in a plastic bag.

"I should explain that your suit has a supply of breathable gases in your backpack so that you can keep your facescreen down for up to four hours. So Sam, don't worry, you won't suffocate. Just

**85**

relax and think 'close up'."

I took a deep breath and thought it. The reality surprised me a little with it's speed. The screen zipped down in about three seconds. I was a bit surprised everything wasn't as blurry as I expected either. It should have been like looking through a clear plastic half-dome, but it wasn't.

"You will notice your vision is relatively clear. It will improve. This is because the suit has eyes and ears which are now linked into your brains through the new nerves we've grown in your necks. You may recall a few months ago having headaches. This was when your brains were growing a few extra abilities. One of them was the ability to connect to these suits. They aren't working perfectly yet. You are partly seeing through your own eyes and partly through the suits. The suit's eyes are located in the shoulder straps of your fake schoolbag. If you cover these you will discover your vision gets a lot worse."

I did. Everything looked blurry like it was inside a plastic bubble.

"The eyes in your suit can see heat like an owl and ultraviolet like a bee. The suit will make things you can't normally see clear to you. The suit also has ears. It will make it possible for you to hear sounds inaudible to your normal ears. It will also present radio signals like sounds as well. So you will hear raw signals like radars as if they were noises, and encoded signals like radio and TV channels or phones if you want to listen for them, like the original sound."

"But now we come to the most important feature of the suit, and the two parts which take up most of the 'schoolbag' on your back."

"You are wearing a gravitational invertor. That means you are connected to the Renwick power core at all times. It allows you to transfer from place to place instantly using the process we call 'bending'. We use this technology to train our own kindergarten children in the art so it's very safe."

"As you've seen already with your lighthouse, it is possible to overlap two three dimensional places, in time along with the other six dimensions. The skin of your suit plays an important role in defining the boundaries of the three dimensional object to be moved.

Normally bending is managed by Control who has a permanent link to your suits. However you will also learn to manage your own bending using the power of your gravitational inverter supplemented by Control. I should warn you that bending slightly distorts time and increases your innate perception of other dimensions. Some find this disturbing."

"The gravitational inverter also has other uses. One is you can increase or decrease your gravity interaction. This is not the same as antigravity. Antigravity is a repulsive force linked to dark energy which does not interact with normal gravity. That's why the universe is shaped the way it is. Lana you might be better at explaining this to them."

"How many of you have seen pictures of the astronauts on the moon?" She asked.

I vaguely remembered some ancient black and white images of some spacesuited dudes bouncing around. We raised our hands – sorta.

"Well, reducing gravity interaction is a bit like that. In effect you are reducing the effective size of the Earth. If you reduce gravity to a third you would be able to jump around like you were on Mars. Reduce it to a sixth and it would be like on the Moon.

What it means is you accelerate toward the ground much slower than if you were interacting with all of Earth's gravity. Notice I am talking about acceleration, the rate of increase of speed. You can still get up to dangerous speeds if you are high enough, it just takes much longer. The other problem is that the more you reduce gravitational interaction the more Cerenkov radiation you will produce. Cerenkov radiation occurs when particles exceed the speed of light in that medium like air or water[†]. Of course nothing exceeds the speed of light in a vacuum like space but in the air if something goes faster than light it gives off this glow called Cerenkov radiation. The physics is complicated but the result is the more you deflect gravity the more you glow."

I immediately remembered Tabika who glowed more brightly when she flew.

"I hope we have wings like Tabika," Tahira wished.

Hekator caught her eye, smiled and just nodded before taking over.

"The combination of reduced gravity and added strength will allow you to run and jump with more agility than any other creature on Earth. And yes Tahira we have also given you wings."

"Yes!" Tahira thought, punching the air and jumping in her seat with excitement.

"They are folded inside your backpacks like beetle wings. They are large, transparent and very strong capable of 100 beats a second but they will only lift you with gravity reduction set at 50 percent or more, so if you want to use them to fly you will have to glow. They also buzz quite loudly, like a huge bee. That's just a side-effect of beating all that air. They can be used as a fixed wing without gravity reduction as well when dropping down but

they won't slow your descent much without some flying tricks."
Lana stepped forward distracting Hekator.

"Just one thing before everyone gets too excited about the wings. The other effect of the gravitational inverter you need to know about is that it will bend all dimensions including those involving ghosts. So when you bend you will attract ghosts. It's something you need to be aware of."

Hekator nodded

"And I should add although your suit has very hard skin if it is penetrated it will bleed. Your suit's blood is red and very like your own but your suit has no major arteries or veins and it will simply close off supply to the effected area, which will die. Untreated this would pose a risk of infection after a day or so. We don't think you will be away anything like as long as that."

"So," Lana asked, "any questions?"

"Do we have any weapons?" Scotty asked.

The pair looked at each other.

"There are a number of other tools and capabilities in the suit which we haven't mentioned yet," Lana said. "Any tool can be used as a weapon. However you are not being asked to fight. If you have a choice between fight or flight you are to escape. Your suit will respond to adrenaline levels in your body and make suggestions where it can."

"I mean like if we find ourselves being charged by an elephant or something," Scotty persisted.

"You should bend out of the way. But if you were surprised there are systems that could deal with something like that Scotty," Lana said.

"But we are not equipping you to be soldiers."

"Well, that's all we are going to tell you about tonight," Hekator

**89**

said. "I believe Gunter and Mariko have organised for you to go up and show your caregivers what your suits look like and they have a game to practise using them."

Hekator waved to Gunter and Mariko who were chatting quietly about something.

"Look after those outfits children and they will look after you," he said and vanished.

Lana stepped forward.

"Have fun guys. Play now because you will need to use them properly soon," she said and also disappeared.

"OK you lrot," Mariko yelled waving us on. "First we going upstairs to show off your new toy. Then we have an exercise. Follow us."

We followed her out of the briefing room into the corridor we'd come in, leaving the other corridors unexplored. Then we went past the sentry statues out into the tunnel and back under Renwick.

The suits were very comfortable to walk in. The shoes provided great support without any rubbing. It was better than wearing nothing because you were warm and felt secure, but it was almost as comfortable. We all couldn't help noticing how much Mariko and Gunter glowed with warmth in the dark tunnel while the rest of us were quite dark. The other thing I noticed was my sense of smell seemed sharper. I could smell things I'd never noticed before. The tunnel smelt slightly of rotten eggs and Mariko smelt much more interesting than I had previously thought.

We climbed the ladder, went through the vault into the cellar and up the stairs to the downstairs lounge. When we came in I think everyone was a bit let down. I think they expected us to look a lot less ordinary. I went over to Aunty Liz, Rewa and Grandpop. I noticed they too smelt in a way I'd never noticed before. It was a warm smell I associated with feeling safe.

"What happened?" Grandpop asked.

I looked confused.

"Did they just give you a new bag coz the thing didn't fit or something?"

"No, Grandpop this is it," I told him.

He did a double take.

"Isn't that what you were wearing before?"

He had a point. It looked very similar.

"No. I don't even know how to take this off. It's like meat on the inside but it sticks to you closer than a wetsuit."

"Ooo yuk, gross," said Rewa.

Grandpop went to put my hoodie down, as he always did. This time however it was stuck to my hair.

"Ow," I said, and twisted away.

"The hoods up so I can do this," I said and asked the suit to seal up. They watched with their mouths open as the clear plastic covered my face.

"The suit has an air supply," I said.

"We can't hear you," Aunty Liz interrupted loudly. I could hear her rather too well and put my hands to my ears. I asked the suit to open up and the facescreen peeled open and folded away.

"It's got an air supply so I can swim in it," I told them.

"How do you control it?" asked Grandpop fascinated.

"It's linked to my brain somehow. I just think stuff and it does it."

He raised his eyebrows at that.

Aunty Liz was touching it.

"It feels like cotton."

"They said it can change to pretty much anything but it's very hard. It's made of diamond they said."

"Well, we'd better see what you can do with it," Grandpop challenged.

"Yeah..."

"OK kids! Outside! Time for a show!" Mariko yelled, clapping her hands.

They led us outside and everyone followed. It was cool but clear with a warm if distant winter's evening sun blazing brightly over the hill and casting long shadows from the trees. Mariko lead us out to the driveway. The birds were twittering nearby. Gunter was waiting for her on the dusty road. She went up to him and took a length of ribbon and then drew back.

"OK, first is race. You have to high-five Ken who's waiting by righthouse. Behind the rlibbon prease."

She bossed us into line.

"Rule. No fighting, no tripping. Use anything you rlike to go faster. Rlun when ribbon goes ... Rweady..."

I immediately thought 'foot claws' and felt them under my feet just in front of where my arch would be if I had one.

"Set...go!" Mariko tugged the ribbon out of the way as Gunter let go, but we were already flying.

I couldn't believe how much faster we could run! I felt like I going at least as fast as a car and I wasn't even gasping. Tarik was winning, as usual, with Ashley close on his heels with the rest of us not far behind her. Suddenly there was a light overhead and Tahira leapt over everyone glowing brightly before bouncing again like a huge rubber ball.

"*Clever bitch*!" thought Tarik.

*"Jealousy will get you nowhere,"* she jeered.

And now we were all starting to leap and glow. I picked quarter gravity which was what the suit suggested and leapt.

The interesting thing about trying to run in reduced gravity was making sure you leapt along rather than up because it seemed to take ages to fall once you became airborne. I experimented with changing the reduction after jumping and discovered I could go faster by increasing gravity again as I got to the top of each leap. That gave me more acceleration and less floating.

We were all so busy experimenting that when we reached the lighthouse we almost forgot to look for Ken.

*"Where is he?"* Ashley asked.

We all got the same feeling from him at the same time and looked up. He was at the tiny window about four stories up, smiling down at us. Scotty ran forward and jumped. It was an enormous jump. At least two stories, but it was still short of his goal. Everyone thought of a different answer at the same time. Tahira was going to fly, Cam was already trying another jump, and Ashley thought of climbing the outside. Tarik rather cunningly thought of the internal stairs. Like Tahira I wanted to see whether I could imitate Tabika and fly.

Cam's leap was too strong and she went over the lighthouse brilliant with light yelling her head off with surprise. As she increased the gravity again she realised she was in danger of landing too hard and unfurled her wings.

Both me and Tahira, had got our wings out and had started them buzzing. They were quite loud, like a huge bee. There were four of them; made of the same stuff as the facescreen; clear like an insect's and quite large. The upper pair were one meter ovals which extended out from our shoulders while the lower

**93**

pair were rounded and extended down about an arm length. But we were both finding them a lot harder to use than we'd hoped. It was easy to hover but if you tipped forward too much you shot off, out of control. We were wasting a lot of time getting ourselves organised.

Meanwhile Ashley seemed to have found a way to stick to the lighthouse walls and was starting to climb them like a spider with Scotty following not far behind her. Tarik was stumped by the lock but was going through the possibilities to pick it while Cam had her wings out too and was trying, like us, to direct her way to the window.

It was Ashley who got there first. She high-fived Ken through the window then increased her glowing and jumped back to drop slowly back to Earth. Her jump was back at me and gave Tahira a chance to buzz in and high-five Ken. From below Tarik gave a cry of triumph and was soon leaping up the spiral staircase like a monkey. Scotty was next to reach Ken followed by me, then Tarik, and Cam.

Ashley was quickly running back, but now that she had got better at controlled flight Tahira was gaining rapidly, and I was just behind her. There was something about flying along with Tahira that felt cool. Like we were Fae or something. Anyway we overtook Ashley who was bouncing below us. We could see Gunter and Mariko holding the ribbon when suddenly the world around Mariko began to distort and a brilliant light appeared. All the adults shielded their eyes and just as Tahira and I swept up, Tarik appeared out of thin air.

It was too close to call between them. I followed a second behind, followed by Ashley, Cam and Scotty. Tahira and me landed, noticing the crowd had been swollen by quite a few ghosts, drawn by Tarik's bending. In a short while we had all gathered together at the finish line. None of us were puffed, as we normally would have been, but we were all excited. The adults came forward making 'ooh' and 'aah' noises about the suits as we chattered excitedly about the race.

"How did you appear like that?" Tahira asked Tarik admiringly.

"I asked the suit to take me back to where I was. It was easy really," he said, as much astonished as everyone else.

"How did you climb the lighthouse?" I asked Ashley.

"There's a sticky pad in the gloves and knees. But I think I could have done it better. How did you fly?"

"Well, it's a bit tricky because you lean to steer and it's easy to overdo it but it's really cool..."

There was another bright light and Hekator appeared dressed as he had been in his hologram.

"Good work all of you," Hekator agreed. "Tarik your bending was excellent. Note it well everyone: you can always go back to somewhere you've been. You still need Control but it's a lot less difficult. And while I think of it Tarik, show them how you opened the door."

Tarik held up his right pinky and a metallic probe about the same length as his finger grew out of it.

"It's a titano-mercury key which flows into any lock. Sets hard enough to act as a key and then liquifies again," Hekator explained. "And Ashley. Explain how you climbed the lighthouse."

"Well, it's like there's these little suckers on the palms of our gloves and knees? But I don't rightly know how they work," Ashley admitted.

Hekator smiled. "They work using tiny hairs. There are more on the soles of your feet and along your forearms. They will hold fast to any smooth, clean surface but not if the surface is very dusty or crumbling. For those you will need your claws and your whips. The whips are in your forearm. You cast them by pointing your arm. That's it Scotty, and then you project them," Hekator nodded at Scotty.

An amazingly thin wire about eight meters long licked out of Scotty's arm instantly like a long tongue and in the blink of an eye had retracted itself again.

"The whip curls around things or can be driven into soft materials. It's mostly for climbing because it's strong enough to lift you when it retracts," Hekator said.

"Well, you are probably pretty hungry after all that, so that's where we will leave it today. Tomorrow we will begin your training."And with that he vanished into darkness.

Chatting and yakking we all went inside to find a large birthday cake with all our names on it waiting on a table surrounded by our presents in the lounge. I couldn't help feeling that I was already wearing the best present I was ever going to get.

We had a brilliant eggplant soup, followed by souvlaki with dolmades. The cake cutting and presents were pretty low key. Our families stayed plus Ken, Gunter and Mariko but there was no sign of Drs Prosperov or Morozov.

My presents were some sunnies and some nice clothes. I was stoked. Not so much with the presents themselves but because I had such a great group of friends around me and all my family too.

Later that night Aunt Liz came in to say goodnight and ask me what I thought of my birthday. Only one word captured it.

"Awesome," I said and fell asleep in no time.

## CHAPTER THIRTY FIVE: LONG DROP

Wait, wait wait!" Sue stops me.

"Hmm?" I reply.

"So ... let me get this straight ...you didn't travel in that little UFO of yours. You had a teleporting suit instead?"

"We got the speeders later. That was when we discovered the limits of what the suits could do and the Fae were convinced we were doing something useful. We got the suits first as a kind of trial."

"And you could just ... teleport anywhere?"

"Yeah ... though it's called 'bending'."

"Anywhere at all?"

"Well, into the air, and if we had to, into water, but you can't bend into anything solid. The molecules are too dense and it won't seed."

"But anywhere on Earth?"

"Yeah ... and the moon too."

"You went to the *moon*?" Sue nods, doubtfully.

"Uh-huh."

"OK ... so let me get this straight ... the fairy queen came, and using tame ants built you a lovely underground grotto, and for your birthdays gave you magic suits with wings so you could visit the moon?" she recites.

I burst out laughing. I'd never thought of it like that before.

"I'm glad you're laughing Sam, because it's completely *nuts*!" Sue complains.

"Yeah," I laugh, "I have to admit when you say it like that it does sound nuts."

"Well, I'm starting to think you're taking the piss," Sue tells the sky from under her shades.

"I'm really not Sue. Anyway you've seen the glowmoss and the glass tunnel made by the Draca."

"Yes, and I've seen your ... what did you call it ... speeder *and* a flying saucer. Those I can cope with. I've heard of flying saucers. There's plenty of evidence for them ... even if half of it is from nutjobs ... there's still enough from pilots and police officers who want to keep their jobs. But fairies? C'mon, it's really hard to listen to this and imagine you really think it really happened. I have to keep reminding myself that you actually think all this is true and not a fairy story."

I sigh.

"I know. That's why I wasn't talking to you when you interviewed me the first time. I knew you wouldn't believe me. Look, am I just wasting our time? Because if you *really* don't believe me there's not much point going on," I ask.

It's Sue's turn to sigh.

"I just keep thinking about work tomorrow, and all the stuff I have to do at home," she admits.

That bothers me. We aren't at Caz and Julia's to spend Sunday in the sun telling fairy stories. We are at Caz and Julia's because Sue's house is compromised by enemy alien powers out to get us. I'm sure they'll have her house staked out by now. I really don't want Sue to go back to there, and certainly not by herself, but if I go on too much longer her frustration will get the better of her.

"Do you want to get a cab?" I ask.

Sue thinks for a moment. Luckily the cost bothers her.

"No, I'll wait til Caz and Julia get back. I need a car."

I'm quiet for a moment, thinking of ways to follow her without annoying her.

"Is there any way of checking out *anything* you're telling me?" she asks.

"No, not til the others come back," I reply.

"Well, at the moment I'm thinking you might need that psychologist after all."

"Yeah, I know."

"What do you mean, 'you know'?"

"I know what you're thinking. You're very easy for me to read."

"Am I?" she asks, a bit worried.

"Uh-huh."

"Why's that?"

"I dunno. Some people are and some people aren't. The closer you are to someone's soul the easier they are to read."

"Really?"

"Yeah."

"And what does that mean? Close to someone's soul?"

"It just means you're close – even before you meet them – you're always close."

"Are you buttering me up?" she asks, looking at me.

"No. You asked. Of course the opposite is also true. People who you're far away from are harder to read."

"Like Doctor Prosperov?"

"Yeah, sort of. He's just slippery. He's practiced being hard to read. Others are just horrible and you feel bad going near them. Of course infiltrators you don't dare read because they can take over your mind that way. And biobots just aren't there at all because they don't have souls.

"Yeah, look I have my doubts about this whole soul thing. When you say 'soul' I think of a transparent person like a ghost, and frankly I don't really believe it either," Sue says.

"Do you think your life means anything?" I ask.

"Not especially, no. It's just a bunch of stuff that happens."

"Did Rachel's life mean anything?"

There's a distinct pause as she thinks about it. She's kind of snookered because she knows I know she almost took her own life over Rachel, so she has to mean a lot.

"Well it does to me. But I don't ... I don't think we matter to the world in any big way. We're just a couple of people living our lives."

"But you give each other meaning?"

"Yeah, OK, I get your point. She meant so much to me I thought I couldn't live without her," she admits, impatiently.

"OK, that's what I mean by your soul. She ripped at your soul. The meaning you give yourself or allow others to give you."

"OK, that makes way more sense than ghosts."

"Not really. Ghosts are pretty much the same, but we'll get to that later. In the meantime ask yourself, could all the people in the world be part of this big network of meaning to one another?"

Sue thinks for a moment, "Yeah, I suppose when you stand back from it, six degrees of separation and all that, they must do."

"And sometimes even people's dreams have meaning?"

"Sure."

"And even completely random shit, like me showing up at your door, or the sun shining or a bird crapping on you ... well ... anything?"

"But only because we give it one."

"Sure, but if you were trying to explain what happens in the universe, you couldn't leave out humans as part of nature could you?"

"No, but obviously we aren't that big a deal."

"But we are part of the universe, so you couldn't leave out what things meant to people when explaining what we people do, could you? I mean all those buildings and wars and stuff, they have meanings to everyone don't they."

"Yeeaah," she agrees unwillingly.

"So meaning is what we get from information isn't it? I mean without receiving information we can't get meaning? Like, if you're blind a picture doesn't mean a lot."

"OK."

"OK, so what if information is a part of space? What if the Universe *itself* remembers."

"Does it?"

"That's Dr Prosperov's whole point; how the conscious dimensions work."

Sue sighs.

"OK, so what does *that* mean?"

"It means that there is meaning in the Universe. We extend into the informational dimension through having consciousness. Rocks, trees or butterflies don't. We do."

"So ... when you said our souls are close ... that's because our meaning is similar or what?"

"Aligned. We are aligned."

CHAPTER THIRTY FIVE: LONG DROP

"I'm going to have to think about this."

"Yeah … we did. It's not easy. And that was before we met Khadiyeh."

"Who's Khadiyeh?"

"A girl from Yemen, but I think we should stay at the shallow end of the weirdness pool for the moment because Khadiyeh is way over *my* head. Shall I go on?"

"Oh all right. Until Caz and Julia show up anyway."

So I go on.

•••

The next morning I couldn't get over the fact that Grandpop had moved in with us. There he was in the morning in the cafe, eating pastries and drinking coffee and chatting with the other adults. It just made me feel totally happy inside.

I talked with Rewa about it on the bus. She said she was happy that Grandpop was back, but she still seemed a bit distracted and sad about something. Maybe I didn't need to be psychic to realise she was sad Grandpop had come for me, and not for her, and she started to chat with Asal to avoid thinking about it.

Emma noticed my birthday clothes and that I was looking happy and distracted. I think she'd also realised that Tahira hadn't been chatting with me secretly since May, and didn't seem to be showing the slightest bit of interest in me either. She even asked me about my birthday, obviously wishing she'd been invited. When I told her Grandpop had moved in she was surprised. She smiled, but I could tell she was thinking what her dad would think about it. I didn't really care. I didn't mind her dad, but Grandpop was my hero.

That night we did our homework as usual, then Mrs Jones rounded us up for cleaning and we did that until five again. Then she sent us down to Mariko in the cellar.

"OK kids. Go get changed and come back to the front steps," she told us.

So off we went at a run. We were all really excited about having a chance to play in our suits again. This time changing was faster than before. We got through changing in little more than two minutes and ran back up through the tunnels, through the vault, up the cellar stairs and out the front door to the steps. We found Grandpop waiting with the other parents and Ken with his cross-country Pinzgauer van. Mariko explained the rules.

"This game is hide and seek. You kids are the hiders, you start at the chapel but...but you have to get to the hericopter without being seen. If you make it, you get extra cake which is ..." she looked to Mr Trân.

"Chocolate gateau," Mr Trân said.

I loved his gateau.

"But roosers get nothing. Hah!" Mariko told us impishly.

"Uhh! It's *our* birthdays," Ashley, Scotty and Tarik complained.

"You got your cake yesterday," Mariko cackled evilly, rubbing her hands.

The other adults smiled and said nothing. I could tell they knew Mariko was just making this up, but went along with her for the moment.

It was getting darker now as the sun slipped behind the hills and there was definitely more scope for hiding. The sky was still light, however, but it was going to get darker soon. I wanted to finish soon because I was getting hungry. I noticed Grandpop and Bernard step forward.

"The seekers are Mr Kahu and Mr Khumalo, and if you can beat *them,* you can beat *anyone,*" Mariko told us.

That was true. A former game warden and guide, and a special forces soldier were about as hard as it could get. In fact I was a bit nervous about Grandpop in the pine wood. He might flip out again. Still, he looked relaxed.

"How will we know we've been seen?" Tarik asked.

Grandpop and Bernard smiled at each other.

"We'll let you know," Grandpop nodded to Tarik, smiling.

Ken called from his Pinzgauer van.

"OK guys," he called, "the sooner you get this game started, the sooner you eat."

We all piled into the van, and Ken drove it up the hill. An immediate discussion on tactics began in the back. The ideas flew silently.

"*Maybe we should gang up on them,*" Tarik suggested.

"*What do you mean?*" Ashley asked.

"*Some of us are a diversion and the others try to get through.*"

"*But then the diversion guys miss out on the cake,*" Scotty pointed out.

"*So we should agree to all share any cake we get,*" Cam suggested.

"*OK,*" I agreed, and everyone else did too.

At the top of the hill Ken drove up to the chapel and turned around. We all got out.

"Good luck guys," he called and drove down the hill again in a cloud of dust.

We gathered in the graveyard in the gathering dark, sitting among the long grass.

"*Let's do this in our teams,*" Tahira said.

I could tell she was less confident than I was, and wanted some help.

"*Yeah, let's,*" said Ashley looking at Scotty warmly.

"*OK,*" agreed Tarik. "*but Cam and me get to go down to the beach and work around from behind because Sam and Scotty know the seekers which gives you guys an advantage.*"

"*OK, but we'll go left,*" Tahira negotiated.

"*Which leaves us down the middle,*" Scotty said a bit bitterly.

"*What you have to know about my Grandpop is you won't see him,*" I warned, trying to be fair. "*He'll be hiding too, setting up an ambush.*"

"*We won't hear, or see, Bernard either,*" Scotty added grimly.

We considered that, looking a bit worried. Although it was a game, I realised we were taking this pretty seriously.

"*Let's see what* we *can do,*" Ashley said standing up. She went over to the chapel and seemed to vanish.

"Wow!" exclaimed Scotty, surprised.

Then we could make out her outline. She turned around. Only her face was normal. The rest of her had the same colour and apparent texture as the chapel. It was almost like she was made of glass, but without the reflections.

"That's *brilliant,*" Tarik conceded.

"Sure evens up the odds a bit," I said. "But remember, these guys use their ears and they can track."

"*So keep quiet. Telepathy only. If you have to sneeze close up,*" Scotty said.

"*I suppose the suit eats our snot as well,*" Cam wondered.

"*Saves you a job,*" Tarik sniggered.

Cam kicked him hard. Tarik grimaced silently.

"*OK? In teams, let's go,*" Scotty said softly.

One by one we all switched on the adaptive camouflage and went 'transparent'.

We *looked* great but I couldn't help noticing how much noise we made in the crackling grass. It wasn't until we entered the pine needle carpeted forest that I felt confident we were quiet. The smells of the place were powerful. Like a perfume I'd never noticed before. I led Tahira to the left moving quickly from tree to tree trying to get a look down the hill to where the helicopter was. We were too high and the trees were in the way. Then Tahira tapped me.

"*We could always climb them,*" she thought.

I wasn't so sure.

"*If you're in a tree you just get stuck up there,*" I warned.

"*Not in these things,*" Tahira 'said' silently.

She extended her long hand and foot claws and stuck them into the bark and started to climb. She went up quite quickly. I wasn't convinced but waited below. I felt sure I'd have to catch her. But she climbed about twenty meters to the top of the tree.

"*Can you see anything?*" I asked.

"*Not really,*" she admitted.

"*I thought not. Come down!*"

"*I want to try something.*"

She fired out a wire from her arm and it wrapped around the branch of another tree.

"*What are you..?*"

Then she leapt.

She swept through the air and slammed into the other tree's trunk. I couldn't help sniggering.

"*Why are you so pleased? It didn't hurt at all,*" she told me off. She was hanging on with her feet and one arm. She released the branch from the whip with her right arm and climbed around the trunk on the left side, put out her left arm, and leapt again.

Now she was ahead of me and out of sight. Worse, it looked like she was having more fun than I was!

I put out my claws and ran up the tree. I was amazed how easy it was. I had both fingers to grip with and claws to hold, plus I was far stronger for my weight than when I usually climbed trees. I climbed up to where Tahira had been, and looked around for her. I couldn't see her at all. There were a lot branches and things that jutted out, so I decided to protect my face by sealing the facescreen. Then a branch moved and focusing hard I thought I saw Tahira swing to the next tree. She looked back and I could see her disembodied head watching me. She had a huge grin on her face.

"*Come on Sam, this is fun!*" she said in my head.

I picked a branch and shot out my whip which looped around it. Then, thinking if I fell I could always reduce gravity, I jumped. The whip was like a having a super-long monkey arm and swinging felt completely natural. It was a rush. That was until the trunk loomed up in front of me. I put my feet out and instinctively withdrew the whip so I could put my hands out to protect myself. Tahira was right. I hit the trunk pretty hard but it didn't hurt a bit.

I climbed around the tree on my claws and thinking harder about where I was going this time, whipped out, grabbed a branch and swang again. Halfway through the swing I noticed another useful branch and grabbed that with my other whip, releasing the previous one on the way. I ended up landing on a large branch.

"*It you retract the whip as you're swinging you can go higher,*" Tahira suggested.

"*Where are you?*" I asked.

"*Two trees ahead and one to the left.*"

"*Wait for me.*"

"*OK.*"

I found her sitting on a branch about twenty five meters up waiting for me. I swang to the trunk and climbed around to her perch.

"*I can see the helicopter from here,*" she pointed out.

It was true. Through the foliage the helicopter was at the bottom of the hill about 300 meters away.

"*Any sign of Grandpop or Bernard?*" I asked.

"*No.*"

"*Grandpop will wait where he can catch us getting close to the helicopter,*" I said

There wasn't even a sign of body heat.

"*I wonder where the others are?*" I wondered.

"*Ask your suit,*" Tarik put in.

"*How?*" I wondered

"*Just think 'situation',*" he said.

I thought 'situation'. It wasn't a map like a picture you could see. It was a like knowledge of trails in my head, as if I knew all the routes around Renwick and simply knew where the others were along them. It was so amazing I sat for a moment marvelling at how clever it was.

"*We're a long way behind the others,*" I told Tahira who was watching the open area below like a hawk.

"*We can catch up,*" she said confidently, "*follow me.*"

She leapt, grabbed a distant branch, swang, and at the top of her swing grabbed another branch and swang again. It looked a bit risky but I could tell she was right. You had to commit everything to make it work. So I leapt too.

Once again I was surprised that, once you were doing it, how easy it was. In the dense pine forest there was always a branch or a trunk to grab somewhere. Of course there were also a lot of annoying branches jutting out everywhere as well. Unfortunately Tahira discovered the hard way that not all branches are healthy.

We'd swung down the hill, speeding, half falling, silently through the forest, when the pine trees stopped and were replaced by some larger bushy ones. They were a bit more open with thicker branches which made it easier to see a route. Tahira was one leap ahead of me when the branch she was swinging from cracked suddenly and she fell at full gravity.

"Hae!" she yelled. Everyone could hear her.

I had my own problems because I had been planning to use the same branch and I had to hastily grab for another one and pull up quick.

Tahira had sensibly reduced gravity as she fell, and grabbed for another branch, retracting herself on to it, but the combination of her yelling, the glow and the waving of the lighter branch she had rescued herself with, had totally given our position away.

And now we were 75 meters from the edge of the trees and 150 meters from the helicopter. Down below I saw a figure move in the gloom.

"*Tahira someone's down there,*" I warned her.

"*Oh great!*" she said.

"*Who is it?*" asked Scotty urgently.

"*I think it's Grandpop.*"

Tahira was hanging from her branch now, trying to keep still, but it was obviously bent.

"*I'll draw him away,*" I told her. I looked around, found a series of lighter branches leading in the direction Tahira had been going and leapt, hoping fervently none of *them* would break.

I swang shaking the trees like some large ape for three, four, five swings until I dropped to the ground and rolled. It was a colossal distraction.

"*He's right underneath me,*" Tahira warned us.

"*Did he see me?*" I asked.

"*Yes, but he is looking around. He is not stupid.*"

"*Bugger. Hang in there.*"

"*We're 50 meters short of the chopper and closing,*" Tarik reported.

I grabbed a branch above me and pulled myself up silently.

"*He's moving in your direction,*" Tahira reported.

"*Has anyone seen Bernard?*" Scotty asked urgently.

"*Yes,*" Tahira replied sourly, "*he's just spotted me.*"

"*If that's Bernard, where's Grandpop?*" I asked.

"*Here,*" reported Tarik. "*Hiding under the sand in the brush by the chopper, he's just spotted us.*"

"*No fair,*" Ashley commented.

I could see the small dark figures of Tahira, Tarik and Cam trudging back towards the house looking disappointed.

"*Where are you two?*" I asked Scott and Ashley, simultaneously finding out from my suit.

"*Slithering toward the chopper and very exposed to Bernard on our left,*" Scotty said.

"*Can you see him?*" I asked.

"*Yeah, he's moving through the trees towards you. He's bright with heat.*"

It was night now but there was a moon and we could still be seen by it – just.

*"I'll keep drawing him, watch out for Grandpop."*
I swung off another branch and scampered away up the hill.
Then silently reached up a tree and hauled myself up it.
Bernard was moving silently through the trees after me. If I
hadn't had the thermal view I'd never have seen or heard him.
He really was brilliant at stalking.
*"Your Grandpop's just passed us Sam, the way's open. Keep
drawing them,"* Scotty called.
I swang to another tree. Even with the suit's eyes it was getting
hard to see. I remembered what Grandpop had said that night I
had followed him into the bush: "there just isn't any light here,
Sam". Luckily they were downwind and I could smell them. I
didn't know where they were, but I could tell they were closing. I
spotted Grandpop moving closer to the treeline watching around
him. Bernard was getting closer again.
*"Twenty meters,"* Scotty called.
I let Bernard get closer and closer. Grandpop disappeared from
view.
*"Ten meters to go,"* Scott reported.
Bernard was looking around about twelve meters below me.
Suddenly there were two big glows near the helicopter.
*"We made it!"* Ashley called out.
I'd had enough. Take me back to the stairs I told the suit. Then
something very odd happened. Time seemed to slow down,
the colour seemed to drain out of everything. My whole field of
view seemed to fold up and distort and I had to close my eyes.
I was falling back, unable to move, falling and spinning, and
then suddenly I stopped falling back and started falling forward.
There was brilliant light all around me. Brilliant light and
presences. My mother and my Grandmother.

Somewhere my magical ancestors Te Whareti, who in legend too, could teleport, and his son Papa-huri-hia, noticed me briefly. Dozens of my people surrounded me, and slowly began to fade. I opened my eyes and I was crouching on the ground in the same posture I had been in the tree. I looked around. Tahira, Tarik, Cam and Gunter were looking at me. It seemed the others had gone in out of the cold. I stood up.

[+]

"Wow," I said, mostly to Tarik, noticing a number of the ghosts, including Corporal Higgins had gathered too, drawn by my bending.

"Yeah, it's pretty wild huh?" Tarik replied. Then he looked up and stopped.

Mariko was looking behind me. I turned. A tall half-man, half-goat had just walked into the light by the house. For just a second I had a strong urge to run.

"Hello everyone. How's it going?" Hekator grinned.

We all greeted Hekator warmly and asked him when he had come back.

"I just got back to the cave an hour ago and came out to watch your game."

Two big glows were floating through the air in an arc towards us, with Ashley and Scotty in the middle of them.

Mariko turned and shouted out into the dark.

"Game's over Bernard! Mike! Hekator's here! Score is Hiders two. Seekers thlee!"

She smiled at Hekator, "I think they a bit rost," she explained.

"If you two are cold, why don't you go in? I'll wait with the kids for Mike and Bernard," Hekator offered.

Actually we wanted to go in too, not because we were cold but because we were also hungry.

Mariko and Gunter looked at each other, then at Hekator, who shrugged.

Mariko turned back to Gunter, "You hungry baby?"

"Ja," he agreed

"Me too!" she said giving him her arm.

And they went in.

"*OK guys gather around,*" Hekator said silently.

"*You played that exercise well,*" he began, "*I was impressed by your teamwork. Tahira you discovered the point of the exercise, which was to exploit your camouflage and climbing tools. Sam, you did well too. I liked the way you tried bending like Tarik. Tarik I'm glad you found the situation function, it's based on a common locational process native to most Earth animals which we hadn't used for a while, so I'm glad it still works. Finally you've been wearing the suits for an hour now. How do you feel?*"

"Great","Excellent","Lekker," we all chorused.

Grandpop and Bernard appeared out of the darkness talking together.

"*Well, you may as well eat in them and then get out of them later. In fact the longer you can leave them on today the better,*" Hekator told us silently.

"Hi Mike, hi Bernard," he said out loud.

Grandpop and Bernard skipped up the stairs and greeted him.

"You kids go in, we'll be along in a moment," Grandpop ordered us.

"See you tomorrow, sleep well," Hekator said.

We opened the door to find Corporal Higgins standing there looking out, aghast.

"What are *you* looking at?" I challenged him.

He looked at me horrified.

"Devils! They're devils!" he said, and faded.

It left a bad taste in my mouth.

As we went inside I asked Scotty because he was next to me what he thought.

"They do *look* like devils," he admitted. "but they don't seem evil."

"What if they turn out to be evil later on?" I asked.

He shook his head.

"You've met bad spirits before. Do they feel even slightly like them?"

"No," I had to admit. I stopped to think.

"Problem is they don't feel like *anything*," I pointed out.

"Don't sweat it." Scotty advised me, "that ghost's stuck in 1919 and he was an ignorant git when he was alive, anyway."

We came into the cafe and started settling down. We had a Szechuan Duck banquet that night. It didn't even suit gateau for dessert but we were still determined to leave room for it. Ashley had been opposite me against the window when she got up and pushed her way out.

"Where are *you* going?" asked Tarik, who was on the aisle opposite.

She looked at him with annoyance. "Bathroom," she said quickly and continued pushing past Tahira.

She got two steps and stopped, realising she couldn't get her suit off in the bathroom.

"You could do it here, no-one would know," Tarik sniggered.

Tahira's face creased in anger opposite him.

"Dzhou 'av no manners!" she told him angrily. She was scary.

Ashley kept walking and went out.

Tahira continued to give Tarik a piece of her mind, while Tarik sniggered. Scotty, Cam and me thought he was being pretty dumb too. Then Ashley came back looking quite pleased with herself and squeezed past to her seat before sitting down.

Everyone at the table looked at her.

"What?" she said.

Nobody dared answer her question. And before the silence was filled she went on.

"Actually it's way cleaner than normal," she said.

Tahira waggled a finger at Tarik.

"Do *anything* in front of me…" she warned. Her warning was so scary I wondered if she'd found some new weapon.

"How do you know I haven't?" Tarik responded smartly.

"Oh, don't be so childish," Scotty said wearily, "I'm going to get the cake."

He came back with two rather large slices of cake and six plates, put them on the table and shared them around.

"You know we should ask Bernard and your Grandpop to explain what we did wrong," he said.

Grandpop seemed to hear that and came over to talk to us.

"Your biggest mistake was thinking that we would be fooled by a diversion," he smiled at us. Bernard came over to join us too.

"In fact we assumed you would try a diversion so we used defence in depth. Bernard was the probe, I was the ambush," he said.

"And you should never assume that just because someone isn't *looking* at you, that they don't know where you are," Bernard chuckled.

"I knew I had one of you anyway," he went on, "because of the branch bending, but I let her hang to see what *you* would do. Someone tried to distract me so I had to make sure I wasn't missing more than just one," he smiled.

"You also need to work on moving silently. I heard Tarik and Cam long before I saw them," Grandpop added.

"Why were you under the sand?" Tarik asked.

"Heat signature," he replied. "I knew you could see body heat. Still, it's early days. You've still got a lot to learn and we've still got a lot to teach you," Grandpop smiled.

We divided the slices of cake, which we didn't really need, and stuffed ourselves on them. Even after the spicy Chinese flavours it was still delicious.

We got changed and went up to the lounge. We were still pretty excited after the game and talked about it for a while. Then we were told to go to bed. When I went in I heard Aunty Liz talking to Rewa. She still felt left out.

For the rest of the school days before the mid-winter holidays we spent the day counting down the hours till we got home. I tried to be nice to Rewa but she just seemed permanently sulky. She and Asal had a secret little world where we weren't allowed to make up for the fact they felt left out from our games. When we got home Mariko would pull on Betty's handbrake and turn around to us.

"OK peepul. You know drill. Homework! Then chores for you older ones."

We went in to the café where one of the parents would be waiting. The parents took turns at homework supervising and they all made sure we did it. We'd eat heaps of Mr Trân's dumplings, samosa, sausages and cakes and complain about our homework as we did it. Then at four Mrs Jones turned up to set us to work cleaning. Tahira and me could do our vacuuming in about half an hour now, but we had other bits and pieces that kept us going until quarter to five.

Our busy schedule now meant *we* were getting jealous of Rewa and Asal who would usually play together or watch TV instead of work. Then, at five, Mrs Jones would inspect our cleaning before we gathered in the cellar, and Mariko led us down through the vault, along the tunnel to the base, where we would split up to get changed into our suits.

We called this "work" – and it was hard physically. That was why we ate so much after school and we didn't have any problem eating dinner as well.

In the short calm days in mid-June we enjoyed the pale yellow sun and played lots of games Mariko made up, in the bush or pine woods through dusk into night. These games were a lot harder when the people you were looking for had perfect camouflage or could jump twenty feet up a tree. It was all pretty easy stuff really.

But on the last day before the holidays things changed.

We walked over to the briefing theatre where Grandpop and Mariko were waiting for us. We flopped into the chairs and Grandpop came down. He waited for a moment until Hekator appeared by hologram.

"Up until now we've been getting you and your suits tuned. But now you are ready for more challenging exercises. Tonight's one is a new and quite important one because it introduces an extra dimension of latitude you aren't used to thinking about," Hekator began.

I was confused. He was thinking about being at right angles to the ground. I thought he meant some sort of mysterious fourth dimension.

"My job is to explain *why* you will need to use it. Mr Kahu will teach you *how* you do it. The technique we are going to talk about is called 'bend-diving'. What you do is bend into the atmosphere about a kilometer *above* your destination, examine it, and then either fly to a landing zone or bend on to it. The main reason for doing this is you may want to take a look over an area before entering it. Being above somewhere provides a better viewpoint to check it out from."

I suddenly felt very worried. It wasn't a different dimension at all. It was just up, and we were going to fall from a kilometer up. I couldn't believe he was serious but he was. My mouth went dry.

"Of course, being a kilometer up means you will fall. Under normal Earth gravity you will have about twelve seconds to look around and make some decisions. If you engage your gravity deflection field you can increase this but you will be pretty obvious – especially at night. So instead of doing that you will be learning to use your wings."

My head had a sudden flutter as I tried to calculate whether our wings could keep us up. They were pretty small. Somehow I doubted it. Hekator nodded at me.

"That's right Sam, your wings are not parachutes. To make them work you will have to dive, then climb into an aerodynamic stall."

He held out a hand, fingers angled down, to show a dive. To be honest in the dark, in my warm comfy suit, it seemed strangely unreal to talk about falling. His hand arced back up so the fingers angled up,

"Which is where you climb enough to lose forward momentum and fall back to the surface from a much lower height than you started."

His hand dropped slightly so the heel of his palm was down like the hand was a figure standing.

"How much lower?" breathed Tarik. His eyes seemed to be bulging a bit. I wondered if mine were.

"If the ground is sloping uphill it could be a few meters."

That sounded insane to me but we all sat there finding it hard to breathe and not sure what to say.

"Of course it takes a lot of practice to get right. However we've programmed your suits to do it for you, if you let them. The problem is most of you find falling terrifying and that will interfere with the suit's functioning."

"So what we will be doing for a while is getting you used to falling for extended periods of time. To make it safer and easier we will run your suits through Control. In other words you won't have to make any decisions tonight. We will put you up, let you drop, and then put you up again, several times over until you get used to it. Then we'll bring you in for a debrief. We will power the bend and you can't bend home out of this."

My stomach hurt. I snuck a look left at Tahira who looked nervous, and right at Scotty who didn't look any better. I caught Ashley's eye as she was doing the same thing. You didn't need to be psychic to know we were all really scared by what Hekator was saying.

"Now to help you we have Mr Kahu who has made over ten thousand far more dangerous parachute jumps who will talk you through the rest of the session. Don't worry, you wouldn't be normal if you weren't scared. You are, however, in no danger whatsoever no matter how bad you feel. Mike?"

Grandpop had been staring at his shoes while he walked around as Hekator spoke. Now he stopped and looked up smiling wryly.

"Hi everyone," he began quietly.

"I have to admit that I've had to think about this a bit because I'm used to briefing soldiers before a drop rather than kids, and they're all ..." and now he barked like a soldier, "'yes sir! no sir! three bags full sir!'"

It made us jump. He stopped to smile, and then he spoke a bit louder, "with shiny shoes and sitting up straight."

He looked at us hard. We sat straighter. Then he went quiet again.

"But you aren't soldiers, you're kids, like my grandson. So what I'm going to talk to you about is something soldiers don't talk about much, but which they face all the time: fear."

He paused for a moment. I'd never heard him talk like this and I was hanging on his words like all the others.

"Being scared isn't hard. It comes to us naturally without any work at all," he grinned.

"It's a physical thing. You feel it in your gut. Your body shakes. If it's really bad you shit yourself."

We laughed nervously.

"... it's not so much fun when you have to do your own laundry," he added quietly.

We stopped laughing. He really meant we might shit ourselves. I was glad the suits could handle that.

"But the worst thing fear does to you is freeze your mind so you can't think. So what we train soldiers to do is react without having to think. We train their bodies to work even when their brains are mush. So that's what we're going to do, a little bit, to you."

He let that hang there. My stomach hurt even more.

"We're going to drop you for about thirty seconds from five kilometers up, five times over. It will be dark but you can still see the sea beneath very clearly. You may have seen pictures of people skydiving looking like they're having fun. Well, they are, but first they have to deal with fear. We aren't birds. Flying isn't natural to us."

"A long time ago our ancestors were like monkeys and the part of the brain that connects our mind to our body is pretty much still, a monkey's standard issue brain. It allows us to walk and crawl and climb, so hey, why change?"

"But like any monkey falling from a tree, our natural reaction is to try to grab hold of something. In the sky there *is* nothing to hold on to, so your monkey brain is terrified. No matter how brave you want to be, you will be scared – you have no choice."

I wondered whether I should quit now but I couldn't – not in front of Grandpop. I wasn't alone. Ashley wondered if the reason her mum had allowed us to train was to see if we would quit at this stage. That thought made us all feel a bit more angry and determined, even though we felt sick in the stomach.

"What we are training you to be able to do, is to keep going when your monkey brain is screaming terrified rubbish at you. It takes time to master but like anything practice makes perfect."

He paused again and went on.

"You will find an unpleasant sinking feeling in your stomach for the first six seconds. It's like falling asleep and waking up with a jerk but without the jerk. That will be because you are going to be weightless like in space and as you fall freely your stomach floats about inside you. After a while you will come to what's called terminal velocity. That's when air resistance stops you

**121**

accelerating and you will feel like you are lying on top of a huge wind."

"At this stage you may like to see what you can do with this wind. Try moving your arms and legs and see what effect you get. We'll worry about wings and low gravity another time so you can't turn these on. Just try and relax. Remember to breathe. It's going to be very hard but that is what we are trying to train your bodies to do."

I realised I hadn't been breathing just listening to him.

"To avoid collisions we'll drop you every four seconds. You will fall from 15,000 feet which skydivers call fifteen grand. You'll fall down to one thousand feet or 300 meters. Believe me that will seem *very* low. Then we'll pull you out and put you up to the top again. OK, let's go to the jumpstation."

With lead butterflies flapping in slow motion in our stomachs we filed through into the control room and then down into the jumpstation while Grandpop and Mariko sat above us at the consul. Mariko addressed Control.

"Control prease take over suit bending on all agents."

"Sure. Don't worry children, we won't let you hit anything," Control said in his warm masculine voice.

It was reassuring to hear him, although I felt totally nervous. My heart was beating like crazy.

"We'll do this alphabetically," Grandpop said. "First Ashley."

"*Damn*," thought Ashley.

"Then Cam."

"*Oh great.*"

I found myself unable to think what letter came next.

"Then Sam, Scotty, Tahira and Tarik. OK, seal your facescreens and retract your hands please."

This was it. As the screen peeled down in front of me I felt my gut clench and mouth dry. There was no escaping this now. I wondered if I was going to chuck. Ashley looked as pale as a black person could look.

Then Mariko and Grandpop came down into the jumpstation too.

"OK, into huddle," Mariko ordered.

We formed a huddle with Mariko.

"Time for a chant," Grandpop said starting us off.

"Go! Go! Go! Go! Go! Go!" he began with a stamp on each "go".

It all seemed a bit quick. I kept thinking 'but what have I forgotten?' trying to think of some way to get out of this. We all were. It just seemed too crazy.

We joined in chanting with Mariko leading us on.

"Go! Go! Go! Go! Go! Go!" Stamp, stamp, stamp.

It was great to hear the voices of us all together. As we heard each other and saw each other's faces the craziness of it seemed to make us laugh and forget what we were about to do.

"Go! Go! Go! Go! Go! Go!" Stamp, stamp.

We chanted for a long time just building the feeling between us. Forgetting what was going to happen and keeping time.

"Go! Go! Go! Go! Go! Go!"

And then as we chanted Grandpop roared a ha-ka, A Maori war dance of defiance of death with stamping and eye-rolling that is barely contained insanity that puts anyone's hair on end.

 "Ka ma-té (death?), ka ma-té (death?), ka ora (life?), ka ora (life?).

Ka ma-té (death?), ka ma-té (death?), ka ora (life?), ka ora (life?)."

It began. You could feel the spirit rising in the room. We were going to do this crazy thing and we were going to win! Then at some signal Ashley folded into darkness.

Instantly we were all hit by her terror and panic. Our chant faltered but Mariko kept us stamping and chanting "Go" while Grandpop kept up the Haka. Then Cam vanished. I felt my gut tense.

"Go! Go! Go!..."

And then the world folded, lost its colour and drained to a line of whiteness, span into the place of light and death and burst around me, and I was falling.

[+]

I flailed around trying to grab something. My gut was a floating ball of terror. I wanted to scream but I couldn't. There was nothing to hold on to. My body was rigid. And around me was nothing but fog as I plummeted blindly through the cloud. I seemed to be falling *far* too long. I was sure I was going to shit myself. Normally I would have hit the ground by now but it just went on and on and on.

It's amazing how long six seconds of terror feels. Time seemed to slow down. I could feel the wall of wind beginning to support me and felt slightly better when a new terror hit me. My comforting blanket of fog vanished and miles below me I could see the big black shiny wall of the sea, racing up towards me like a black wall of death. It was awful. I could see everything with total and complete clarity. Below me I could see Cam and Ashley like little toys rushing towards death. We were all transfixed with fear. The sea seemed to get closer and closer. I felt panic rising. And then a miracle! Ashley vanished. I watched Cam feeling the seconds pass like hours. Then she too vanished! Could I too cheat death? Or would the system fail *just for me* and I would splat into the shiny black wall below? I was so close I could see the smallest waves. My heart was hammering in my chest.

And then the world folded, lost it's colour and drained to a line of whiteness which burst around me and I was falling again.

[+]

I really hated the falling stage as I accelerated up to the wall of wind. My sweat was cold and my limbs ached with stress. My blood was still hammering in my ears. I felt out of control, sick in the stomach, and lost in the fog. I reached out for the wind wall and felt it.

"That's right Sam. You can play with it," Grandpop's voice said softly in my ears.

Suddenly the fog was gone and the sea was below me. I could see Ashley sliding sidewards below me. I began to experiment with moving my hands in the blast. It just didn't support you like water.

"Look at the horizon guys. It will help stop the vertigo," Grandpop said again.

I looked out and noticed Aotea far to the right of us for the first time. I started looking around realising you did get quite a view to look at. I started reshaping my body and finding how it effected my direction.

The horizon was getting lower and closer. I looked down just in time to see Cam vanish. It was funny I couldn't help thinking the system would only fail for me. And then it worked again!

[+]

"Third time round try diving and pulling up," Grandpop told us. It was weird I'd been falling for over a minute now and although my body was tense as a stick, I was finding the sickening yawning feeling in my stomach less scary than I had the first

125

time around. The wind-wall came up and I started playing with it again.

I went around two more times. Each time the terror of the drop was reduced. On the fifth time around I fell flat on the floor back at base. I only fell half a meter but it hurt more because I was expecting nothing. I picked myself up to find Ashley and Cam looking as shocked as I felt when there was a bright light behind me and Scotty fell on the floor. I was shaking inside and found it hard to believe where I was. I looked at Ashley and Cam.

"How are you guys?" I asked opening my facescreen and retracting my sleeves.

"OK," they gasped vaguely; as vague as I felt.

We helped Scotty up and then Tahira fell on the floor in a blaze of light. We all felt shaky inside, although our bodies were tense as guitar strings. I looked up at the control desk and saw that all the parents plus Rewa and Asal were watching us. They were clapping. I'd wondered what that noise was.

There was another flash of light and when Tarik had picked himself up Mariko and Grandpop led the other adults down among us. They came down still clapping and high-fiving and hugging us. When he got to me Grandpop grabbed me in a big bear hug.

"You did well," he whispered.

There was something about his hug that turned me to jelly and I found myself shaking and crying a bit but somehow also so happy. Aunty Liz came and hugged me too.

"I'm proud of you Sam. You're brave boy," she said.

Rewa came up and threw her arms around me.

"Sam. I don't feel jealous of you guys *any* more," she said earnestly. We all laughed.

All of us seemed to have tears in our eyes but we also felt good to have our parents there for us too. Grandpop went up a few steps and turned to talk to us.

"OK, so what you have just experienced is the equivalent of about ten parachute drops. Those are always the hardest and I have to say for a bunch of thirteen-year-olds you guys were brilliant. I was really impressed. Now that you've started to calm your monkey brains and get used to the fall we can move on to more techniques. Next time we'll practice using wings and then we'll start working in groups. But I think Mariko has another game to round off the night."

Mariko stepped up next to Grandpop.

"OK this game is called grlow tag and it's veeery simpul. Evelyone gets a grlow-stick duct-taped to their butt. You aren't allowed to take off your own grow stick. If you roose your grow stick to another prayer you have to stop, and come home and have your grow sticks counted. Whoever takes the most grow sticks wins."

So we went outside to play. It was a good game. And all the jumping, fast running, flying and dodging seemed to soak up the fear that had drenched our bodies. We came in to a fabulous mixed roast dinner feeling hungry, tired and more than a little pleased with ourselves.

The holidays had begun and we had faced a huge fear together. We were buzzing with a sense of achievement. Little did we realise we had only begun.

## CHAPTER THIRTY SIX: MY HOLIDAYS

I had been happily asleep when I was woken by Aunty Liz. It was still dark.

"Sam. Grandpop's getting everyone up for more drops before breakfast."

I felt sleepy and warm.

"What time is it?"

"Six."

"Awww cripes."

But with a big sigh I dragged myself out of bed, got dressed and went downstairs to the cellar where I found Grandpop and the others waiting for Tahira and Ashley. Finally they appeared looking grumpy and rebellious.

"Five drops to see in the dawn and then breakfast. It'll be fantastic," Grandpop enthused.

There were grumbled mutterings about Grandpop's definition of 'fantastic' as we went down to the base. I felt a bit better about falling but I was still scared. I half wished I could go back to sleep in the changer and hide but it tipped me out as usual.

"You may as well stay in your suits today. We're going to be busy," Grandpop told us.

Then he herded us over to the jumpstation.

We were feeling a bit more awake now as we realised we would soon be plummeting over the ocean shortly. We all looked a bit sick.

"We've got you set to arrive in the sunlight and leave, out of it. It's clear up to twelve grand. Take a look around and enjoy the view," he advised.

"*You enjoy it*," was the thoughts of more than one of us.

"Now this time we're going to send you down all together," Grandpop went on happily ignoring the looks he was getting. "So Control says form a circle and hold hands."

We formed a circle. I had Tahira to my right and Scotty to my left. I liked this a bit better. At least we'd have something to hold on to.

"Now grip each other's wrists like this," He said showing us. Then he walked around checking and adjusting. I was feeling very tense in my empty stomach.

"OK seal up."

We sealed up.

"Blend camouflage."

We seemed to go transparent.

"OK, scream!"

We made a mumbled noise.

"No! I mean like you wanna wake everyone up screaming! Like this ... Yeeeeeeeeeaaaaaaaaaaaaa!"

And he screamed so loud we flinched.

"That sort of scream," he added.

"Yeeeeeeaaaaaaaahhhhh," we screamed.

Grandpop cupped his ear, "Louder."

"YEEEEEAAAAAHHHHHH!"

"And again."

"YEEAA..."

And then time slowed, the world lost it's colour and folded to a line. We fell forward, then backward, span, went into the place of light where all our presences were, now including Scotty and Tahira's dads and then faded to find ourselves in the brilliant blue sky, over the dark, blue sea.

**[+]**

Falling.

"... aaaaaahhhhh," we continued all feeling the awful drop and the fear in our tummies, but at the same time a huge sense of relief that we were all together and had each other to hold on to. We looked like pieces of the sky but with green outlines around us. It was funny we could see each other, and through each other.

I felt Scotty and Tahira holding me very hard and thought I must be doing the same. As the wind wall came up we started to relax more. It really was a nice day. Cold but beautiful with Aotea still in darkness below us.

It was Tarik who discovered the suits could adapt so that a thin skin extended down between our legs. It unbalanced the circle as Tarik started falling slower but then we all did it.

"Break up and see what you can do," Grandpop suggested.

We were a bit unwilling at first but one by one we released each other.

*"Hey! We can do it with our arms as well!"* Ashley said, and she had a skin between her wrists and her hips."

"Going around guys," Grandpop called

**[+]**

Time slowed, the world folded, we passed through the presence world and then we were falling again. This time separately. The panic rose, my heart rate soared in my chest.

**130**

"Fly apart," Grandpop instructed.

I closed my legs and arms and then the suit told me it was ready. I opened my legs and arms and I had skin there filling with air. I started seeing what I could do with it, slipping and sliding around. It felt good. I started to feel a bit more in control.

"Everyone head for Aotea," Grandpop said.

I was going exactly the other way. I found by lifting a leg and closing an arm I could turn quite quickly. In fact I spun a bit before I was headed in the right direction. I could see the others ahead of me. But the angle was low. I always wondered if the system would fail and we'd plummet to our deaths.

"Going around," Grandpop called.

**[+]**

And when the world came back we were way up in the air again. We had been falling for over a minute and we were starting to get used to it.

"See if you can pair up. Don't fly at each other. That's dangerous. Fly in the same direction, then hold one hand and swing around." Grandpop suggested.

It was harder than it sounded. The trick was to match speed and direction. It was easy to head in the same direction, but hard to match speed and angles. I dove past Tahira, then she dove past me, when I pulled up. By the time we got to the bottom we still didn't have it.

But halfway around the third time we finally linked up. We tried to link up with Tarik who was nearby, but by the time we were brought to the top again we decided just to have fun and cut each other loose.

"OK guys bringing you home this time, see if you can land on your feet. In ... five, four, three, two, one."

Time slowed and the world folded, we span and passed through the quiet place of light and then we hit the jumpstation floor hard. None of us stayed on our feet.

[+]

Grandpop was standing, smiling at us from the control area. We must have looked quite funny sprawled as we were.

"Good work guys! Who's hungry?"

I have to admit I was. Grandpop led us upstairs to the café. Mr Trân wasn't up yet. He didn't bake on the weekend usually. The sun was just up and starting to paint the windows in pink and orange brilliance.

Grandpop made us six cooked breakfasts with eggs, bacon, hash browns, and thick slices of heavy white bread with different teas (for Tahira, Ashley and Cam), coffee for Tarik, and juice for me and Scotty.

We gobbled that down in no time and then he put us to work doing the dishes.

"What I'm trying to teach you guys to do, is be invisible," he said as we dried our plates.

"You should be able to act in the world but nobody will notice you were ever there. That won't be because you *are* really invisible but because you are never out of place, and never leave anything out of place. At best they will not notice anything happened. At worst they know something happened but all they may vaguely remember were that there were some kids around somewhere. That's the ideal anyway. Which is why we are doing these dishes."

Sounded like a con to me. Still, when we finished he had a new suggestion.

"OK, this morning we're going to do some swimming."

"But Sir ..." Ashley began

"Mike."

"We just had our breakfast," Ashley objected.

"You aren't going right away Ashley. We're just going to the beach to have a little chat about it."

So he dragged us outside in the early morning light.

We crunched over the gravel, past the tussock and down to the high-tide line where we sat down on some big driftwood logs.

"Hekator's been telling me more about what your suits can do. He says they work just as well in water as they do in the air. For a start if you put your legs together you can ask it to join them together. Try it out."

I put my knees together, thought "join" and the skin that had joined our legs at the back when we were skydiving appeared at the front as well.

"Now, you turn your feet out. Don't worry about keeping your knees together, because you can't."

I twisted my feet out and found there was a skin between them now like a scoop-like fin. We laughed and compared fins. Tarik managed to scoop some stones with his fin. It was impossible to walk like that so Ashley slid off the log and couldn't get up again. We dragged her back.

"To get rid of all that, you do it all in reverse."

I pressed my feet together again and felt the skin disconnect. Then I pressed my knees back together and the same thing happened again.

"You also can also make your suits form a sharkskin which is rough like sandpaper. That will speed you up a bit too. Hekator says you'd swim twice as fast as you usually would like that. But to make up for the drag from your backpack your wings work

**133**

underwater. These will drive you at up to thirty kay which is as fast as dolphins, seals and sharks but not tuna or swordfish. To go that fast you need to be extra slippery. To do that you use your ultrasound. Ultrasound agitates the water to create tiny bubbles. It's called cavitation. Using that you can get up to sixty kay which is up there with swordfish."

We all agreed this was pretty cool.

"But there are limits. For a start you can't really go that deep. If it's dark in the daytime you are too deep. Your suit feeds you ordinary air and if you are too deep for too long you could get nitrogen narcosis, where you fall asleep, or worse the bends, when you change pressure too fast, In general stick to no deeper than thirty meters. You are faster closer to the surface than in the deep too."

"Sir ... Mike?" Cam asked.

"Just 'Mike' Sweety. The knighthood's a state secret," he smiled.

"Could we go faster by reducing gravity too?"

"Good question," he paused.

"I say 'good question' coz I asked that too," he smiled, then went on.

"Hekator said the answer is not much. The problem in water is drag not gravity. You already have the water holding you up to reduce gravity. So even if you have more power to your weight the real problem is pushing water out of the way and that isn't affected by gravity much. And because the speed of light is slower in water, apparently, the glow will be brighter."

"Which brings me to another problem. The other limit on speed is knowing where you are going. There's no point going like a bat out of hell if you're going to hit something before you know it's there. As any of you who have done it will know, eyesight is pretty hopeless underwater. You can see maybe fifty meters in the best conditions but when there's turbulence or mud, visibility is zero. Thermal vision isn't much better."

"So to help out your suit has extra sensors. The first is the whole surface of your suit can act like both a speaker and a microphone to detect vibration. It makes loud sounds ranging in frequency from deep, deep subsonic rumbles below human hearing up to very, very high pitched squeaks also outside human hearing. Using this you will be able to see all around you even in water so muddy you can't see your hands in front of your face. This is your situational sonar and it's good out to fifty meters depending how noisy you want to be. Remember you can turn it on and off because it will give away your position to animals and fishfinders. It also won't work if you are using cavitation."

"You also have a directional sonar in your backpacks. Directional sonar works the same as dolphin sonar. You send out clicks in a specific direction like a searchlight through the water. The echoes light up the distance ahead. This is what you would use at high speed because it has long range out to hundreds of meters. Directional sonar does work with cavitation – although not so well. It's also easily heard by animals and fishfinders, miles away."

"Your last sensor is electromagnetic. This is really cool. I liked this one. It uses an electric field to detect movement in very dirty water. It is very short range. No more than five meters, but it's completely silent. Some animals will affect it and it will upset fishfinders. You can't use this with cavitation either."

"So let's sum that up. You have three speed modes: ordinary swimming, swimming with wings, and cavitation. And three sensor modes: passive, where you use your eyes or electromagnetic sensors; noisy, where you use locational sonar; and long range, where you use directional sonar. You guys got that?"

We repeated them back to him.

"OK, one final thing. Hekator reminded me the sea is where the largest predators in the world live. I'm talking Orcas and white pointers for example. Most of them eat seals – which is exactly what *you* will look like. So you need some defences. The defences you have are an extension of the sensors. Your locational sonar can be very loud. This will make you seem bigger and scarier than you actually are. So you can sound like a Sperm whale or an Orca. In air it can also be used to make a subsonic frequency that spooks out people out to fifty meters away. "

"The directional sonar can also be used as a sound weapon. By shouting you can magnify your voice to a level of volume that will stun others for about fifteen seconds. At the right pitch you can also use ultrasound to shatter glass. It will work better in water and it can be used at very close range in air. Also you'll find you can change your voice so you sound deeper or higher if you want to. It won't change your voice pattern or accent but it will allow you to sound like other creatures or people."

"Your last defence is an electrical shock. It is powerful enough to knock out a shark or an Orca and it can kill fish as large as a tuna or giant squid. It uses a technology similar to the electric eel."

Grandpop stood up and smiled at us.

"Have fun," he grinned and walked off, leaving us on the beach in the early morning sunlight. We watched him go. We looked at each other for about two seconds and then raced each other to the sea.

It was weird getting to that beach we'd known from the summer wearing what looked like ordinary clothes. Of course we felt warm and almost naked. The sea which we knew was freezing barely seemed wet. We walked into the surf, sealing our suits, feeling the pressure of the waves, which were chest height, pushing us back to the beach. Then one by one we dove under the water.

Our vision under water was pretty poor and if our breathing had been in any way worse we might have panicked. But our air supply was good and we sank into the bright blurry world under water exploring our senses through the suit. The suit didn't float naturally but it didn't sink like a stone either, it just took a little effort to kick back to the surface. I joined my legs as I bobbed in the surf and dove under again.

The sounds of the sea seemed louder and more meaningful than I had previously known. I could hear the channel that separated our bay from open sea; the waves on the beach; and the others in the water more clearly and precisely than I could remember doing with my own ears.

A lot of light clicks started and not only did they make the location of the others more obvious they also picked out the shape of the bay in my mind and made the presence of a small shoal of fish nearby clear. I was focusing on swimming around using my whole body and arms. The added strength of the suit made rolling, turning and dashing much more enjoyable than with a wetsuit and flippers. You really did feel like a seal.

In the shallows of the bay it was still quite easy to see one another like murky shapes in the swirling water. We looked kind of odd in our jeans and hoodies. I asked the suit to change me to look more like a fish. I made my tail blue and my top light gray and changed to sharkskin.

"*Woah! Check out Sam!*" Ashley told the others.

"*He's The Thing!*" Tarik agreed.

Then they all changed. Tahira went for green scales and a white pale top. Cam had gold scales and a gold body. Ashley went for adaptive camouflage so she looked transparent with a brilliant blue stripe. Scotty copied me while Tarik copied Tahira.

"*It's a pity we can't do long hair,*" Cam said.

"*But you have short hair,*" Tarik pointed out.

"*So it would be nice to try something different,*" she shot back.

"*The gold is lovely,*" Ashley said.

"*I love the clear and fluro blue,*" I told Ashley.

"*Thanks Sam, I saw it on some fish in a goldfish bowl once.*"

We swam around the bay a bit testing our bodies and practicing with our sonar. It was funny. The sonar just fed into your sense of awareness. It just meant you knew where everyone else was, and where they were headed without having to see them.

We started playing with the directional sonar. It was sort of like having a lantern and a spotlight on a dark night. The spotlight gave you an intense view of the sea beyond but it was narrow so you still wondered what else there was.

After about ten minutes of playing around. Grandpop spoke to us.

"Hey guys how about you head out to sea and see if you can catch us something for dinner."

There were a range of responses to that. Me, Cam and Scotty were into it, but Tahira, Ashley and Tarik were less keen. Tahira because she thought fish smelly, Tarik because he thought it would attract sharks and Ashley because she hated the idea of

killing anything. Me and Scotty lined up on the channel and
started our wings. The increase in power and speed was great!
By listening carefully you could hear the rocks and small islands
that dotted the big bay and the rest of it was the big wide ocean
that stretched halfway around the world to South America.

It was different to any other experience of swimming I'd ever
had. It was effortless. You could breathe without having to worry
about getting a lungful of water. It wasn't cold at all, just like
wearing an extra layer of warm muscle. The power of the suit
meant you could move more like a seal than a diver, but you still
had your arms free. We swept out over the rocks and seaweed
towards the deep water, chasing and dodging each other.

There were Ka-whai and butterfish flitting about among the
seaweed. You could see about twenty five to thirty meters but
everything after that disappeared into the blue gloom. Our sonar
was telling us there were bigger fish further out.

Then we spotted a couple of snapper and chased after them.
They were very pretty: maybe half a meter long, silver and
flashing as they dodged and twisted. It was Scotty who first
got close enough to grab one and hesitated, pointing out the
problem with fishing this way.

"*So if I catch one, where do I put it? I mean do I have carry a
dead fish around with me until we go in?*"

"*Exactly,*" Tahira agreed.

"*Maybe we grab one before we go in,*" I suggested.

So we played some more chasing games and experimented
with cavitation. It was amazing how much faster it made you.
We zoomed further out leaving a wake of tiny bubbles like
underwater jets.

The seafloor dropped away beneath us into a dark blue-black

nothing below. You got the definite feeling we were now out in the sea where the big fish live.

Not having heard them before we picked up some clicks and wondered what they were. Some large fish loomed out of the gloom and swept past and then we realised they weren't fish at all but some of the local dolphins. They were about a meter longer than us and fast, but now we could keep up with them easily.

If Ashley and Tahira had been holding back a little before, the dolphins changed everything. The way they started gushing anyone would think dolphins were cuddly bunnies. We played around with the small pod of three for a while. They certainly seemed to be quite curious about us, but even so I knew from my trips out on Hua Kai that dolphins are not pets. They are wild animals who are clever and quick. They don't live by being cute, but by killing things.

Still I was surprised how Ashley and Tahira seemed to be able to communicate with the dolphins. They got them to jump or follow them with surprising ease.

*"You just think it. They seem to get the idea,"* Ashley said.

Me, Scotty and Cam meanwhile had spotted something more interesting. It was a large Kingfish about half as big as us. We chased it and the dolphins lost interest in playing games and joined in. It was Cam who darting after it got her hand to it. Suddenly the fish jolted and was floating lifelessly in the water. The dolphins closed with it, nosed it around and then started tearing it to bits. The sea swirled red with blood.

Cam, Scotty and me were a bit grumpy. We'd caught the thing and now the dolphins were chowing down on it. Ashley and Tahira also found the dolphins a little less cute now that they could see their razor sharp teeth.

Still they certainly seemed happy for the free meal and swam around us like playful dogs. Then in the distance we heard the unmistakable sound of an outboard engine. It was getting closer. "Guys. We don't want any spearfishermen reporting mermaids near Renwick. Better come in," Grandpop instructed.

We set off in a zigzag pattern in the direction of home. Me and Scotty increased the range of our sonar and that seemed to make the dolphins a bit nervous of us. We started moving so fast they were left behind with Ashley and Tahira.

"*Hey Cam, come and look at these,*" Tarik called to her.

Me and Scotty found another Kingfish and chased it. It was tricky but we were too fast. The chase only lasted half a minute before Scotty grabbed it. It shuddered and stopped swimming. It was a good size. Not as big as the other one but still at least half as big as us. My map told me Ashley, Tahira and the dolphins were headed this way so I told Scotty to make for the beach while I headed them off. I took off at an angle to Ashley and Tahira. The boat was definitely getting closer.

I zoomed about but the dolphins seemed to be stuck on the girls, so with the boat throttling back about half a kilometer to the south but closer to shore, we dashed back for the channel at high speed leaving the dolphins behind us.

We got back into our home bay and started separating our legs and reshaping them to be like clothes again while our wings carried us in. Ashley and Tahira had raced each other in and zoomed up the beach to leap out of the surf like a couple of penguins. I followed and discovered what they already knew: landing on your feet and staying on them was hard. Ashley and Tahira were face down in the sand giggling together.

**141**

It turned out we'd made a good haul. As well as the Kingfish Cam and Tarik had taken a couple of lobsters. We dragged the big fish back over the beach to Renwick House in time to meet Grandpop coming out the front door.

"Not in the *front* door! Mrs Jones'll have kittens! Take it around the side," he growled.

So we dragged the fish around the side.

Mr Trân looked a little shocked to see the size of the Kingfish, when we brought it into the kitchen, but he was very pleased with the lobsters. Grandpop got out a plastic apron and set to work chopping up the fish.

"What should we do now?" we asked him.

"Take a break," he advised. "Or better still go have a shower, you're all a bit smelly."

It felt weird to go back to our apartment and take a shower with my suit on. Aunty Liz was in her room and came out to see who had come in.

"How did it ... oh where have you been?"

"Swimming."

"Oh ... just swimming?"

"No, we caught a Kingfish. Grandpop's chopping it up. He told us to take a shower."

"Oh ... OK."

I got into the shower and sealed up. The water splashed over me. It was like standing in the shower in the driest most leakproof coat you could imagine. I tried to use a bit of vanilla bodywash because it seemed like a good idea but the suit gave me a prickly feeling so I didn't. Then I turned the shower off.

If taking a shower in your clothes was weird, drying yourself in them was weirder. The suit was covered with short fur which resisted water. If you rubbed it the wrong way you looked like a weird fuzzy creature. The suit *hated* that. All you could do was dab yourself. The suit absorbed the rest of the water.

The rest of the day was nothing like as exciting. After lunch we had to do our cleaning. But after that we played more hiding and sneaking games. We experimented with hiding in the sea, climbing trees, and different kinds of camouflage. Then in the evening we did another jump before changing and eating our Kingfish for dinner.

And that was the pattern for the whole holiday.

Our skydiving improved quickly. We learned how to manoeuvre together and individually. We jumped over different parts of the country from different heights all the way up to 90,000 feet at the edge of space and we learned to use our wings.

The wings were made of the same stuff as the facescreen so they took a moment to work. When you were behind someone you'd see their "schoolbag" pop open and wings fly out trailing in the slipstream. Then they would straighten, angle and if you hadn't deployed yours you would go shooting past the others as their wings allowed them to do more flying and less falling.

We were still falling though and it became hard sometimes to judge speeds as we practiced diving down, swooping up and stalling as a way of landing without bending. Control started giving us imaginary hills to practice landing on. The suit (and therefore, we) could see them as if they were floating in the sky. At first they were transparent, but the lower we got the more solid they looked.

The detail was very good too. Even when you were rushing up an imaginary slope at two hundred kilometers an hour you could see every detail of the imaginary land below. Sometimes there were even animals on them just to distract our attention and make us 'crash'. When you 'crashed' into the imaginary hillside it was good to know you were really still a kilometer up with plenty of room.

By the end of the holidays we pretty much had got stalls sussed. We had two main patterns: falling leaf and spirals. In falling leaf we'd dive, then pull up, and either go horizontally as long as we could, or fly a big arc like we were on a big swing. Finally we'd come to the end of the arc, then we'd fall again, and do it back the other way.

Spirals were like falling leaf except we added a curve to our levelling out and climbing. Spirals had to be quite large or you'd just fall. But it was huge fun putting your head down and diving then spreading your wings, flapping carefully and using the speed to pull out first into level flight and then into a climb up.... up until that awesome moment when for just a second you weren't falling anymore at all. Then you'd plummet and could do it all over again.

A few days into the holidays Dr Prosperov announced he had to make a business trip and would be back in eight days. We paid no real attention when he left. We were just having too much fun.

We did a lot more underwater diving. Ashley and Tahira loved playing with the dolphins and went out whenever the weather was bad – which was the only time that the fishermen certainly wouldn't be.

We had found a few more pods of dolphins, including bigger ones; seals and even some smaller whales as well. Ashley and Tahira were still blissed-out by dolphins. They would gush and goo about them and have to be reminded not to talk in front of

Rewa or Asal who would get jealous-as again. Personally I felt the dolphins deserved more respect. The big ones were much bigger than us. Scotty was sure there would be trouble.

He was right. Their fantasy was ruined by the dolphins themselves. They were not just bullies but pervs as well. Ashley was shocked to see a big dolphin bullying a smaller one and they were also a bit quiet when they watched a few of the older ones playing a fairly mean game involving tug of war with live Kingfish which they ripped in half.

But the real clincher came a bit later. We were fishing and Ashley and Tahira had gone off to frolic with their dolphin pals when there was a big vibration like an earthquake through the water and every living thing except us seemed to vanish. A bit later Tahira and Ashley swam past heading in.

"*What was that*?" Tarik wanted to know as we caught up.

"*Me*," Tahira said shortly.

It turned out two of the bigger teenage male dolphins had got a bit too fresh with Ashley. As I said they are big animals and could be pushy. They were somehow aware Tahira and Ashley were girls and starting to herd them away. Tahira said judging by the way their boy bits were showing, she doubted it was to show them their seahorse collections. Tahira had used infrasound at low power to warn them off. What we had felt like an earthquake was not even sent in our direction.

"I used low power," Tahira said later to Hekator.

"I only wanted to scare them a little."

"You probably sounded like a whale to them." he smiled. "but good work Tahira you used the defence system the way it was intended."

We did see the dolphins again and they seemed friendly enough but Ashley and Tahira were a bit less gushy about them now. Under water we were going further out together. Rather than swim out, we bent out. Control said it was easier to arrive over the water than in it. Then we'd check out schools of tuna or marlin. Sometimes we'd see whales. We had to blast a bunch of barracuda who definitely had us sized up for lunch.

The weirdest moment was when a boat showed up suddenly near the Three Kings Islands and a diver came into the sea where we were. We used adaptive camouflage so we were incredibly hard to see and he was fixated on the lobsters we had also come for, but Grandpop's voice was in our ears.

"Come home people."

One by one we winked out. I was last to go. He saw nothing. We also explored Aotea in our suits. We talked about stall landing on to it but when it came down to it the cliffs seemed a bit too big and the trees on the ridges too tall to make it work. We went caving. This was when we discovered the three ducks in the caves we'd explored over Summer. Normally caving and cave diving are the most dangerous thing you can do, but of course we had the huge advantage that we could bend out if we got into trouble. We all had to do that at least once too. It was scary realising that without our suits we would be dead underground, rotting in some freezing, dark water. But we also learned more about working as a team.

Grandpop sent us to explore different places around New Zealand. The easy ones were places like mountains in snowstorms. There was nobody around to see us, we were warm and we didn't even need to worry about avalanches especially. What was hard was dealing with deep snow and high winds. If we reduced our weight the wind got us and if we didn't we were in waist deep snow which was too slow. Grandpop said he'd pass on the problem to Hekator.

Marshes and bogs were similar. We slimed around in a few of those for half a day and came to the conclusion the only way we could deal with them was with gravity reduction. Without the high winds there was less of a problem and the trees and grasses reduced the effect of the glow. But we sure looked spooky, especially at night.

The strangest trip was a weekend visit to Auckland. It was only fifty kilometers away from home but it seemed like a strange new world. We walked about the city, went into shops and checked out the cinemas but when we bent home again from a forgotten doorway it was something of a relief. There just hadn't been anything to *do* there except watch other kids on the skateboards.

The last weekend of holidays before we went back to school seemed like a strange path back from an adventure playground to such boredom it was hard to imagine it could all be on the same planet.

We celebrated our last night of freedom by skydiving over Auckland. With the suit's vision we had the whole city below us. We could see in people's windows who would never have guessed in a million years that a kid, out in the night sky forty kilometers away, was falling from the stars and could see them drinking wine by the fire.

Then Dr Prosperov came back and set the cat among the pigeons by announcing our first guests were arriving at the end of the next week. We had six days to be ready.

●●●

## CHAPTER THIRTY SEVEN: SIR MICHAEL STRIKES BACK

At four o'clock after six hours of talking I finally stop my epic storytelling session because Caz and Julia come back home. My throat is raw and totally sore. I've taken Sue through half a year of my life from escaping Ax to the start of our training. We get up and go in to greet them.

In a funny way the story I've told Sue still hangs over us. It feels like it's there, around us, suspended. Like a movie you're in the middle of watching and it's still on your mind. I get some yoghurt to soothe my throat. It feels so good; all cool and runny. I sit at the table inside, just letting it slide down. Sue seems distracted.

"Julia can I borrow your car? There's a few things I need to do," I hear her ask.

"Sure Sue. When do you want to eat?"

"Uh, I dunno. It's your house. If I'm not back could you keep something for me?"

"Sure," replies Julia and tosses Sue her keys.

I'm not sure what Sue is going to do but I have a feeling she wants to go back home and get ready for work tomorrow, and then maybe go to her work and check out my story when there will be fewer people around to hassle her.

My worry is that if she goes home *they* might get her, but she's decided she's a trained police officer and can handle anyone who might cause problems. I think the weirdness of my story has lost her again.

She's gone back to thinking most of my problem is in my head. She knows nothing of the dangers facing her, but I also know if I try to tell her any different she'll just get grumpy with me. Caz comes over and casually sits down at the long table opposite me.

"Howd'it go today Sam? Sue give you the third degree?" she asks.

I shake my head.

"I never talked so much in all my life," I gasp and take another cool spoon of yoghurt.

"Do you think you gave her any clues?"

I shake my head again. She watches me intently through her sharp Chinese eyes.

"I told her about half of the first year but the real action was all in the second."

"It took you *all day* to tell her about six months?"

"It was a pretty special time. We made some huge discoveries."

"What sort of discoveries?"

I'd love to say, "oh we just made first contact with an advanced alien civilisation and got trained as superheroes," but I can't. So I just lamely say, "About the world, about ourselves and ... stuff."

Caz thinks about that for a while.

"Yeah, I s'pose a really big half year could take all day ... maybe ... if you were being detailed."

I don't know what to say to that so I finish my yoghurt.

"Did it help *you*?" Caz asks suddenly.

"What?" I ask, confused.

"Did it help *you*, telling her all that stuff?"

I had to think about that.

"I guess so. When you've had to keep a secret so long you tend to half forget it. When you tell, you make sense of it. So I guess letting it out did help a bit, yeah."

She bends her head down lower to look me in the eyes under my hoody.

"Go on tell *me* !" she smiles. "I'm dying to know."

I laugh. She's lovely. Then I stand up and pause.

"If you want to know," I whisper, looking into her lovely brown eyes. "I became a super secret agent. Ask Sue about it. My throat's too raw to say it all again."

Then I take my bowl into the kitchen, rinse it, and Julia shows me where to put it in the dishwasher.

"*Chi di gin* (see you later)," I say to Caz in my best Cantonese, and go up to my room.

Upstairs I close the door and plug Qi into my phone.

"You have new messages from para.no.ID at the dead drop," he announces.

"Good! Let's hear them."

"The first message is timestamped at twelve ten UTC. Decoded message header is 'About Sian'. Decoded message body says 'Michael emailed Central Bank asking for time to land fish. He requests Sian email code phrase three'."

Central Bank was our code name for the main email address the Administration used. Dr Morozov had got Para.no.ID to watch it for us as a way of putting more distance between us and the Administration. The message meant Para.no.ID had intercepted Sir Michael emailing the Administration and asking for more time to convince me. That, I had expected. What I hadn't expected was that he was asking his daughter to send a safety code. That could only mean one thing – she had been kidnapped and was being held hostage.

"Second message is timestamped at twelve thirty eight UTC. Decoded Message Header 'About Sian'. Decoded message body says 'Sian emailed Sir Michael from Yahoo account SHS93 from a Swiss connection via cell account registered to Erich von Streicher. Her message was 'wish u were here'."

The second was Sian's message from a yahoo address accessed via a mobile. At face value it meant Erich von Streicher had Sir Michael's daughter, Sian Hamilton-Smythe, with him as a hostage somewhere in Europe – probably Switzerland or Austria. The interesting thing was Von Streicher was a member of the infiltrator group 'Die Bruderschaft'. I thought he was wanted by the Administration for questioning about their conspiracy. When we last looked, the whole Brudershaft gang was. But here was 'Central Bank' or the Administration passing on messages to him.

That could only mean the Center was taking this whole operation against us very seriously. Someone in the Administration wanted us, and the Fae, so bad they would work with the infiltrators.

It might explain Sir Michael's apparent change of loyalty too. Baron von Streicher is not someone you leave your daughter with if you can help it. He'a tall, pale, white haired man who looks to be in his sixties. In fact he is at least several centuries old, drinks blood, and regularly eats the raw crushed marrow of fresh young human bones. It keeps him young.

"Third message is timestamped one forty UTC. Decoded message header 'make your woman happy'. Decoded message body, 'Von Streicher cell geotrace streaming channel opened, updates ten minutes, and then an RSS address. Car registration MNS 0778 Qo. Good luck'."

The third message is the web address for an RSS data stream to tell me where von Streicher's mobile is every ten minutes and the numberplate on his car.

That last message bothers me on a whole bunch of levels. It's telling me what to do. Dr Morozov had traded information in exchange for our information with para.no.ID. They'd never presume to suggest we *do* anything. They didn't even really know what we did anyway, so giving me a geocode feed was not something para.no.ID would even think of.

Obviously a geocode feed could easily lead me anywhere convenient for *them* or the infiltrators to get me. Hiding out, somewhere in some unknown house in Auckland with a police officer and a couple of lawyers on my case I was pretty hard to get extract. Flying around Europe looking for damsels in distress in Ka-rea-rea would mean I would be a sitting duck if a scout was waiting to catch me.

So all these messages were all wrong. They sounded more like Sir Michael telling me to rush off and rescue his daughter, not the para.no.ID we knew. Although the codes were all good that just suggested the whole para.no.ID network was compromised. So far our enemies had compromised two of our allies: Sir Michael and para.no.ID. Everyone I had called for help on Wednesday had actually been an enemy out to get me!

If para.no.ID was compromised that suggested how Ashley had been tagged. Nathan had left messages for Ashley through the para.no.ID dead drop system. No one else had. It was a simple system: coded messages were embedded in one or more spam messages and broadcast to the entire internet. They looked

like the usual emails offering fake watches or sex treatments
or chances to make heaps of money from Nigeria but inside
them were the real messages. We could even make messages
out of real spam. The key to the code was sent separately, not
as a normal email but hidden in network control messages. The
theory was the sheer volume of spam and the unpredictability of
the messages made it impossible to find the hidden real message
in the mass of emails. Even better, there could be more than one
hidden message in any given combination of emails. Because
the spam was transmitted to everyone in the world there was
no problem with anyone monitoring the content. There was
mountains of content but without the key it was useless, while
the coded key looked meaningless unless you knew what to do
with it. We'd assumed the system was secure. Maybe it wasn't.
But if Ashley was safe, what about Nathan?

Our whole mission was to keep kids like Nathan safe and it
looked like we had endangered him. The simplest way to see if
he was OK was to just phone him at his grandmother's house.
But if *they* were on to him (as they certainly were) it would
be hard to know if I was actually talking to Nathan, or some
Cybermind tapped into the exchange and imitating him. The
only way to know for sure was to go to Washington and see him.
I didn't like that idea at all. First Washington DC is a big busy
city which the US Air Force protects fairly seriously so getting
close and landing Ka-rea-rea there without being spotted would
be harder than normal. Then, even if I did get down, Capitol
Heights, where Nathan's grandmother lives, is not the safest
DC suburb. Out of Ka-rea-rea I'd be as vulnerable as any other
smallish teen there. It was OKish during the day but gangs run
rampant at night there and anyone out of their home block is

fair game (as Nathan had found out the hard way). DC wasn't somewhere I liked the idea of being caught out without a suit or back-up.

Then the question was whether *they,* or the infiltrators, had tapped Nathan as bait and were just watching him in order to get to us. I needed to see if Nathan had posted anything lately. I also needed to see how he responded to random phone calls. As far as I knew they had my voice prints from my dinner with Sir Michael so I couldn't be on the phone to him or they'd trace me faster than the National Security Agency.

The best I could come up with was to get someone else to call Nathan and see how he was. I immediately thought of Lana Vilenskaya. She was on the wrong side of the continent in L.A, but she may know someone who could call Nathan locally.

It was Saturday night her time. I had no idea where she would be on a Saturday night in L.A. The safest thing to do was to call her on her mobile from my mobile. If they were tracking voice prints they'd take a while to work out where I was. If I used Caz and Julia's phone they'd know *exactly* where I was. Qi had Lana's number.

I dial it. There's a long, worrying, pause and finally an American ring tone. It rings for a while and goes to messaging. I'm not doing *that*. I hang up and try again. Again it goes to messaging. The third time I try someone answers.

"Hello?" a man replies uncertainly.

"Hi, is Lana there?" I'm suspicious and ready to hang up.

"Uh ... are you a family member or relative?"

God! I knew immediately why he asked that. Only police talk like that. Lana was dead. I could feel a cold lead weight in my stomach.

"What happened?" I ask urgently. I should disconnect but I need to know.

"Uh ... look, who are you?" he asks.

"How did they do it? Did they shoot her?" I ask.

There's a loud siren whooping in the background.

"Hang on a minute."

He's in the street but I have his attention. The sound stops.

"Son, where are you? What do you know about this?"

"If you guys think this is an accident think again."

I'm reading him. He's just got to the scene. She's on the ground, face up, with blood coming from her head.

"Who are you?"

"I'm a friend of Lana's. They used a car didn't they?"

"It's a hit and run. Look son, if you know something you should tell me about it. I'm Patrolman Larry Johnson LAPD. It's just a motor vehicle accident unless there's a lead to follow."

"Yeah, I wish I could help, Sir ... I really, really do."

I hang up. I've been on too long as it is.

I can't believe it! They've killed Lana! The evil, murdering criminals! They're so determined to get us. Sir Michael mentions her at the restaurant two nights ago and now she's dead.

It's a reminder of the stakes I'm dealing with. Their Service is out to kill all of Fae. A whole planet. One more or less of us doesn't matter a damn to *them*. I have to wipe my eyes a bit. I'm getting emotional. I can't help it. The whole mission is failing. Nathan's in danger and I can't help him. I'm all alone and in hiding and my own survival is not exactly certain. I start to wonder how long I can keep this up. The stress is getting to me. I need to calm down.

I decide I need to breathe and pray for Lana. She was a good woman. She should have stayed a Fae. I take deep breaths and think about Lana. I remember her laughter, her funny clothes, her clever designs.

As I focus I feel a presence. Lana is free. She isn't so unhappy. It had been an unlucky life anyway. And a new impression settles over me. It wasn't murder. She'd done it herself. She'd stepped out in front of a car because *they* were chasing her. She had chosen death over capture.

I open my eyes and take a deep breath.

Death over capture! It's coming down to it now. *They're* drawing closer. *They're* breathing down my neck and any minute *they'd* reach out and I'd find myself in the same position as Sir Michael or Lana. I'd face a simple choice. Give in and do what they want like Sir Michael, or die like Lana.

I feel so hunted. They have all the power and I've got nothing to work with! It's so f___ unfair! I'm only fourteen! I don't want to do *either* ! Why is it all up to me! Where the f_____ is everyone? I take some more breaths. I need to get a grip on myself. I need to focus. I think about my situation.

I know I've taken my eye off the ball, relaxing in the garden with Sue. Of course, after a week on the run I *needed* to relax. How many times over the last year had we just stepped away from stressful situations so we could keep our heads together? You just can't keep going on adrenaline forever. You need some down time or you'll crack up and make a mistake.

But while I've been relaxing my enemies had not been pausing. There is no doubt about it. They are definitely out to get me. The pressure is stacking up and even though I'm drawing Sue in, I still feel very alone.

I'd known the risks as soon as the others had evacuated but now everything is stacking up around me. Sir Michael is working for *them*, the para.no.ID network probably is too, Lana's dead, and Nathan is in danger, and of course innocent Sian Hamilton-Smythe is also in danger of being murdered!

I'm panicking. Exactly what Grandpop said was the worst thing we could do. I need to take stock. Think. Breathe. Make a list. Doctors and pilots use lists. That's how you turn panic into a logical steps.

The first problem is Sue has gone home. Sir Michael's minder Antonio Rossi will almost certainly be after her. So my first step is to protect Sue. But I can't do that forever. I have to make them chase me instead. The best way to draw them away from Sue is if they think I *have* fallen for Sir Michael's para.no.ID 's trick and head north. Then they have no need to bother Sue, because they can focus on catching me instead. If I give them the impression I've fallen for their trick, I can take off and go somewhere else giving me a head start before they realise I'm not going to be caught that way.

But first I have to make sure Sue is OK.

Outside, the sky is still light and the weather is good. I can see houses all around us. Flying out the window will be tricky. I'm too close for warp invisibility. Anyone nearby would see a halo around nothing. The other option is adaptive. Adaptive camouflage in bright environments is nowhere near as effective as in the dark. Still, I have no choice.

I open the window as wide as it will go, then open Ka-rea-rea, hop in, and quietly slip out the window under the big oak tree. I switch on adaptive camouflage. If I'm slow people might notice me and take pictures. If I'm real fast they might notice some sort of movement but it will be over before they know what they're seeing. I go inertialess and shoot out the window and up two kilometers in about three seconds before levelling off. It's so fast even I find it hard to understand as I fly over Parnell in the afternoon light. Then I switch off inertialess and switch on warp camouflage because now I'm outside halo range.

Invisible, I head west for Sue's house. I'm over it in about five seconds. I can see Julia's car in Sue's carport so I tap Sue's house windows with the beam mike. All I can hear is snatches of Sue singing, a radio in the background, a vacuum cleaner and the washing machine.

After being so keyed up do I feel dumb! I'm flying tactical air support for vacuum cleaning. But it's so nice to be wrong. They aren't as close as I thought they were.

I decide, now that I'm up here, to go and check out Sir Michael's jet. Within a minute I'm over Auckland International Airport. The radio traffic is busy and there's a lot of radars about, but none of them can see me because light and radar signals wrap around Ka-rea-rea's hull like a stone in a stream. It looks to them like there's nothing here.

Hovering two kilometers above Sir Michael's Falcon I set Ka-rea-rea to work checking his plane for transmissions. Ka-rea-rea tells me the Falcon has an Inmarsat data channel open so I ask him to intercept it.

It's a slow link and it takes a while. About five minutes into it I get a sense of unease. Something is happening with Sue.

I want to continue my tap but I daren't leave Sue unguarded and I whizz back over her house and lay my beam mike on her windows again.

The vacuum cleaner noise has gone. There are two voices: Sue's and a man with an Italian-Spanish accent I've heard before. It

**158**

sends a shiver down my spine. Of all the evil bastards Sue could get caught by this is the one I had *least* wanted her to meet: Father Enrico Rocelli.

There's a silver Ford parked in the road I didn't see before. Sue's voice is sleepy but Rocelli's is soothing and calm.

"He has it in his room," Sue tells him.

"Where is that Susan?" Rocelli's voice is gentle with a soft sing-song accent. But I know this monster well and my guess is Sir Michael's personal secretary, Antonio Rossi, is really Father Rocelli. He is practically everything that is evil inside the Roman Church.

"Upstairs first on the right."

So much for the security of Caz and Julia's. Now there is no safehouse! I'm on the f__ run again!

"And what have you been doing today Sue."

"Listening."

This is very bad news. I've told Sue enough to make her interesting to him. I have Ka-rea-rea spoof the cell network and place a call to Sue's homeline.

"Listening to what?"

"Him. He told me about last year."

The phone starts ringing. It's my call. There's a pause. Father Rocelli gives Sue instructions with gentle calmness.

"Susan, I'd like you to answer the phone, act normally but remember you're alone and haven't seen me ever in your life."

"I'll just get the phone," Sue says automatically.

She picks up.

"Williams," she says in my ear.

"Sue, it's Sam," I reply.

"Oh, hi Sam."

"Sue what is the name of the man in your house?"

"Uum..." she says.

She's now focused on the very thing her subconscious has been told not to reveal. Hypnotism is about suggestion to the relaxed unconscious. If it's interrupted by focus on the same topic by the conscious mind the internal tension starts to break the suggestive state.

"Sue you just told me it's Antonio Rossi or Father Enrico Rocelli."

I say that because he explicitly instructed her not to say that. Even the unconscious mind recognises that its instructions have become redundant.

"No I didn't!" she argues.

"Indirectly, Sue you just did."

"But that's not fair," she complains.

I was pretty sure she was now fully conscious.

"Exactly. Look the man in your house is extremely dangerous. It's very important that when you hang up, you run out into the street suddenly screaming for him not to touch you. You'll be OK if you do that immediately. Don't worry I'm overhead."

"Sam, for Christ's sake give me a break! I can't spend all day listening to your crazy stories. I've got work tomorrow! Now let me get my house tidy and my uniform clean without being constantly harassed with your bloody stupid, teenage fantasies." Then she hangs up.

It's so convincing that her sudden dash out the door catches both me and Rocelli by complete surprise. I see her run out of the house from above. She runs under the carport and into the street below and I'm amazed to see her mouth moving. She really is screaming and looking around.

The first I see of Rocelli is his face at the door. He looks up, I think he's looking for me. He looks angry. Sue's yelling at him now. Her next-door neighbour's come out. I can see Rocelli think about holing up in the house but then he realises he simply can't stay. He has huge powers – way more than me – but this is getting embarrassing, and out of control.

Sue ran at him yelling something. He sees his chance and shoving her aside, dashes out of Sue's house for his car. Emboldened, Sue runs after him shouting at him through the windscreen. She tries to stop him but the car pushes past her and drives off, up the street. Sue chases vaguely, yelling at him. I climb higher so Ka-rea-rea can track him.

At first he drives quickly but soon he looks like any other driver heading home after a Sunday afternoon drive. I call Sue as I watch him head towards the central city.

"Williams."

"That was amazing Sue."

"What are you doing?"

"Watching him."

"I still don't know what he did to me. All I remember is waking up, and finding myself getting angry with you on the phone, with a strange man in my house."

"I think he's the guy behind Sir Michael at the moment."

"Is he coming back?"

"No, I don't think so. He's heading towards the motorway. You can do your washing in peace."

"How did you know he'd come?"

"I told you they'd send someone. That's why we were hiding, remember?"

"Yeah, well what are you going to do now?"

**161**

"Take him out if I can."

"Sam!"

"Sue, we aren't playing tiddlywinks here. You remember Lana, the Fae who became human and designed our suits. Well, she suicided an hour ago to prevent the information *she* knew falling into their hands. The stuff I'm telling you isn't stories to keep your mind off your old girlfriend on a sunny afternoon. It's intelligence in a very old and very dirty war. Don't stay at home long. *They* will probably be back soon with numbers. I'll see you back … home," and I disconnected.

I didn't say Caz and Julia's on purpose. We didn't usually attack but we weren't usually under so much pressure and right now attack made sense. If Rocelli was taken out, and Sian whisked to safety, then Sir Michael had more freedom. Plus only Rocelli would have the key phrase needed to activate whatever he'd embedded in Sue's head.

*And* I was angry. *They* had killed Lana and I wasn't so damn noble that I was above taking out an international child abuser to let *them* know I had teeth.

Of course I wasn't going to burn his brain out. For a start a two millimeter cauterised hole in Rocelli's head would be a bit of a giveaway. Police would consult experts, the experts would recognise a high energy laser and then everyone would get excited and the investigation would become enormous – probably involving Sue. There are far better ways to get rough, nobody even notices. For example people put a lot of faith in tyres. Millions and millions of people the world over drive along at 100km/hr or faster on pumped up walls of rubber and steel only five millimeters thick on the side. That was my target.

I wait for Rocelli to get onto a median separated motorway. I

could have put him under a truck but why hurt a truck driver?
I'm not actually going to kill him with a car crash in a new car
stuffed with airbags close to a hospital. He's much more likely
just to be injured, but that would slow *them* down a bit.

He enters a single lane on-ramp at 70km/h. There's no-one
else he can hit. He's accelerating into the curve. My beam's on
his front wheel and I carve the tyre. The car stops following the
curve of the on-ramp and hits the side wall head-on, nose first,
bouncing off. The next car smashes Rocelli's passenger side door
and the car behind joins the pile. I always wonder why people
drive so close they can't stop.

He had no time to brake so that was a big hit. The front is
crumpled and there's steam from the smashed radiator. There's
no movement from inside Rocelli's car. Cars are stopping and
people rushing to help. I watch for a while to make sure Rocelli
isn't going to get up like some movie monster that won't die. But
no, I can see him slumped in his seat surrounded by deflated
airbag. My instruments can detect breathing and a pulse. He
probably hit his head on the B pillar with that second impact.
*They* will be angry but I may have bought some time so I can
relocate Sue. The trick will be doing it and not getting her all
ansty on me. The other option is I just f____ off.

I zoom back to Caz and Julia's to see if they've been visited yet.
The shadows are long and the light yellow, in leafy Parnell as I
stooge around overhead two kilometers up. I check the house
and hear Caz and Julia chatting away to each other about me.
They're wondering where I've gone and whether taking me on
might prove too much for them. It certainly will be if some men
in black suddenly bust in looking for me, that's for sure. That
isn't their cup of tea at all.

I consider surprising them by flying back into my room and pretending I've been there the whole time but there's a problem. The window to my bedroom is now shut. I can't fly Ka-rea-rea back inside without smashing it.

Sue isn't back yet. That's strange. She should have got there by now. I wonder where *she's* got to. I hope Rocelli hasn't sent her somewhere. I try reading her and get the impression she's popped into work. I decide to make sure by calling her on her work cell.

"Sam?" she picks up immediately.

"Hi Sue. Are you becoming psychic too?"

"No. Did you do anything to that man …?" she begins.

"You haven't checked?" I ask, thinking the police must have some sort of internal news service.

"Check what?"

"I dunno … police radio."

"No. I can't," she admits.

"Don't worry. He's alive. Hopefully a bit injured though."

"What did you *do*?" she asks mingling telling me off and worry.

"Don't ask Sue so you don't know. It could create problems later," I tell her, thinking that she doesn't need her colleagues linking her with an accident of a recent visitor. She can see my point.

"No, maybe not," she agrees.

"Hey Sue, Caz and Julia have closed my window. I can't get this thing back inside."

"Yeah, they called me saying you'd run off."

"What did you say?"

"I said you were doing something for me."

"Thanks Sue. I didn't need a lecture."

"Tell you what would be nice: if you got them a gift for having you."

"Where did *that* come from?" I ask.

I'm a bit suspicious of Sue having new ideas given she was hypnotised only half an hour earlier. There's something funny about this suggestion though. Something's tingling and made me feel it was weaving.

"It's what I would have got you to do and explains why you went off secretly," Sue says.

"Oh," I say, catching on.

"Something pretty for their house."

"Yeah ... Uh, OK,"

I wonder where I can find something like that at five on Sunday.

"Sue?" I ask.

"Yeah?"

"When will you be back at Caz and Julia's? We need to talk about security. Rocelli's down for the moment but his finding you has implications."

"Oh, about an hour. I've still got a few things to do. Look, I'm OK I'm in the biggest Police station in the region."

The 'few things' involve checking out what I'd said but she isn't telling me this yet.

"OK. Look, I might come back at the same time as you, so you can distract Caz and Julia a bit," I lie. Actually I want to cover her, just in case.

"Can I call you on this number?" Sue asks.

"No, it's a hack. Shall I call you back at six?"

"Yeah, OK."

We sign off.

A present for Caz and Julia's house!

Practically, where was I going to get a *present* at five on a Sunday? All the shops are shut. Sydney is probably open but how do I explain anything I might get from there? Plus that only gives me an hour to get over there, find a shop with something small and get back by six.

Girls and their damn presents!

That made me think of Emma and the diamond I'd given her. What about something from my treasure collection? That meant Renwick. It was the easiest, safest and most *obvious* solution. Unless of course *they* were watching Renwick. What if Sue had been hypnotised to suggest a problem easiest solved by returning to Renwick? After our last run-in with the Scout I was a bit nervous about going back. Still, on the other hand, Rocelli had just been told I had Ka-rea-rea in my room. Had he passed the location of Caz and Julia's before I got to him? If he had *they* would be focused on the safe house in Parnell. If he hadn't they might still be watching Renwick. And did Rocelli have back-up available?

There was no safe test. I just had to do it and find out.

So I zoom out to Aotea island with the sun setting behind me. I round the southern end over Port Carlyle and head out to sea for a few kilometers. Then I dive underwater, switch from warp invisibility to adaptive, and sneak up on Renwick's sheltered bay. Even if *they* have a survey craft overhead they won't spot me. I'm too small and too well hidden in the water. But if they're watching the hole we made in the floor closely they may well notice the tiny disturbance I make flying in.

Renwick's ruin is in shadow and the sky pale above the ridgeline. It makes the whole bay look dark and mysterious. I watch it for a while. It's very dull because nothing is happening. The waves crash onto the beach, the police tape ripples in the wind and the ash is flying around. I decide speed is best. If I get into the vault as fast as I can, even if they *are* watching, I'll be safe inside. Well, sort of.

I wait for ten minutes, building up my nerve. If *they* are watching, this would be over damn fast. After another five minutes I realise I'm huffing and puffing but not really doing anything.

There's nothing for it. I can feel the sweat on my hands making the grips inside Ka-rea-rea slippery. If I'm going to take the risk now is as good a time as any.

Ka-rea-rea erupts out of the waves, we skim over the water and beach in seconds, and drop into the hole I'd jumped into the previous day. I land, jump out of Ka-rea-rea, heart pounding, run to the door, do the security, and open the door. Then I dash back, leap into Ka-rea-rea and fly him inside. Inside the vault I jump out again and slam the vault door behind me, panting with the effort.

I'm breathing hard, trying to control my breath, listening intently through the door. There's a noise behind me. Two humanoid figures step out from the shadows behind the shelves. My heart stops. I'm going to faint. To be caught now, like this! Totally with my pants down.

"Howzit Bra?" Scotty's voice calls out.

Ashley just runs forward and hugs me. I slump into her arms. Then laughing Scotty joins in.

I can't help it. I just cry my eyes out with relief. There's a series of bright flares of light and Tahira, then Cam, then Tarik appear. It's so incredibly good to see them all again. I feel weak with relief.

**167**

Then we're all talking. Dr Prosperov has a new base. I tell them para.no.ID is probably compromised and tell them about the mission they sent me to rescue Sian. They all agree the message is highly suspicious.

"That's serious," Tarik says. "I'd better warn Morozov," and he vanishes.

"Hey. You have new suits!" I notice.

It's true. The bulky old schoolbags are gone. The hoods go down and the jackets are longer. They look much smaller than the old ones. They might even fit inside Ka-rea-rea, which the old ones couldn't do.

"Lana and Hekator had just finished them. Dese ain't no kindergarten romper suits but made jus' for us. Da Fae are stepping up support," Ashley tells me.

That reminds me of the worst news of all.

"Guys! Lana's dead! They killed her a few hours ago," I tell them.

"What!!?" they gasp. They're all really upset.

"Sir Michael's been compromised, Lana killed herself to escape capture, Para.no.ID are probably compromised, Nathan Robinson may well be too."

They're all shocked. They had no idea how fast things have been moving over the week they've been away. So I tell them what I've learned. Like me they're sad and angry. Then they tell me what's happened to them.

"The pod took us to a base in some moon that was pretty close to being a prison. It was all tunnels and doors and scans. We all had to change into these skimpy robes and all our clothes were destroyed. Then we had to have baths in this oil and pass through all these field analysers and things. We didn't get any food until that night and then it was mostly strange fruits, nuts

**168**

and raw fish. Their plant loos are pretty weird too. Like big Venus Flytraps except you have to sit on them and they have tongues instead of paper." Scott says.

"Oh *gross!*" I wince.

"There was this female avatar like Control who smiled a lot but kept telling us to be patient," Cam adds.

"We slept on bushes in a series of rooms with flowers and stuff but still felt like cells. The next day – it was hard to know what the time was – we finally got to see a hologram of Hekator. He told us we were in quarantine. Apparently nobody goes straight to Fae. Not even the Fae themselves. Quarantine is very strict. But he said they were getting ready to receive us," Scotty goes on.

"Your Aunt and sister were so worried 'bout you so Hekator promised to start searchin'," Ashley puts in.

"When we got to Fae Hekator said you were very hard to track. He found you but lost you again several times. No sooner were you in one place you were gone to another. It was only one night when you wanted to be found he had you for long enough to show your Aunt and sister." Scott continues.

"Yeah, in the hotel. I remember that!" I tell them.

"After three days in prison it was so good to get to Fae. Sam you have to see dat place! It's incredible! Rewa and Asal met a flying unicorn called Secret who took them all over," Ashley tells me.

"They made even Mariko look boring," Cam smiles at the memory.

"I like crystal spires best," Tahira says.

"Coral city was my favourite," Cam nods.

"Anyway it was amazing, but they made no secret of the fact they wanted us back on Earth," Scotty goes on.

"So we're working out of Vimana Ashanti while they set up the new base but this is our first trip since we've been back."

"Great. So where's the new base?" I ask wanting to see everyone again.

They suddenly look a bit sheepish.

"Sam, we'all been screened but you ain't. You cayn't join us til you are. We ain't even meant to *talk* to you," Ashley tells me, looking bothered.

I can't say I don't feel bad about it, but the fact they are talking to me anyway means a lot. I do understand.

"Hey don't worry Sam. It's just three days of boredom. At least you're safe there. Then you can join us again," Scotty says comfortingly.

"But what about Nathan?"

"We'll take dat over. You done enough already!" Ashley says.

"What about Sue?"

"What about her?" Ashley asks.

I explain my worries about her having been hypnotised by Rocelli.

"We might 'ave to erase 'er memory," Tahira concludes.

"What!? Why?" I explode.

"You said yourself. She is risk," she shrugs.

"But she's the best chance we have to come back to Earth."

"How do you work that out Sam?" Scott asks doubtfully.

"Look you guys weren't here but Renwick was all over the news for days. I mean worldwide. Everyone thinks you guys are dead! They're still looking for your bodies. I did my best to cover up but well ... if we all just disappear the mystery will just grow. They'll find the tunnels. They'll dig the place up. People will investigate. I mean the police are already investigating, but others will want to make TV shows and write books about the Renwick mystery. We don't need that do we?"

They look at each other, surprised and worried.

"We can't leave a mystery behind us. We need the cops to solve the case and find us again. It has to become boring or it'll turn into a legend like the Loch Ness monster or something," I warn them.

"I don't think Dr P has caught up with that yet," Scotty admits.

"Well, we need him to get it," I tell them.

"We'll tell him. So you reckon this cop is ok?" Scott asks.

"Sue? Yeah, she's been good. The Administration scout sure got her attention."

"What scout?" they all ask.

So now I have to tell them that story as well. By the time I've finished they sort of understand why Sue's become important to me.

"Was zere time for Rocelli to bug 'er?" Tahira asks.

"I dunno. Probably," I admit.

"If dey accept her, den she'll have to be screened too," Ashley says.

"She might not be too keen on that," I admit.

"Well, it's either dat or we erase her memory," Ashley says grimly.

Their faces are set. The Fae have obviously demanded a new level of security and they aren't going to let them down again.

I have no choice. They're my family. Sue either played it our way or she was out. There's a bright light and Tarik reappears.

"Look at it this way. If they let her come. At least you'll have someone to talk to in quarantine," Scotty says punching my arm.

"Sue's going to find this hard."

"She 'as a choice," Tahira shrugs.

"OK Sam, mate, I've got something for you to put on," Tarik says holding out an oval piece of leather with a violet jewel set in a silver mount on the front, like a necklace some old hippy might wear.

"It's a communicator. You'll be able to talk to us and we'll know where you are."

"Man it's ugly," I say, taking it and putting it on.

" 'old it against your neck," Tahira says coming forward to fuss.

It feels so good to have my friends around me again I nearly hug her.

Then I feel a strange sensation – the necklace is gluing itself to me and something is worming its way to my suit interface under my skin.

"It feels disgusting," Scotty nods.

It does.

"Tuck it under your clothes. It looks weird like dat," Ashley says.

I hide it away against my body.

Then I get a weird feeling. It's a bit like wearing a suit but without the comfort that normally came with it. I was online with the others.

"How are you boy?" Grandpop asks.

I couldn't help breaking into a big grin.

"You OK big brother?" Rewa asks.

"I need a hug as soon as you're out Sam," Aunty Liz tells me.

"Me too," says Rewa.

"Ay, and me three Sam. You've been badly missed here," Grandpop says.

I tell them I've missed them too. I had to wipe my eyes over that. Scott and Tarik pretend not to notice but Ashley and Tahira have moist eyes and big smiles too. Cam just smiles.

"Sam we need to bring you in soon so you'd better wrap up whatever you've been doing," Grandpop says.

"OK,"

The others are looking at me cautiously.

"*So what's the plan?*" Tarik asks silently.

It had been so long since I had used telepathy I took a while to catch on.

"*Is the food in quarantine really that bad?*" I ask them.

"*Well it's OK but not as good as Cam's dad makes it,*" Ashley says.

"*I have so missed his food,*" I nod to Cam.

"*I really want Sue to come too. I don't want to be there alone plus it'll give her a chance to really get up to speed.*"

"*That's up to Hekator,*" Scott warns.

"*Yeah. And Sue. If she just freaks out then it's all off. OK, look I've been staying at this safe house, but Rocelli found out where it is from Sue. Trouble is they're a couple of lawyers so it's all official and I can't just vanish. So I'll have dinner there and tell them that you guys are back and pretend to get a cab to the airport. I'll get Sue to come with me and she can decide how far she wants to go. So I should be out of there by about eight.*"

"*OK that's cool. But if you haven't called us in by eight we'll come and get you,*" Tarik says.

"*I'm looking forward to it … uh hang on,*" I say, remembering Sue's gift. I grab a pair of solid silver candlesticks from a box of lesser treasures.

"*For the lawyers,*" I explain.

"*Your share,*" Tarik shrugs.

I look at them all and speak.

"You know when I came in here I was planning to piss off overseas because *they* were closing in. All my safe houses were blown. Sue was in danger. You have no idea how good it is to see you."

"We really missed you, bra," Ashley tells me, for all of them. They give me another group hug.

"*What's it like outside Grandpop?*" I ask.

"Clear to a thousand kilometers. If they're watching they're using something pretty small," he replies.

"*Cool. See you guys soon,*" I tell the others.

I hop back into Ka-rea-rea while Cam and Tarik open the door. I nose out into the dim hole and the vault swings shut behind me. If it weren't for the necklace I'd worry I'd been hallucinating. It's like a dream come true. Then I turn Ka-rea-rea for the darkening sky and shoot out inertialess into the gathering dusk. The island is dark but I quickly zoom up over the ridge and head for the city. Auckland looks very pretty as I speed up and over it two kilometers up. The sodium orange lights and the signs reflecting in the inky harbour under a dull copper green sky look familiar and friendly. I am sooo relieved and sooo happy!

I'd been thinking about a lone last ditch flight to escape when I'd flown out, but now as I fly back in I'm linked back with my best friends. It's so great I roll and loop just for the fun of it. Finally I swing back over Parnell. It's evening and adaptive camo is enough. I have Ka-rea-rea land on a spot in the back garden under the oak tree.

Inside, I can see Caz and Julia in the kitchen through the big glasshouse. They're drinking wine and talking about Sue. Most of it is speculation about Rachel and whether they might get back together again. That annoys me because I know that it would be the worst possible thing for her.

I go to the back door of the glasshouse and knock quietly so they don't get a shock. Their heads turn and they look a little grumpy. Caz comes to the door and opens it.

"Where have you been Sam? We were getting worried about you."

"Sorry Caz, sorry Julia. Hey guess what? I've got you a present." They look a bit surprised but pleased.

And I take out the candlesticks and put them on the table.

"Sorry, I didn't have anything to wrap them with. We think they're 17th Century. Spanish of course. Peruvian Silver. I could have made it a silver spoon but I thought a pair of candlesticks looked nicer."

Caz looks a bit worried and steals a glance to Julia. I know what they're thinking. Maori hoody equals thief. It's a bit of a downer but I bury the anger behind a helpful smile.

"Sam, where did you get this?" Julia asks quietly.

"Renwick house. That's where I went. We have heaps of this sort of stuff in the vault. Ask Sue. She's seen it."

Caz looks at the candlesticks like they might leap up and bite her.

"*Sam,*" Julia smiles fakely. "That *really* is a lovely, *lovely* thought. It really is. Isn't it Caz?"

Caz is looking at me carefully.

"Uh ... ah yeah. It is!" she says catching Julia's eye.

"You really are a kind kid aren't you Sam?"

I smile at them, though inside I knew this was why I couldn't stay here.

"I hope you like it. It's sort of a thank you and a goodbye present really," I confess as I sit at the table next to Caz.

**175**

That gets their attention.

"Goodbye? Sam what do you mean? You said this morning you might live here," Julia begins.

"Where else would you go?" Caz asks.

"You offered to let me stay here ... which was very kind ... so I got you this gift," I begin.

"But you have to go to court first," Caz interrupts.

"Nah, I don't! Not any more anyway. They're back!"

"Who's back?"

"My Aunt and Grandpop. *And* everyone else. They're back. They're picking me up about eight."

"Sam!" explodes Julia, "*Oh*, that's *fantastic* news! *Oh* I'm *so* pleased for you!" she says and she really means it too. She rushes around and hugs me.

Caz is all smiles and leans forward and hugs me lightly.

"I just wanted to give you something to remember us by."

"Us?" Caz asks. She's sharp, this one.

"Me. Me and the others from Renwick."

"So how did it happen Sam. Did Sue call you..." her excitement falters.

"No, Sue doesn't know."

"So ... you found them?" Julia guesses.

"Yeah. They were emptying the vault. So when I got there, there they were."

"OK," Caz agrees doubtfully.

"But ... why didn't they call you dear?" Julia asks.

"Because I haven't slept in the same bed twice this week. I've been hard to find."

"But why not call the police?"

"Ah ... I don't know ... maybe you can ask ..."

The front door opens.

"It's Sue and her mystery dinner guest," Julia says.

Caz gets up and goes out to them.

"*What* dinner guest?" I ask.

"Caz this is Sir ..." I hear Sue say in the hall.

"Just call me Michael," an English accented voice says outside.

## CHAPTER THIRTY EIGHT: STEPPING OUT

I instantly let the others know what's happening.

Caz leads Sir Michael into the room. He's carrying a large bunch of flowers.

"For the cook," he announces passing them to Julia.

Sue has this enormous fake smile on and shoots me an angry and worried look. I'm a bit relieved. They're still reeling me in gently. They don't think they need to go hard. If they did there would be a whole gang of men in black.

"*Interesting,*" Dr Prosperov says inside my skull.

"*Start with gambit that you are falling for para.no.ID instructions. May prove illuminating.*"

"*It sure helps to know you guys are backing me up again,*" I reply silently.

"*Got your six brother,*" Tarik says.

"*Do you* have *to say stupid things like that*?" Ashley asks.

"*Shut up,*" I suggest.

"And Samuel," Sir Michael says turning to me, his eyes check me out carefully.

"You are certainly a remarkable young man! I never dreamed anyone so young could be so resourceful. You give me a lot of hope for our future," he smiles carefully and offers his hand.

That *was* a strange thing to say. I pause and then shake. His big fleshy hand is firm, but a bit clammy.

"I hope we can put any unpleasantness in the past behind us. I think you realise the pressure I'm under," he mutters.

"When your loved ones wish you were with them it stretches anyone's patience," I say quietly.

Sir Michael looks a little unsettled at my exact use of the code phrases he and his daughter, Sian, used, while the word "stretches" sounds similar to "Streicher". But I'm also giving it to Dr P as well. He'll know.

"Uh...yes...quite," Sir Michael says uncertainly.

"Well, I hope everyone likes lamb because that's what we're having," Julia tells us.

"Would you like a wine Michael. We're trying this Australian Shiraz. It's not bad at all," Caz puts in.

"Thank you Caz, it sounds splendid."

I slip around the counter.

"Would you like a drink Sam?" Julia asks.

"Me? Oh, ah...yes please. Apple juice would be nice."

Julia turns to the fridge.

"Sue, I think Sam has some news for you," Caz says .

I'm not sure how this is going to work and I notice Sir Michael catch me looking uncertain. This is going to take some serious acting skills. I have to convince Sir Michael I'm lying because I'm following Para.no.ID's tip, but I also have to keep the faith with Sue and my hosts. Luckily my hesitation helps me.

"Yes. Ah ... well," I stumble. "I got Caz and Julia a present this afternoon ... a goodbye present ... because I, ah I, have to go ... you see I met the others and they're back. And so ... They ... well, I'm going to go back home with them."

I say this with as much cold dread as anyone going to battle the

Bruderschaft might have. Sir Michael's glass is frozen to his lips. His blue eyes are scanning me like a bomb detector. Sue's looking shocked and confused but it's she who chokes out a few uncertain words first.

"That's ... ah ... great Sam. You met them today?"

"Yes, It was completely out of the blue when I got the present from Renwick. I'm no longer marooned. They're picking me up tonight," I say, using the code words again and still looking as uncertain and nervous as anyone planning to go half the way around the world to do something dangerous could.

"Tonight?" Sir Michael repeats.

"Yeah, I dunno how. I just gave them this address."

"You have seen Dr Prosperov?" Sir Michael checks.

"No ... no not yet. Just some of the others."

I needed a lie that Sir Michael could detect, but not the others.

"At Renwick?" Sue asks.

"Yes."

"But none of the adults?" she persists.

"Uh apart from Ken, no," I lie. I was trying to look as sus as possible.

"What were they doing?"

"Emptying the vault," I say truthfully. "It's not really much use where it is."

Sir Michael is thinking carefully.

"So you can get into the vault?" he asks.

"Yeah ... that's how I got these candlesticks for Caz and Julia." I point to them.

"Thanks Julia," I say taking an apple juice. It feels good on my throat which is still sore.

Sir Michael and Sue look at the candlesticks.

"Huh ... Gennady gave me some just like them," Sir Micheal nods with recognition.

"Seventeenth century Spanish design in Peruvian silver."

Caz and Julia's eyes turned to me with surprise and appreciation.

"Never did tell me where he got them, although the chap who valued it for me said they were worth around a thousand quid," Sir Michael adds.

"So Sam, uh where is Dr Prosperov? I have quite a few questions for him." Sue asks. If she'd had a tail it would have been twitching.

"*Say am on superyacht,*" Dr Prosperov told me.

"He's on a superyacht with everyone else. They're out to sea."

"*Is it Shulyagin again?*" Sir Michael asks.

"I don't know Sir Michael," I reply honestly.

"Did they tell you why they left you behind?" Sue asks.

"Ah yeah, well they were a bit grumpy with me for taking off that day. I'd arranged to see someone and ..." I trail off.

Sue is looking really pissed off. Sir Michael is smiling craftily. He's decided my story is so thin I need help.

"Well, all's wells that ends well anyway," Sir Michael says. He seems to have concluded I am making all of this up so I could follow the instructions Para.no.ID fed me. It's working.

"So after they pick you up when will you be back? There's a lot loose ends to tie up you know," Sue says, annoyed.

"Oh about three days. We'll be back before the court hearing don't worry about that," I tell both Sue and Dr Prosperov. Then I turn to Sir Michael slightly and catch his eye.

"There's just a few things I have to take care of first," I have to think rescuing Sian is going to be tough and keep a straight face.

He nods slightly at the hint.

"Of course … I suppose you'll be needing to find a new place to live," Sir Michael suggests.

"Yes. I guess I … I mean *we* will," I agree.

"Well, I'm ready to serve if you're ready to eat," Julia announces. There's a kind of flatness to the mood. Where you'd expect me to be celebrating I seem distracted and withdrawn. Caz and Julia are confused but aren't sure what they should do. Sue's wondering whether everything I've told her all day is a pack of lies and she's pretty annoyed.

"Can I help? Set the table or something?" I offer.

"Yes Sam, thank you. The cutlery's up here. The settings underneath."

"Two courses?" I ask.

"Yes, thank you Sam."

I set the table while Julia and Caz dish up. Sue and Sir Michael try to make friendly, if stiff, conversation. Finally we all sit down to roast lamb, roast vegetables and the usual greens with gravy. I sit next to Sue and opposite Sir Michael with Julia on the end of the table. It's great eating and I get more than a hint of envy from my mates.

"*We need a mission to get dad some ingredients,*" Cam says.

"*Tomorrow,*" Tarik agrees.

"*Pig out Sam, there won't be anything as good in quarantine,*" Scotty says.

"*Will you guys let me focus here?*" I tell them, smiling as Sir Michael says something about wanting to meet Dr Prosperov as soon as practical. I agree shiftily, avoiding his eyes on purpose to make it look even more like I'm lying.

"*I think I'm going to have to exit this in a cab to the airport,*" I tell them.

"*Agreed,*" Dr Prosperov says.

I keep watching the clock in the corner.

"So how did you end up coming home with Sue?" I ask Sir Michael.

"I called her," Sir Michael replies. "There was a ... shall we say 'misunderstanding' between Sue and one of my staff today. I wanted to make sure the message hadn't become ... confused, by the messenger."

One of *his* staff. Ha! Rocelli was calling all the shots. Michael here, just can't help big noting it even when they have his arm up his back.

"Sir Michael was so charming I just *had* to invite him to dinner," Sue says smiling fakely, giving me the impression he'd been as charming as an angry rattlesnake.

"You see Sam. I think underneath it all, we're really on the same side. We only want what's best for ... well, everyone really. But you especially."

"Thanks Sir Michael. It's ... encouraging to hear *you* say that. We do need to remember *where our hearts truly lie* sometimes," I say thinking of Sian, and looking grimly into his eyes for the first time that night.

He get's it straight away and I'm astonished to see his eyes water. Then he covers his face with his hands and begins to shake with suppressed sobs. It's only then I realise how much stress this poor man is under. How much he fears for his daughter.

Caz turns to him smiling and then recoils in shock to see such a powerful man reduced to tears. Then she put her arm around him. He turns aside, curling up in grief.

**183**

Sue is looking shocked and Julia bewildered.

"Michael? Michael what's the matter?" Caz is asking him.

"I will free her, Michael," I add into the confusion.

The others look at me without understanding. I don't know what to do with myself. The last thing *I'd* expected was for *him* to collapse. I knew this was as big a shock for *them* (as they monitor him) as it is for us.

"*Time to call the cab mate,*" Scotty suggests.

I make noises about needing to go to the toilet. I slip from the room and dash up the stairs. I put on Qi and get my omnicard out of my sock putting it under my wrist. Then I call the cab company for a pick up at 7:20. I come down to find Sir Michael heading upstairs for the loo. His face is a mess.

"I will get her out, Michael," I repeat.

"Sam, I fear you are badly underestimating what you're up against," he says. And just for once he looks genuinely concerned for me. Then he winces, clutching his head.

I think they're hurting him.

"What difference does it make? My family's gone, Lana's dead, Rocelli's attacked Sue. I'm seriously running out of things left to lose around here!" I tell him angrily, heading downstairs

But when I arrive at the table I switch back to 'happy Sam'.

"Oooo is that apple pie?" I ask, spotting Julia putting it on the bench.

"Apple and Rhubarb pie with custard and ice cream," Julia smiles proudly.

"*Oh,*" moans Scotty, "*this is* torture."

"*I'm going to Saigon* tomorrow!" Cam declares.

"*Austria I think,*" Dr Prosperov corrects her.

"*Yay!! Apfel strudel!*" Ashley says.

**184**

"*Torte*," Tahira drools.

While they're going on like this I carry bowls to the table. Sir Michael told the women he was worried because his daughter has an eating disorder and is starving herself. He said he needed to fly home soon. When he comes back to the table he seems a different man, somehow. The confident front is gone. He just looks tired.

He talks about Sian a lot. I learn she both modelled and designed clothes and had fallen in with a crowd of girls who competed to be the thinnest. She had been in competition and not done as well as expected so now she was punishing herself by putting herself on a starvation diet. She'd done it before and Sir Michael said she had looked like a concentration camp victim.

Knowing a real concentration camp victim and having seen unchosen starvation in Dafur I admit I found it pretty hard to sympathise with a messed-up rich person who didn't know what was good for her. The women, however, are far more sympathetic and ask Sir Michael about his background.

Sian's mother, it turns out, wasn't so stable either. She'd killed herself with pills. Sue and I don't quite look at each other after that, but we both think the same thing. Sir Michael says the pressure of work meant he hadn't been as supportive a father as he should have been. Sian had become very close to a teacher at her boarding school in Switzerland, but when she had left to get married, Sian had become very depressed.

Maybe all this should put me off my pie – but it doesn't. I keep imagining that I'll be flying to Europe soon and that I need to focus on my body.

Julia made coffee for everyone and at seven twenty on the dot there was an unexpected knock at the door. I race everyone to answer it.

"Taxi to the airport for Mr Kahu," the driver, another Maori, asks.

"I'll be out in a minute," I reply.

I go back in. I feel a bit lightheaded because, although I'm not going to the airport, I *am* finally going home.

Everyone has got up.

"Taxi's here. Ken's chopper must be at the airport. I'll just get my stuff."

I climb the stairs and gather up a small collection of clothes in a pillow case. Then I come down.

"Do you mind if I borrow this pillow case? I don't have a bag? I'll bring it back," I ask Julia.

"Sure Sam," she says. Then she comes forward and gives me a hug.

"You're a lovely young man, Sam. It's been great having you," she says.

Even better, now I'm going, I think to myself.

"Thanks. Thanks for having me," I reply.

Caz hugs me too.

"Come back and visit," she says.

"I hope to," I say, thinking "*I'll be back a good deal sooner than you think*".

Sue comes up.

"Well ... I don't know what to say. I didn't expect this," she says, her fake smile covering her annoyance at me for what she now thinks was a wasted day. I just look really worried (for Sir Michael) and she gets it completely wrong and melts.

"Oh come here," she says, and just gives me the hugest hug.

"Come back and see me eh? At least you distracted me from Rachel," she smiles.

"I definitely hope to, Sue," I say, still trying to look worried.

"Ah Sam? Would you mind sharing your cab to the airport. I want to get back to my plane," Sir Michael asks.

I'd expected that. This was the way I had hoped to get Sir Michael out of the house.

"Sure."

"Thank you so much for a wonderful meal, Julia, it's been so very good of you to invite me. But my business here is finished and I must get back to Europe as soon as I can," he tells them. Caz and Julia seem a bit put out by this sudden rush for the door, and Sue just looks grumpy as he shook their hands and said a quick farewell.

With the women waving us off, we head for the cab. I make sure I get in the front seat next to the driver to avoid the potential danger of rear seat child locks. The driver seems a bit surprised by that. We wave goodbye and the driver takes off.

"Just up to Ponsonby Road for me thanks driver," I tell him. It's barely a hundred and fifty meters. He looks at me, annoyed.

"So is anyone going to the airport, then?" he wants to know.

"Yes, driver, I am. Thanks for calling the cab, Sam," Sir Michael covers. He pauses, and then asks, "Sam ... I have to know. Is Prosperov really back?"

"No. But Rocelli going after Sue means I'm out of here, and I'll do my best to get Sian away from Streicher too. How is Rocelli anyway?"

"He's hurt ... He's gone too, actually."

That meant *they* had taken him in.

The driver pulls out onto Ponsonby road.

"Just over there would be good," I tell him.

"Where is it Sam?"

"Hidden nearby."

"Yes, I saw it wasn't in your room."

The car stops. I'm about to get out.

"Sam ..." he pauses. His eyes are warning me I'm headed for a trap, but then he winces again. He smiles and asks, "would you mind indulging me with a little flypast."

"So *they* can get me?"

"At Auckland International Airport?"

He partly wants to be sure I am going but I think he also just wants to see my craft in action.

"Oh, OK. I'll even make it visible this time!" I smile.

"Good luck, Sam ... you really are a remarkable young man."

"See ya," I say and get out, slamming the cab door behind me. I walk back and watch Sir Michael drive off. He waves slightly, lit by the red tail lights, before turning to the front again. I feel sorry for him. He's in way over his head and it wasn't his fault. In fact, it's probably *ours*.

As I walk back I wonder if there could be a double-cross and agents waiting to try and jump me while my guard is down.

"*You guys watching this?*" I check.

"We're with you Sam," said Grandpop.

And I noticed a few sparkles of violet next to me.

"*Could you scout around I'm worried about a double-cross.*"

"Sure."

"*How's the road ahead?*" I asked before heading down the hill into the dark shadows of the narrow street.

"The road's OK but there's two guys sneaking into the back garden of the place where you were just pigging out," Grandpop tells me.

*"Shit! They're after Ka-rea-rea! What do I do? I can't fight them!"* I'm a bit worried.

"Nothing we can't handle," Grandpop growls.

*"But we don't want them to know you're back do we?"*

"No. Good point. But don't worry boy, I'll just have Mitra call the boys in blue. She can sound like Ponsonby matron if she wants to. But you better get back there quick or they might grab you on the street," he points out.

I jog back down the road with my pillowcase in front of me. A minute later I was at the door.

*"What's everyone doing inside?"* I ask Grandpop

"Hang on ... They're sitting at the table talking. Our friends outside are watching and searching around the garden," Grandpop says.

I ring the front doorbell. A few seconds later Julia answers it.

"Sam! What happened? Won't you miss your flight?"

"No Julia. It's a helicopter, they're waiting for me. Sorry to be a pain but I really need to talk to Sue."

Sue's already halfway to the door. Her head's up, like a horse curious about something in the next paddock. Julia stands aside to let me in.

"What is it Sam?" Sue asks.

"Um ... can I have a word?" I ask awkwardly.

"Sure," she replies a bit confused and surprised.

I look a bit uncomfortable.

"It's a bit private."

"Here, use the office," Julia says helpfully, a bit confused by me, opening the door and switching on the light.

We go into a largish office with two desks and two computers and heaps of papers, filing cabinets and law books.

"What's the matter? Where's Sir Michael?" Sue asks.

"He went on. Look, I had to trick Sir Michael into thinking I'm off to rescue his daughter."

"From bulimia?" she asks, bewildered.

"No Sue, from infiltrators. The bulimia's not what's bothering Sir Michael. The Bruderschaft are holding Sian hostage. If he doesn't do what they want, they'll kill her. That's why he broke down."

"Oh?" she said, doubtfully.

"Look, I have to ask you to come with me for a few days."

"What? Sam, I'm a police officer! I can't just take off for a few days. I've got a lot of stuff to get through tomorrow."

"Sue, it's your choice. Come with me to meet Dr Prosperov or lose all memory of the past week."

"What? What are you talking about?"

"I'm sorry Sue but we really were just lucky with Rocelli today. He could have turned your brain to mush if we hadn't taken him by surprise. You see what I've been telling you is valuable. Either we wipe your memory or you come with me."

"*We*? Sam, how can *you* wipe my memory? Look Sam, is Prosperov back or not, because I'm getting the feeling I'm being played here and I don't like it..." she went on blathering on about how she didn't like being dicked around. I wasn't listening.

"*Who are the bad fairies*?" I ask.

"*We are*," Tarik and Cam tell me.

"*Cue for this room behind her.*"

"Go," I say, suddenly out loud.

There's a flare of bright light behind Sue.

"What the?" she asks, turning.

Cam and Tarik are in ordinary looking hoodies but you can't see their faces. Sue glances around. I'd forgotten how spooky the face-screens look, all blacked out. Sue opens her mouth but no sound comes out. She looks weakly around at me. Surprise doesn't begin to cover it. She's stunned! Gobsmacked!

"Sam? What is this?"

"Open up guys, you're scaring *me* !" I grin at them.

Sue watches fascinated as the facescreen unpeels.

"Sue. This is Cam and Tarik who I think I've told you about. Guys, this is Sue. She's the cop who's been helping me."

"Hi Sue," Tarik and Cam say evenly. They're eyeballing her in a way fourteen-year-olds normally don't eyeball police officers.

"Uh... Hi," Sue says uncertainly.

"You may recall the suits give us a wide range of abilities," I remind her.

"Cam and Tarik are here to either help you join us for three days or erase your memory of the past week."

Sue looks back at them somewhat fearfully. Her eyes are roving over their suits reminding herself about them. Her whole brain is doing somersaults recalling everything I've told her – which she'd almost decided were crazy stories. Cam and Tarik look back at her calmly and without any of the normal awkwardness teens show when an adult looks at them. Sue's freaking.

Suddenly, outside, there's the sound of sirens. Sue looks around, confused.

"It's just the cops. We called them because there's some guys outside waiting to jump me."

"Outside?"

"Yeah. Those men in black I was telling you about. They usually have a few helpers."

"They're here?" she asks.

"Yeah. Well, what's left of them. Taking out your visitor has knocked them back a bit. The two outside are probably all they had left."

"But won't they? ..." she wonders if they'll overcome the cops.

"No, they'll run. They're probably just biobots. They don't have any special powers."

Sue's eyes flick back to Cam and Tarik who haven't moved.

"Sue, My story was never just a way to fill in a Sunday. Do you remember me telling you about the former Fae, Lana Vilenskaya? She designed the suits?"

Sue finds it hard to remember, but does well in the circumstances.

"Yeah, I even checked her out. She really is a Prof at UCLA."

"She *was*," I tell her. "*They* got her today. She's dead."

"What do you mean?" Sue asks, a bit worried.

"She walked under a car to avoid being captured. She's dead," I repeat.

Sue is trying hard to catch up. I go on.

"We can't leave you vulnerable to the likes of Father Rocelli. Besides before they kill you they mine your brain. So you have two options. Erasing the last week from your memory entirely, or coming with me to meet Dr P. You're only getting a choice because I asked for you. Normally you'd just get the amnesia."

Her eyes are wide. She gulps.

"Where are we going?" she asks, confused by too much information.

I point up. Her eyes widen, even more. She points up in a questioning way. I nod.

"OK," she says in a squeaky voice.

"Call in to work," I suggest. "Tell them you've found Prosperov but you'll be out of communication for a few days. It'll be big news. You'll be fine."

She takes a long deep breath and sighs. She starts to speak, then coughs and manages to squeak out.

"I don't suppose they have fags up there?"

I shrug. She looks to the others who shake their heads.

"I could sure do with one now," she exhales.

She takes another deep breath.

"What do we do now?" I ask the others.

"*Wait a moment. The dog's chasing your friends.*" Grandpop says, sounding like he's enjoying a funny movie.

"*Sam, only Hekator can bend you to quarantine,*" Cam says.

"*Is he around?*" I ask.

"*Not yet,*" Cam replies.

"*How long?*" I ask.

"A few hours. He's at the new base. Oh, they got to their car. Pity." Grandpop tells us.

Sue's looking at me. I look at the others and think for a moment.

"Sue. There's a small hold up. I suggest we go back to your place and wait 'til they're ready for us."

"Is it safe?" she asks.

"I dunno," I admit, "but they don't seem to be doing so well at the moment. Anyway it will look more natural to Julia and Caz."

"OK,"

"*Guys, could you check out Sue's place for us?*" I say, giving them the LZ.

"*Sure.*"

We leave Tarik and Cam in the dark to bend as we come out.

**193**

"Hey Sue! Some of your lot are out the back," Caz called from the greenhouse door looking out into the dark.

"What?" I say, acting all surprised, and run forward to look. Outside, Julia is talking to a big man in dark blue overalls with a dog back on a leash.

"Some peeping tom, or something. One of the neighbours complained, apparently," Caz tells us, still watching Julia.

"Did they catch them?" I ask, as Sue comes to join me.

"No, he beat it when the cops showed up."

I glance at Sue. Caz was still looking at Julia.

"Sam's asked me to come and meet the missing people from Renwick," she tells Caz.

"Oh ... that makes sense. It is your case isn't it?" Caz says looking at Sue.

"Yeah, I guess it is," Sue reminds herself.

Julia comes back inside, saying goodnight to the dog handler and locking the door.

"Well, that was exciting!" she says, and she seems a bit excited by having had a visit from the police. "Still, it's good to know they can get here so fast. Apparently they only had the call five minutes ago."

"We're only five minutes from Central, at most," Sue points out.

"Yes, but it's nice to know if there was any real trouble how fast they could be here," Julia says.

So we say our goodbyes all over again and call another cab. Then we go to wait outside. Julia and Caz stay a while but Sue's change in mood has made her antisocial so they go inside again complaining about the chill. It's about nine now, and the sky is clear. Sue's looking up at the stars, blown away she's about to leave Earth, and thinking about her life.

"How are you feeling Sue?"

She tips her head down and looks around at me.

"Bit lightheaded actually Sam. I can't believe what's happening. It's a total, total trip."

She looks back out at the stars.

"I guess it must be," I say. "We had two years to get used to it. You've only had a week."

Sue laughs. It's genuine delight.

"What?" I ask.

"I'm just thinking what an incredibly dull life I had with Rachel compared to this."

"You haven't even met Hekator yet."

"He's the ... goat-man eh?"

"Yeah. He's going to be taking us from your place."

"Wooo hooo," Sue laughs.

"That'll make two aliens in my house in one day."

And she seems to find that extremely funny. The taxi noses down the street. Sue gets in and I leave her. I sneek around the house, into the garden, and find Ka-rea-rea. They tried to move him but he's heavy and they didn't get far.

I get in and take off. It's a fine night and I fly around a bit to let off some steam after the stress of managing all these adults. Then I fly over Auckland and pick up Sue's cab, and track it to her place. She arrives, pays and goes inside.

When the cab's gone I land under the carport, get out and knock on the door. Tarik and Cam appear in a flash of light behind me. Sue opens the door to let us in.

"C'min," she says walking away.

We all go inside. Sue asks what she should pack. Tarik looks at me.

**195**

"Uh, Sue the place you're going is a quarantine," he tells her. "They burned everything we brought. They give you clothes."

Sue looks a bit deflated.

"So what do we do now? Wait for the mothership or something."

"They don't need spaceships. They come and get you," Tarik tells her.

"So my neighbours won't notice anything?"

"Nothing."

"How long do we have to wait?" she asks sitting down in her lounge.

"Well *you* have to wait for an hour or two. But *I* have to pretend to fly to Europe for Sir Michael," I say.

"Why?"

"I dunno. That's the story we're spinning so they think I'm feeling the heat and going to rescue Sian."

"I don't understand. Why do you need to do that?"

"Because we don't want them to realise everyone's back and we're on to them. Why don't you get to know Tarik and Cam? Tell them about yourself. You already know a lot about them. I'll be back in a mo."

I go back outside and jump into Ka-rea-rea, I shoot up at enormous speed and whizz to the airport. It's still busy. I zoom over at one kilometer up and then drop straight down.

Sir Michael's plane is in a dark corner of the airport by some hangars. Cars come around the corner occasionally but apart from the sodium lights on the road and the lights from the cabin in Sir Michael's plane it's quite dark.

I land Ka-rea-rea in a pool of shadow. Then I call Sir Michael on the number he'd given me.

"Michael," he answers.

"Are the others with with you?"

"No, I sent them out for a spot of shopping before the flight home."

"Good. I'm outside. Bring your phone," I tell him and disconnect.

I open Ka-rea-rea and get out, then walk into a corner of lamplight. It's breezy and aircraft are taxiing around making noise. I see a head at a porthole and then Sir Michael breaks open the inward facing door.

"Sam?" he calls out to the dark.

"Come and have a look," I call, my voice echoing off the concrete runway and in the open hangars. A jet rumbles in to land behind us.

He comes down the stairs. I make sure he can recognise me. Then I go back to Ka-rea-rea. I wait for him to get close enough to see he'd never fit in the little speeder; then I hop in, pull the lid, and lift off; hovering at head height.

I hover around him slowly and call him on the phone. It rings loudly in the dark, still corner of the tarmac.

"Yes?"

"It's me."

"I very much appreciate this Sam. I suppose I'm just fascinated by your aircraft the same way you were by mine a few years ago," he gives a little chuckle.

"Perhaps underneath the exterior of a 56-year-old silk there's a fourteen-year-old boy who wishes he could fly it too."

"Unfortunately you wouldn't fit. Would you like to see what she can do?" I ask.

"Well, yes, I would rather."

"She goes up," I say.

Then I zoom straight up into the stars to two kilometers very fast.

"and down."

And I come down just as fast, stopping instantly.

He smiles, shaking his head.

"Incredible! Simply incredible!"

I can tell his mind is still ticking over with schemes.

"Well, I hate to go, Sir Michael but it's a long way and speed is life as they say."

"They do indeed Sam. And it may be especially true in this case. Just a small favour though, you couldn't show me some of that speed by any chance?"

"Sure, I'll buzz the field. Keep watching."

Then I head east out into the dark beside the taxiway and off the end of the field toward the approach. It's all dark countryside with cows and trees and stuff. There's a 737 landing so I wait for them to get down.

"It's a long trip even in this," I tell Sir Michael to pass the time.

"My hopes are resting on you Sam," he says. He meant whether I was caught or I rescued Sian, he hoped to win.

"Here I go. Goodbye Sir Michael."

"Goodbye Sam, and God's speed," he replies, as I hang up.

It probably looked like it anyway. I shoot over the airfield lit up like a silent blue rocket at about Mach point ninety nine passing over the 737 as she taxies back to the terminal."

I'm visible and accelerating for about sixty seconds. Of course I'm listening in to air traffic control to avoid hurting anyone.

I like the 737 pilot who remarks, "looks like the swamp gas sure is in a hurry tonight."

Of course as soon as I'm out of sight I switch to warp invisibility and return to Sue's.

*"Is Hekator back yet?"* I ask Grandpop.

*"Yep, he's there."*

*"Where?"*

*"At your pal's place."*

*"How can he be?"* I asked surprised.

*"The house's fine. It's wood. Wood and plastic roof tiles. He's OK with wood. He's waiting inside for you."*

I land outside. It's dark but I can hear the thump of a stereo. I open the door and go in. The lights are out except for a few lamps and the music is quite loud. Cam, Tarik, Sue, Scotty and Ashley are all dancing in Sue's living room. Hekator is in the corner smiling. In the low light he looks sexy but strange and scary at the same time. The others' suits are flashing and fluorescing. Sue's smoking and drinking heavily as well.

*"What's happening?"* I ask silently.

"When she hoird how boring da quarantine was your frien' decided to party!" Ashley grins, dancing.

"I've got Ka-rea-rea outside."

Hekator bends down and comes forward to give me what looks like a bowling ball with a flat base.

*"Put it under the cerebral interface. It will make him remotely controllable,"* he says silently.

I take the bowling ball outside and put it where my head would normally rest. Then I close Ka-rea-rea.

*"Ka-rea-rea?"* I ask.

*"Sam?"* he replies.

It's almost like being inside him.

*"Up to twenty kilometers. Then warp invisible to Europe. Pacific polar route."*

And he shoots straight up and vanishes into the night heading for the North Pole. I go back to the party. I find Hekator looking completely out of place but quite amused.

*"Hekator? Is bringing Sue to quarantine OK with your people?" I ask a bit worried.*

*"We have looked at it. Raman has advised in favour. She has not been tagged with any spatial tracking devices which will work in quarantine, and in general we like to keep your kind either very close or very far away. So close it can be."*

*"Thanks Hekator."*

He smiled. *"Sam, Sue is no accident. Raman is sure the deep weaving that entangles us has her as well."*

I watch her stomping around to the beat. It is strange. Just as it had been with the others, I feel I've known Sue a very long time. Then Cam pulls me up to join in and it felt good to just relax for a moment.

At ten the others announce they're going home for dinner and fold into the dark. Sue turns down the stereo and puts on something more restful. She changes into old clothes. She's smoking a lot. She seems nervous. I'm just very glad of the company. The thought of being quarantined by myself does not appeal.

"Well, I'd better get you two ready to go," Hekator says out loud, so Sue can hear him.

Sue's fascinated with Hekator, which doesn't surprise me because he is very good looking.

Two brilliant columns of light flare casting harsh shadows and making us look away, then two hugely tall, shiny black, columns appear in the middle of the living room. They're just short of the ceiling, about a meter by a meter square.

"Normally these land flat because we use them for medical evacuations. But as there's limited space and you two are well you can stand in them. But first I have something for you Sue that will give you a better idea of what's going on."

And he produces a metallic tiara with a green gem on the front and earpieces.

"What do I do with it?" Sue asks. She seems quite drunk.

"Put it on and in a few hours you'll be able to communicate telepathically."

"OK," she says and puts it on, "How do I look?"

"Scruffily pretty, with a tiara," I tell her.

She smiles at me and goes to a mirror.

"It's a tool, Sue, not a fashion item," I call after her.

The big black boxes open silently. The inside is like the inside of our suit drawers. All meaty and wet looking with tentacles.

"*Shouldn't we be naked?*" I ask Hekator silently.

"*It doesn't really matter. There's no need. But if you prefer?*"

Sue comes into the room and sees the two coffin-like black things with their meaty interiors and tentacles.

"Ooooooh my God! I am NOT getting into that! That's the most disgusting thing I've ever seen!" Sue slurs, revolted.

"It's an ambulance for carrying wounded people Sue. It's built to provide intensive care," I explain.

Sue looks again, and the wrinkle disappears from her nose. She can see how that might work.

"It's still disgusting," she mutters.

I go and get into the nearest coffin. Nothing happens.

"How do you close it?" I ask Hekator.

"Just ask it to close. That's how you open it too. Now because you're arriving in these you'll arrive in the hospital. They'll send you through to the decontamination centre and then on to the accommodation block. It's just what you'd expect." Hekator says out loud to Sue.

Sue looks both nervous and amused.

"*None* of this, is what *I* expect goat boy!" she slurs.

Hekator smiles.

"You'll be fine," he reassures her.

I decide to move things along.

"See ya there," and I close my box.

The lid is actually transparent and I can see Hekator get Sue into her box.

"*Hey, I can see out!*" Sue thinks.

"See you in a few days," Hekator says.

**[+]**

Time seems to slow down, the colour drains out of everything. My whole field of view seems to fold up and distort and I have to close my eyes. I'm falling. There's brilliant light all around me. Brilliant light and presences. My mother and my Grandmother. Dozens of people surround me. I spend longer among them than I ever have before. I even notice more distant people like my dad and Lana. I wonder how Sue will take this. I've told her about it but I haven't warned her about it. Then slowly the light and the presences begin to fade, flattening to a line which bursts around me.

I'm lying on my back. I can see a blue ceiling. It's a brilliant blue like the sky. I open the box and sit up. The whole area is a garden of pretty flowers, hedges and bushes. It's like an indoor garden. The light is bright and warm, and the air fresh, and clean.

A female Fae who looks a bit like Tabika, but more angelic, with a woman's breasts, white wings and short blond hair approaches us.

"*Sam and Sue*?" she smiles, greeting us silently.

"*That's us*," I reply.

I realise she's a hologram but it's almost perfect.

"Did we die?" Sue asks looking at the hologram and the garden.

"No Sue, we're alive. I told you this is what they look like."

"Yeah but it's kind of weird actually seeing it," she mumbles.

We're wet and sticky where the liquids in the boxes have soaked into the back of our clothes. It makes our wet clothes warm although the air temperature is warm too.

"*Please follow me*," the hologram says. So we do.

It's a bit of a strange process. We have to get undressed in the same room which we both find hugely embarrassing. Then we go into a dark tunnel up to my chest in clear oil, then under and over a series of waterfalls. Then we pass through a series of round gates where the air buzzes with static.

Finally we arrive in a small room where some robes are waiting for us. Scotty was right but they aren't exactly large. An old male avatar who looks surprisingly human appears and leads us to the sleeping chambers. They're dark with small glowing lights, a pool of warm water with a cool waterfall and a warm waterfall, a large bed bush and a couple of plants hidden away behind long grasses I suspect of being the toilets.

The old man shows me to another room. I have to use the toilet plant. It's weird but clean and not as disgusting as I'd expected. I settle down on the bed bush and the next thing I know I wake up.

It's dark and Sue's crept in too. It's nice that she's here although a bit disturbing because her robe doesn't cover her very well. It makes me feel a bit pervy. Then I realise why I'm awake.

"*Sam wake up! We're five minutes from Norwegian airspace,*"
Ka-rea-rea tells me.

I focus on the craft with my eyes closed. It's like a dream.

It's dark over the North Pole. Below is the ice, cracked and
majestic glowing white.

"*Head for Montreux, Switzerland.*"

"*OK. ETA 17 minutes.*"

It's afternoon in Europe and the sun is setting. I doze as Norway,
cloaked in cloud, slips by 30 kilometers beneath me. Then we're
over the Baltic which is covered in fog. A few minutes later we're
over Germany descending towards Switzerland in the sunlight.
As we approach Ka-rea-rea slows to Mach two and descends.

"*I want to find a deserted spot above the town to wait in.*"

"*How close?*"

"*The Alps will do.*"

Ka-rea-rea begins to spiral down. I can see Lake Leman below.
The Alps are looking magnificent in the pink and gold sunset as
we descend into them. Ka-rea-rea spots Montreux but I tell him
to head over to France for Mont Blanc. We close quickly and
soon find a deserted ledge (safe from rockfalls, goats, climbers,
and avalanches) to settle on, and wait for the others. The view is
snowy mountains in all directions.

I doze and must have fallen asleep because I start dreaming
about black coffins sprouting trees which in turn grow people
I know, like they're apples. Then some of the apples, like Sir
Michael, begin to go bad and fall off. I'm raking them up into a
bag. It's a confusing dream. After a little while I wake up.

I feel a bit funny lying next to Sue while she's asleep so I decide
to leave her there and go look for breakfast. I go out into the

next room. There's a table with food on it. I try all of it. The flavours are weird. Like cherry-vanilla and cucumber-orange. Still, once again it isn't bad. So I eat a breakfast of strange fruit, and hot nuts, with thin slices of sashimi and cups of a soup that's closer to miso than coffee, but different to both.

"*Sam, where are you?*" Sue asks silently.

"Out here." I reply out loud.

"*Wow!*" Sue thinks.

"*The telepathic interface must have sorted out your language centres while you slept,*" I tell her.

"*Hey this is weird. And I know where you are too!*"

"*I told you it's much faster and better than talking.*"

"*Wild!*"

She comes out to the dining room.

"What's all this?" she says.

"Food. All sorts of strange stuff. See what you think."

"Hmm not exactly full of fats is it?"

"Is that's what's missing? I wondered."

"No real carbs either. Is this what they usually eat?"

"I have no idea to be honest Sue. I've never been to Fae either."

"Is that where we're going?"

"No...well, I don't know. All I know is we're going to where my family are and we have to go through decontamination and quarantine first."

Sue collects a breakfast together and sits down opposite me to eat it.

"So what are we going to do here for three days?" Sue asks.

"I don't know exactly, but it sure beats any of the alternatives back on Earth. Up until yesterday afternoon I was right in the shit. Rocelli had got the location of Caz and Julia's out of you, and he was going to start finding out what you know. I had no safe house to hide at. My legal guardian worked for *them.* It was looking grim."

"What do you think would have happened if you hadn't bumped into your friends at Renwick?"

"I would have gone somewhere else. That was my plan."

"Where?"

"Anywhere away from Emma and you."

"To draw them away?"

"Yeah ... After I learned they'd got Lana I realised I couldn't hide forever. And I couldn't protect you from agents like Rocelli either. If the infiltrators have penetrated our network I needed proof for the others. And if they didn't come back I was going to take out as many of them as I could before they got me. So when you sent me to get a present for Julia and Caz I was in a pretty dark place. But it didn't happen. Out of the blue you suggested I get a present and the only place I could think of was Renwick and there they were. The Fae would say there was weaving in that coincidence."

"It just seemed the right thing to do. But I had no idea you'd go to Renwick," Sue smiles.

"Where else could I get a present at that time on Sunday?"

"Oh!" Sue exclaims.

"What!" I ask.

"I never called Kevin!. It's Monday morning and I'm Awol," she says her voice rising urgently.

"Why don't we get Dr Prosperov to call in for you?" I suggest.

"Would he do that?"

"We can only ask."

"Can we ask now?"

"OK."

I think the best person to ask would be Mrs Jones. I concentrated on her hard.

"That jewel is really bright when you do that," Sue says looking at my necklace.

But Mrs Jones doesn't seem to notice, or, if she did, she was ignoring me, so I focus on Tahira instead.

"*Sam?*" she responds dozily, "*how nice of you to think of me.*"

"*What's happening Tahira?*"

"*I am having a nice dream.*"

"*Dream on dreamy girl,*" I smile.

"They're asleep," I report to Sue. "I noticed the guys were eating later than normal. I'll try them again in a few hours. What were you going to do at work? And how did Sir Michael get in contact with you anyway?"

"Sir Michael? He chewed Kevin's ear off about police denying him access to his legal ward. Kevin put him on to me saying he was ordering me to assist, and if I didn't I could expect the Police Complaints Authority to rip my career to shreds. So I had to call him up and eat humble pie. He insisted on seeing you last night; said it was extremely urgent. Until you told me about the hacker thing I couldn't understand what he thought he was doing. Still he didn't exactly blurt out a warning did he?"

"It's not his fault Sue. You have to realise *they* have him completely wired now. They hear and see what he sees. They can't quite completely read his mind but they can torture him or kill him wherever he is. They don't see our pain as particularly important. It's because they're biobots. All they live for is their mission. If killing or torture are logical ways of achieving that, it's what they will do."

"There's nothing scarier than a fanatic. That's for sure."

"Yeah. So now Sir Michael's tapped, plus the infiltrators have his daughter. Everyone is double crossing everyone else. *They* probably want me to get Von Streicher. Sir Michael really wants my rescue to succeed so he gets his daughter back and possibly gets Ka-rea-rea into the bargain. The infiltrators want to see me caught by Administration."

"But you told us all Prosperov was back?"

"Did I look relieved and happy?" I ask, a bit worried.

"No, not a bit. I'd have expected you to be really happy. I think that confused us all."

"I wanted Sir Michael to think I was making up a story so I could get away. He's in a real jam. He had to send me into a trap but his best hope was that somehow I might escape and rescue Sian. Anyway, you saw him crack. He wasn't acting that."

"No, he sure wasn't. He was a mess. But why are *you* meant to be doing this?"

"Not sure exactly. But Dr P will have some scheme. The big question he'll be worrying about is how did they break our security in the first place? If we don't know how they almost caught us the first time we might not get lucky a second time. It's been a big worry for me ever since we evacuated. Ashley went to visit Nathan and came back with a trace on her. That shouldn't have happened. It could mean all sorts of bad things."

"Like what?"

"Like they're on to our mission, or we have a traitor, or they've tracked Ashley in Washington somehow."

"Is a traitor likely in a houseful of psychics?"

"Nah. We could read everyone ... well, everyone except maybe Dr P."

"So you think either *they* are on to your mission or they tracked Ashley?"

"I think so."

"Hmm. OK, but why would you fall for this scheme to rescue Sian?"

"Well, maybe they may think that if I've no friends left I might take orders from Para.no.ID, and imagine I'm well enough armed, and dumb enough, to think it would be a good surprise counterattack."

"Do they think you're dumb?"

"Probably."

"OK, but to walk into an ambush knowing it's an ambush. That's still pretty risky. Won't your Aunt worry?"

"Nah, not if I'm all backed up. She knows the team. We don't take dumb risks."

"Well don't. I'm feeling pretty nervous already. If you left me here I'd panic."

"Chill, Sue. The Fae are cool, they really are."

"Sam, I'm barely handling any of this. A week ago I was a cop whose biggest challenge was coping with Rachel, dealing with macho blokes with too many forms and some fairly snotty teenagers. Now I'm half-naked, living on nuts, somewhere in the Universe surrounded by aliens who look like they belong in a kid's story book. My weirdness limit is totally maxed out here – seriously."

"That's your problem with thinking you're in charge. Us kids don't. We just go with the flow."

Sue sighed, long and hard.

"You're probably right. It's fear of the unknown."

"Yeah, take it easy. The Fae won't hurt you and Rocelli and the

**209**

men in black can't get you. You're safe as houses here. It's me that's gotta watch out."

"I thought you would have back-up?"

"Well I will, but we all have to keep our eyes open. These dudes already showed they play for keeps. They're seriously evil. Most of them were Nazis..."

"That priest guy wasn't old enough to be a Nazi," Sue objects.

"His official name is Rocelli and he's over a hundred, Sue. Probably several hundred or maybe even more years old."

"Like Mrs Jones?"

"No, not like Mrs Jones at all. Mrs Jones doesn't need to eat stem cells from the blood and marrow of kids to live."

"What?"

"Rocelli needs a supply of fresh stem cells to live. He gets them from kids. He kills them."

"That's ... horrible. Why does he need stem cells?" Sue asks.

"They keep him young. We think it was an early genetic experiment at immortality that went wrong. That's why they came to Earth. Eating us was better than eating their own."

"So they ... ohh *noo*! *Sam*?" she looked at me like I'd said something disgraceful.

"No Sam! That's *not fair*! I really am in an alien ... whatever this place is! I told you my weirdness limit was maxed out and now you tell me the enemy of these space fairies is a bunch of f_____ alien Nazi vampires! You're *totally* taking the piss!"

I laugh. It's ridiculous. She half laughs too.

"So you finally *are* bullshitting me this time aren't you?"

"No," I laugh. "No, I'm not."

"Well, why are you laughing then?"

"Because it sounds really funny when you say it like that. It's like the moon fairies you said before."

"Because it is," she insists.

"Well it is," I agree, "but that doesn't change anything. I thought Scotty's elephants were pretty funny too, but in reality there's nothing funny about a pissed off elephant when you've met one."

"OK, but that's an elephant. You're talking B-grade movies here. C even."

I calm down.

"It's like the Fae on Earth, Sue. All over Europe, Asia and even the Pacific there are legendary magical people who come out during the full moon and do stuff with humans, like give them gifts, have romances or steal children. Not just in one culture but dozens and they are mostly the same. Most people say it's just old stories. It's bullshit. Where are they? Well, the answer is they're *hiding*. They don't want anyone to see them and they can make damn sure we don't or those that do don't remember afterwards. But we act like humans are the most intelligent and greatest power in the Universe. Nobody can fool us, eh? "

"Yeah, OK I get it. You said the same about UFOs."

"Yeah that's right! And the legends of vampires in Eastern Europe are not just stories either. Countess Elizabeth Bathory of Slovakia killed over three hundred women and girls in the seventeenth century[†], drinking and bathing in their blood. There are legends of vampires all over the world going all the way back to Mesopotamia[†]. But because these guys won't sit still for scientists to check them out under their microscopes, they don't exist either, apparently."

"But Nazis?"

"I know it sounds stupid now, but seventy years ago Nazis weren't a joke. They were running the police in Germany and a bunch of other Eastern European countries too. What would a vampire do? Run away? Hide in his castle? Yeah right! He'd take advantage. It gave them ideas."

"What sort of ideas?"

"Well if you have to get stem cells to survive when's the easiest time to do it? When there's peace and order and the police investigate every suspicious death? Or when there's chaos, war and mass murder all around?"

"Yeah, I guess war would make it easier."

"Plagues too."

"Plagues?"

"Yeah, it's another way to make sure they can have victims."

"We haven't had any plagues."

"We've had three. Remember the Spanish flu killed the soldiers at Renwick after World War One. It killed fifty million which was more than the war did."

"Are you saying they made Spanish Flu happen?"

"We're not sure. That strain of H1N1 was a strange disease because it didn't affect the old or children as much as young adults who usually are the least affected by illness, and it moved very fast[+]. Hekator's looked at the DNA but he said it was impossible to tell if there was genetic engineering involved in creating it."

"So what were the other plagues?"

"In the 1950s there was an outbreak of H2N2 influenza which killed four million[+]. And of course there's HIV/Aids which has killed twenty million[+] and Scotty and Ashley have seen up close. Hekator said after the Sverge were largely wiped out thousands of years ago, the Fae adopted a policy of assuming disease is a weapon, regardless."

"Thinking like that could work both ways. A disease might hurt you but might be used as a weapon too!"

"Yeah, except viruses are more accurate than bullets. They can kill one person and not another coz they target by DNA. Or one race of people and not another. That's why they're so dangerous. That's why we'll be in this quarantine for a few days."

"Fair enough I guess."

"I know it all seems weird and scary but think about Tabika. She ended up in our world. That was way more dangerous than the other way around. She knew Fae had been killed by savage Earth people before but she didn't hurt us. The Fae may have teeth but remember what I told you about Tabika? They like us! They are more likely to want to kiss you than bite you."

Sue looks around again.

"Yeah, I suppose this is more like some weird kind of Japanese hotel than a prison. OK ... I guess you're right. I've got to loosen up and go with the flow."

There's a pause as we look at the strange furniture and eat our strange food.

"Still, space fairies versus Nazi vampires is funny," I giggle.

She smiles too. Then she looks around and calms down again.

"Except I really am a long, long way from home."

"Chill," I advise. "It was the only way we got through and you're doing it way faster than we did."

"Yeah ... I have a habit of doing dumb things like that," she says.

"It's your way of making commitments that makes you so cool," I tell her.

"Oh gaawwsh!" she grins. "Go on ... You better tell me more about more about your training," she says.

So I do.

# CHAPTER THIRTY NINE: FORTUNE COOKIES

After skydiving, diving and exploring, having to go back to school was a total let-down. We had had the best holiday ever and we didn't want it to end. The idea of sitting in a pokey classroom listening to Mr Wakefield drone on for another six weeks did not appeal.

Everyone compared their holiday stories. Some of the rich kids had gone skiing, and some had gone to the Pacific Islands, but most had been at home. Emma definitely wanted to know what we had been up to. She had rung a few times but Mrs Jones had told her we were working. So we all had to act like we had been helping our parents get ready for the guests. Somehow she seemed to think we were lying.

Marshall, who had spent his holidays skiing, was full of stories about his cool snow boarding skills.

It was so much crap. He was such a rooster, but all the others lapped it up. We had to fight down our natural instincts to keep from telling him his adventures were no biggy. I think that our knowing looks and small smiles were the thing that pissed Emma off the most because it proved we weren't just working. Of course training continued. Sometimes we went after dinner to train at night. We had a number of games. In one, each team had to defend their glow stick in a nest while trying to steal another team's. If you were tagged you had to go back to your nest. With three teams and our suits' sensors, and stealth equipment, the games soon became very complicated. When it was dry Bernard and Grandpop would make up a fourth team. Although they didn't have our tools they taught us a lot of sneaky tricks. It was fun.

Two days before the first guest was to arrive Hekator announced he was going home. He appeared as a hologram in the briefing room next to Grandpop.

"Well children, I think I can now safely leave you," he told us. "You have now fully adapted to your suits and there are only a few more things for me to tell you about. Your language interface and your weapons."

The word "weapons" made everyone sit forward a bit.

"Over the past few months your brains have been growing a new channel to connect with your suits. The suits have language processors built into them. They can interpret fifty of the most common human languages fluently and two hundred to a basic level, both written and spoken, into what we call common representation. Common representation is the basis of telepathic communication. You have been using it to communicate simple commands to your suits since you first started wearing them. But that only needs a narrow interface. To translate a lot of material simultaneously you need a broader interface and that's what you have now grown. Listen to this." Then he played us five sound clips of people saying "I'm hungry."

"That was Hindi, Mandarin, Spanish, Swahili, and Arabic. The interpreter can easily handle this level of language. But it struggles with customary sayings, slang or where the words don't match the intention. For example when Scott says 'shame' about something cute. So while it may give you an idea of what a person or sign says, it may not get all of it."

"Can it 'elp us speak?" Tahira asked.

"It can output your ideas into grammatically correct language through the sound projector in a number of voices but it will still sound unnatural to a native speaker. You are really limited to very simple grammar so don't try and act like a local. Nobody will believe you. For languages you know, you are far better off speaking yourself. Now we come to weapons."

This had us excited.

"Your main weapon is mounted on the imitation chest buckle of your bag's imitation straps. In fact the imitation straps link the weapon and the suits eyes to the power unit in the bag. Now you have to realise the suits you have are to protect *our* children when they go on family trips. So not surprisingly we don't give our children lethal weaponry."

"But there are times where even a child may need to protect herself from wild animals which may be unpredictable. So the weapons you have are short range but very quick and accurate."

"The main one is a stun ray. It works a bit like lightning but is obviously lower powered. It is both invisible and silent in dry conditions. It will not work as well in heavy rain or snow. It's practical range is fifty meters and it can engage three different targets each second. All you have to do is identify the targets. The suit will aim the weapon and calculate the power dosage to knock out the target. It will also work on some machinery such as internal combustion engines. I must stress the stun ray does not work in any medium other than the air, and then better at sea level than altitude."

Scotty put up his hand?

"Yes Scotty, it can stun any animal on Earth including a charging bull elephant. Obviously it can't stun an orca underwater."

"At closer ranges the stun ray can paralyse instead of stun. This means the animal is immobilised but remains conscious. You may not be able to do this from all angles. You need to be able to see the target's neck."

"In addition to the stun beam you can also dazzle. The dazzle beam will temporarily blind those looking at you up to a kilometer away. It would also work on cameras. When I say 'temporarily' I mean for about a minute. It's long enough to escape."

"At close range – about ten meters in air – your sound projectors can be used to stimulate a gag reflex in humans which induces vomiting and can stimulate loss of control of the bowel and bladder."

"*Ewww*," thought Ashley.

"*I'd love to use that one on Marshall*," thought Tarik.

Hekator stopped, and looked at him severely.

"Just kidding," Tarik gulped. Hekator frowned and went on.

"Your sound projectors can generate very loud noises up to 120 decibels at one meter in air and twice that under water. This can be used to imitate things your suit hears. It's mostly used in the sound frequencies you *can't hear* to scare animals. Underwater they can also be used to stun smaller creatures like fish or snakes. The transducer can target high power ultrasound which will certainly give larger sea animals a headache. It can also be used to heat water if you need it."

"At very low frequencies you can generate a sense of fear or dread in humans in the eighteen Hertz band. At high frequencies

**217**

you can generate unease and nervousness in all mammals. They can be used together and will work around corners and through walls up to fifty meters away."

"Your final weapon is the electric shock. If you touch or are touched you can stun your prey or attacker. The suit will let you kill small animals for food."

"Safeguards. The suits you have are for kindergarten aged children and as they can't be trusted to be responsible there are some controls. None of the weapons will work if you show some kind of pleasure at using it. In fact the suit will shock *you* instead. I'm afraid we have to stop our kindergarten kids torturing animals too, you see. It's a stage some seem to go though."

"Finally, your weapons are intended to help you distract, not fight. The suit will alert Control when weapons are used and Control will alert Mike, or whoever is on the desk."

"So that is really all I have for you now. I'm going home but you will be able to send messages through Control. We expect to look at your suits again after you've used them a bit more. Say in about three months or so."

Grandpop stood up.

"Thank you Hekator. I think we all appreciate your need to get back home," and he started us clapping.

Hekator smiled at us.

"Thank you Earth children. Farewell and good luck."

And with that he vanished.

That night we played an awesome game where we got to use the weapons in training mode so they simulated the effect the weapons would have temporarily. It was huge fun and we played til ten o'clock.

But the day before the first guests were due to arrive we got another kind of weapons training that was a bit more intense. We got changed and found no Grandpop waiting for us. Instead Control sent us to swim out to one of the small islands about a kilometer off the coast from Aotea.

We landed in a small sandy beach surrounded by a bay of rocks and bushes. It was an awful day with pelting rain and thunder. Visibility was about two hundred meters and the sea was rough and choppy.

Grandpop was waiting for us in his big brown coat with the hood up so his face seemed to be in darkness. His gray stubble and dark brown face seemed mysterious and unreadable as he stood on a rock slightly above us. He waved to us to come up and join him so we knocked back the gravity and bounced up the rocks to where he was waiting in the shelter of small bank.

As we gathered around, with the flax leaves slashing and rippling about and the bushes cowering in the blast of the wind. We couldn't help noticing that Grandpop had brought something with him. At his feet was a sack and in the crook of his arm, his 'Friend', the AK47, with its black barrel dripping water.

"OK, today we're going to do some firearms training," he told us. He had headphones and a microphone wired under his coat which was just as well as the wind carried away his deep voice before it reached us.

"And what that means is you're going to see, hear and feel how dangerous these things are."

"You ain't goin' ta shoot us, or nuthin are you Sir," Ashley asked, her eyes fixed nervously on the gun.

Grandpop looked serious.

"I sure hope not. And that is exactly why we need clear communication. Now first rule is if I say 'freeze' you all freeze. Nobody moves, no matter what. I don't care if there's a seal trying to bite your foot off, *nobody* moves. Second, when you freeze I want you to go bright red. I'll call "red" to remind you. That way if I can see you I can avoid mistaking you for a rock." "Third, when I call 'safe' you can stop freezing. Fourth if I yell 'cover' I want you to find a place behind a rock which will protect you from bullets. And when I say 'a rock' I mean a big, thick, rock at least a meter thick not a little squitty one. If I've called 'cover' and you are behind cover I want you to number off. So if you are first you call 'one' and if someone's called 'one', you call 'two' and so on until the last one to find cover calls 'six'. At that point I will issue the command 'freeze' and 'red'. If I can't see you then I will fire. You will stay frozen until I say 'safe'.

"*Anyone* who moves when they are meant to be frozen and lives will have to repeat this training when the others are operational. So if you don't want to be on the bench, or worse, injured, you will follow these instructions. Got it?"

We all nodded and said "yes".

The gun scared all of us and I'm not embarrassed to admit it.

"OK 'cover'!"

We started looking around.

"Stop! Come back." Grandpop called.

We came back curiously.

"When I say 'cover' imagine that I'm a guy with a gun who isn't going to wait until you're ready. Imagine I'm a maniac who wants to shoot you because if you ever do have to look for cover that's the situation you'll be in. So run! OK?"

"OK," we nodded.

"Cover!"

We ran. We all ended up crouched behind the same rock wall which was about ten meters from Grandpop.

"One," called Cam.

"Two," called Scotty.

"Three," called Tarik and me.

"Four," we both said again.

There was a pause.

"Five," said Tahira.

"Six," said Ashley.

"Freeze and go red."

We froze and went red. There was a pause. Then Grandpop fired.

I jumped. I think we all did. It was unbelievably loud and scary. Not like the little stutter machineguns make in the movies but a sound that ripped the air with deep gut wrenching violence. Then I was cringing low against the rock as stone chips and dust flew. It was a short burst. Just about one second.

"Safe," Grandpop announced.

We hesitated.

"OK guys, out you come."

We slowly got up. And gathered around. My knees felt a bit shaky and my legs quivered.

"OK, that was just a start. What did you think?"

"As bad as I remembered it," said Scotty.

"'Orrible," said Tahira.

"Now I know why folks on da news look more frightened dan dey do in da movies," said Ashley.

"Very scary," said Cam.

"I just hugged the ground," I admitted.

"Me too," said Tarik. Tarik looked a bit pale.

Grandpop nodded gravely.

"Good. So now you know what being shot at is like and that it's *not* like the movies. Now the problem is that while the noise of a gun, especially an automatic weapon like this one, makes you want to hide in a hole that is part of the reason soldiers shoot. It's not always to hit the target. Sometimes it's to suppress the enemy to stop him shooting or moving while other soldiers get close enough to chuck in a grenade or catch them in a crossfire. So what I'm coming to is sitting still under cover is *not* the safest thing to do. Keep moving."

"That *doesn't* mean breaking cover like a headless chicken. Just remember guns need reloading. Most can only fire continuously for three seconds. That's why professional soldiers tag team it. They call to each other when they're reloading so nobody rushes forward without covering fire. But if there's just one guy there are moments when you can get a chance to get away. "

"Now don't be confused. *Never* risk being shot. The safest place is always behind the shooter. Always bend if you are trapped. But if you can dodge, blend in and remember the gun. It's a simple machine with limitations."

"OK, so this is a training session. Once I've said freeze, you freeze. But in real life you want to get somewhere safe and the safest place is somewhere where they don't expect you to be. Behind them or anywhere they aren't looking. Above is always an option if you can't think of anything else."

"Now to get around the problem of people calling the same number we'll call out in alphabetic order: Ashley, Cam, Sam, Scotty, Tahira, Tarik. OK call it! Go!"

We called the names.

"Again."

We called them again.

"Faster."

We did it again.

"Faster."

And again.

"Faster."

We were so fast they were run together. Grandpop picked up a rock.

"OK that's better but you mustn't call out if you aren't under cover. So to test that if I toss this rock to you, catch it and you *don't* call until you've tossed it back and I've got it again. OK ready."

We did that drill about ten times until he was satisfied. All the time the pace was getting faster and faster. Then

"OK. Cover! Go!" he roared.

We ran. We dived for cover. We checked. We named off. He called 'freeze' and 'red'. There was another blast but two seconds this time. We flinched as the bullets cracked overhead and clutched each other feeling ourselves clench inside again. Unlike jumping I was pretty sure this was one scary thing I was *never* going to get used to.

"Safe. OK, now İ have to reload but I'm coming forward looking for you. Go find a new place to hide. Cover! Go! Go! Go!"

We ran like rabbits. I looked back and saw him walking forward reloading casually. We rushed to hide. We started naming but he stopped us.

"I can see your foot Ashley. Start again."

We called our names again.

"Freeze."

This time there was a long three second burst. Now we were a bit more sure of ourselves and waited for it to end.

"OK, this time before I say the unfreeze command I want you to use your suits to get to cover as close to me as you can, but I don't want to see you get there, and I'm not going to be closing my eyes. You have two minutes. Safe."

I switched to blend but I was trapped behind a small rock. The others had cover to make their way around behind Grandpop.

"*Circling to the south,*" Scotty thought

"*Moving back to follow,*" Ashley thought.

"*Going for the sea,*" Tarik thought.

"*Following Scotty,*" Tahira thought.

"*With Tarik,*" Cam thought.

"*Gotta bend back to beach,*" I thought.

"*Hey! Why didn't we think of that,*" thought Tarik and Cam.

## [+]

The world flattened to a line as usual. Then I found myself on the beach in a flash of light. There were two flashes and Tarik and Cam were there too. We couldn't see Grandpop but we blended into the background anyway. We were damn hard to see as we stalked slowly closer.

Tarik and Cam took a cautious approach and went behind him. I snuck along under the small cliff beneath him.

"One minute," Grandpop called.

I snuck closer. He was right above me. I realised how scary this would be if he really did want to kill us.

"Thirty seconds."

I got in position and out of sight under a lip of rock.

"OK freeze and red."

I went red. I couldn't see anything. All I knew was Grandpop was right above me.

"OK stay frozen. Here we go."

With a gut wrenching blast bullets pumped a line in the sand about two feet from where I was crouching. I hugged the wall. I heard two more short bursts.

"Safe! OK, everyone come out and stand by the nearest bullet marks if there are any, or just stand up where you are. Good work! I only saw three of you."

I came out and stood by my marks.

"Scotty! Brilliant. That's about ten meters. Very good. Cam! That's what? fifteen! Also good. Sam – footprints behind you, look!"

I looked behind me. I was disappointed to see he was right.

"Too close son!" he was chiding me.

"Never get closer than ten meters in daylight. That goes for you too Ashley. Tarik you moved that bush. Big giveaway. Tahira safe but miles away. OK, come in and we'll finish up."

We got up and came over to him.

"Tarik, mate, this is for the others really. It's about the effect of bullets on flesh. I think you already know more about that than any kid should ever know so if you want to go, that's OK," he said softly to him.

Tarik looked around at us. We all remembered him telling us about finding his mother and sister. He thought about it but then wanted to stay with us.

"It's OK. I'll stay with the others," he said in a small voice.

Grandpop walked over to the big sack he had brought with him. Then he upended it and a pig's head fell out. We were all disgusted but Ashley and Tahira made more noise about it. Grandpop picked up the head and took it about ten meters away and put it on a rock. Then he walked back to us.

"Tarik if you don't want to watch this that's OK. This is for the others."

"I'm OK," he insisted, again in a high voice. But he looked pale and sick.

"Freeze," Grandpop told us.

Then he cocked the gun and fired a short burst into the head which shattered and splattered as it was knocked about by the bullets. Ashley, Tahira and Tarik couldn't look. Finally it was over.

Grandpop removed the magazine, ejected the cartridge, and put on the safety catch.

"OK, no more shooting today. I wanted you to see this. It's what a gun like this can do to you. Tarik you wait here, you don't need to look at this, mate."

He made a small squeak. We walked over to the head. It looked horrible. The skull had been smashed in. Brains were splattered about. The snout had a huge graze in it. One eye socket was smashed and eye reduced to goo.

"I'm going to hurl!" said Ashley. And she meant it. She ran away and puked twice. Tahira didn't look too well either.

"Hekator tells me your facescreens will take *one* bullet from an AK47. The second one would smash it like wet paper. Most machine guns or assault rifles fire three to ten bullets *per second* so if they shoot you in the face this is what *you* will look like. As Lana said you are always safer escaping. Never take risks. It isn't worth it."

Grandpop picked up the shattered head and carried it along some rocks to the sea and threw it in.

"The sea creatures will eat that up. OK, everyone to the beach.

We walked to the beach and gathered around in a group while the wind blew and sea crashed.

"What have we learned?" Grandpop asked.

"Guns are 'orrible," said Tahira.

"Good. If nothing else I wanted you kids to realise guns in real life are not like the movies. Guns like this were made to chop people up. They aren't cool and they aren't fun. They are tools for making people miserable. That was the main point. What else?"

"Remember to bend," said Tarik, who looked pale and shaky.

"Good too. You have a huge safety advantage. Use it. What else?"

"Don't get too close," I said.

"Yes. That's right Sam. You don't need to stick your head in a lion's mouth to know lions are dangerous. Keep your distance it gives you more leeway."

"Mr Kahu?" Ashley asked.

"Yes Ashley?"

"Should we use our own weapons?"

"Not if they are shooting *at* you. You move first. I never want to see you get into a shootout. It's dangerous and unnecessary. If you have to knock someone out, do it first, do it fast. Otherwise you get them from behind or you ambush them. You are *not* to fight. Understood?"

We certainly did. The idea of fighting it out with anyone who might shoot us might have been an idle fantasy once but no more.

"Last thing," Grandpop said. "You all need a hug. Come here."

He gave us each a hug. It was funny hugging in the suit because we were so much stronger. But even though we had an extra layer between him and us, it still felt good to get a big bear hug.

"OK, swim home it will help you feel better and tell Ken to pick me up. It's getting dark and I don't want to spend the night out here."

We swam home enjoying the cool sea and the feeling of strength we had in the water. We felt like a family of dolphins, safe from the vicious technology of killing Grandpop had shown us.

The next day started as normal. Conversation on the bus was more about guns than the visitors we had been warned about. Rewa and Asal were impressed by the grim way we talked about the dangers of being shot at and what we might have to do about it. There wasn't a lot of silly boasting about it anyway.

Then that night when we came back we heard the first guests had arrived. We didn't see them at first because we were doing homework and cleaning. We did underwater night training that evening but met the first fortune teller that evening in the lounge.

Solomon Rosenberg called himself, "Solly, an old Jewish guy from Noo York". He had old glasses. He smoked cigars constantly which really annoyed Mrs Jones who he seemed to enjoy teasing. He said he was a professional gambler but he and Dr Prosperov were thick as thieves when it came to talking about financial markets. He talked in a low gravely voice and was always making jokes about himself. He was the only person I ever saw make Dr Morozov really laugh.

The next day three more arrived. Professor Robert Lee from Hong Kong was a quiet small man who wore shabby looking jackets and clothes. He was quite old although he didn't look it. He was a bit of a nerd really with a bland face and glasses. He was a history professor. He was very humble and didn't talk about himself although we later learned he had a huge international reputation.

Unlike Solly, who smiled at us but hardly ever said anything, Mr Lee was very friendly. He played chess with Tarik and geographical history games with all of us. He would challenge us to find him a place he didn't know the history of. We ended up finding some pretty out of the way places in order to stump him. Professor Lee was also very interested in the older people, especially Nergui, Aunty Nea and Mrs Jones. He was also interested in our parents. I could tell he just loved collecting stories more than anything.

The other two visitors were Lobsang and Tashi whose last names I forget. They were old Tibetan monks. They wore brown and purple robes, sandals and beanies and were very cheerful. They were big eaters and avid sports fans, always watching games in the lounge and eating popcorn. They were pretty messy too. It was hard to believe they had anything special to contribute. If they had been Maori instead of Asian, drunk beer, and worn ordinary clothes it would have been hard to tell them apart from some of the old men back home. They got on well with Grandpop, Mariko and Gunter, Khenbish and Mr Trân especially. They also enjoyed playing soccer with us kids, and despite the fact they were as old as Grandpop, they were surprisingly fit.

The next day we were introduced to VJ Pra-bhu-des-ai who everyone called Mr Prabhudesai or sometimes "VJ" to his face, or "His Highness" when he wasn't around. He was accompanied by his assistant Mr Parag. VJ was a rich fortune teller from Mumbai in India, about the same age as Dr Morozov. Mr Parag was a similar age but smaller, thinner and treated badly by VJ who shouted at him angrily in Hindi and then smiled at us and spoke to us in fancy English. He was rude to everyone who he thought was a servant and polite to Dr Prosperov, and Drs Morozov and Gursoy. He was completely blind and walked with a stick when Mr Parag wasn't guiding him. I often wondered why Mr Parag put up with it.

It turned out VJ had amazing hearing and also played the sitar which was interesting. The strange thing about him was that while he was blind he constantly saw things. The images were of places and people he didn't know and things he'd never seen before. This isn't so rare apparently. Many blind people see odd visions we learned.

But what was rare and what made rich Indians seek VJ out was that he often saw things which happened later. Nobody really seemed to like VJ very much but he seemed pleasantly disconnected to everyone else anyway and made many rude suggestions for improving things. He didn't like the Tibetans who made jokes at his expense and he didn't like Solomon either. He acted as if he was very important to Dr Prosperov who was friendly – but not too much. His efforts to charm Dr Morozov and Mrs Jones were met with long cold stares.

The last visitor to arrive was an Australian woman named Golda Farrow who was even more dumpy than Mrs Jones. She wore some of the ugliest dresses I have ever seen. She said she got them for cheap from the Salvation Army and seemed very pleased with herself for it. She had black curly hair and was coffee coloured like Tarik.

But Golda was special for two reasons. First because she wore a lot of gold. Big earrings, rings, teeth, bangles and "beets and borbs", as she called them. And second because she claimed she was Romany royalty, or as she put on her business cards "Golda

Farrow, Gypsy Princess, Tarot Reader, Fortune Teller".

In a lot of ways Golda didn't fit in very well either. She was cheap and nicked things. Mrs Jones would find them and take back them back. It was almost like she couldn't help herself. She also couldn't help calling anyone who wasn't white something rude. VJ in particular called her "common" without caring whether she heard or not.

But the weird thing was,Golda *was* extremely good at fortune telling. And I don't mean vague promises to make people feel better either. I mean she just did things that showed she expected things to happen a certain way without any way of knowing that they would.

For example she always knew what the weather would do – and on Aotea the weather changes *all the time*. She told people who would be ringing them *before* they called and was nearly always right. But for some reason, unlike Mr Rosenberg, she would not gamble at all. She would just say "Oi wusn't geeven thees geeft to maike moiney" and refused to have anything to do with Dr Prosperov or Mr Rosenberg's plans, while pocketing silver spoons from the kitchen. It was pretty weird.

We kids had no idea whether these seers or "fortune cookies" as Rewa called them, helped Dr Prosperov work out where the children he was meant to find were or not. All that went on during the day while we were at school. During the weekend we didn't have much to do with them either.

They were hard work for our parents though, because Dr Prosperov told them they mustn't be allowed to compare notes. He spent an hour with each of them every day, taking notes on a computer like a clipboard. Then Dr Morozov would put them into a program she had written that searched for common themes and connections between the stories. The idea was to see if independently they had common visions which might help us. Of course they were not to be told about the Fae or the base and I think most of the time they had no idea what they were doing at Renwick. They never realised what went on when we slipped off to the cellar before dinner because Dr Prosperov would host them for drinks in the upstairs lounge and acted as if we went off somewhere to practice sport or music while the adults chatted. Nobody seemed to notice Grandpop wasn't there.

They stayed for roughly a month and were a drag for all of us. But Dr Prosperov worked them all quite hard. He told them it was a kind of competition to see who could predict the most and whoever won would be paid more. I have no idea whether he was lying or not. Still the presence of the others certainly made them all more competitive.

It was also interesting which of them noticed the ghosts. Solomon and Professor Lee didn't. They didn't seem to be psychic at all – but they did have sharp minds full of facts and connections. VJ and the Tibetans noticed something but said nothing. It was clear that while they were sensitive they weren't as psychic as we were.

But Golda complained about the ghosts a lot. Worse they seemed to pick on her. Appearing while she was in the shower or breathing down her neck in the mirror. Mrs Jones had to have stern words with them to make them stop. Even then, she claimed they were the ones who planted the kitchen silver on her. She was the strangest combination of liar and psychic we ever met.

Gunter, Ken and Mariko made jokes about the seers and Dr Prosperov listening to them. Us kids had our own too.

"I am seeing money, lots of money in my suitcase, going to the airport," Scotty said in an Indian accent, shaking his head like, VJ. Then he frowned. "Hey Mr Parag, you lazy good-for-nothing, you must carry me and my suitcase."

Ashley started smoking an imaginary cigar and doing a pretty good imitation of Solly's Brooklyn accent.

"OK Gennady ahl telya what oyl do. Just fer you, oyl tell you what the woyld will be like in fifty years tiyme, in retoin, you tell me the winner of next week's darby in Lexington. Ya cayn't say fehrer thayn that."

But Tahira really cracked us up with:

"Oi see a buig poile of seelva enn moi fuutcha," doing a brilliant impression of Golda.

Gunter and Ken had some of their own versions of these sketches as well. Dr Prosperov would smile when he caught us telling them to the others. But it didn't stop him continuing to work on the information the fortune cookies had provided.

He just said, "just because someone is a thief doesn't mean they lack foresight."

It was a long month. Our training switched to hanging around different parts of Auckland in the evening for a week. Grandpop would give us people to follow at random and we had to watch them without being too obvious about it. Then he'd ask us questions about what we'd seen.

At first we were pretty bad at it. Part of the problem was we didn't really know much about adults or what they did. But we built up our teamwork changing our groups and clothes so we might have a group of girls then boys, then mixed, then couples. We discovered adults ignored us. The only ones who didn't were shopkeepers who watched us very closely.

But older teens were a bigger problem – especially some of the homeless ones who hung around the square. Some of them tried to hassle us for money. It was a bit of a problem. We were stronger, better protected and better armed, but they were just taller and in our faces. We didn't want to start fights but sometimes they interrupted things so we had to leave in a hurry. That was when Grandpop decided that we needed self-defence lessons in the hall and Mariko joined in.

It wasn't as much fun as using our suits but it gave us a good grounding in understanding simple ways of overcoming others who might grab us. Mariko had learned Judo as a child and impressed us all by flipping Grandpop. We learned about balance, steps to put others off balance, holds and joint twists. Just for once Rewa and Asal could join in too – although they weren't really into it and gave up after a few days.

After a month of hosting the fortune cookies they finally went home and we had a bit of a party to celebrate. It was great to have the house back to ourselves again. Then a few days later Dr Prosperov called us together in the lounge to "announce results of experiment".

"Total of three thousand eight hundred and forty seven observations. All observations weighted by observer for strength. Strong correlation of three or more observers on eighty four observations, weak correlation of two or more observers on two hundred and twelve further observations. Was four hundred strong individual observations."

"Important political drivers identified by Mr Lee and Mr Solomon include growing strength of Brazilian, Indian and Chinese economies; slower growth in US and Europe; Growing unrest in the Middle East; Stabilising social democracy in

South America; Aging populations in US, Europe and Japan; continued political turmoil in Africa, Middle East, Pakistan and central Asia. Is nothing special.

Important concerns under business-as-usual scenario are nuclear war in Middle East, very likely; Asian pandemics, almost certain; successive US credit crises, almost certain; successive oil-driven recessions, almost certain; autonomous craft and robots, almost certain. Growing internet demand and use of genetic technology, almost certain."

"Other points of interest include US military to contract but continue to lead technologically; Chinese space exploration to overtake US; Chinese Navy to expand; European decline to continue; EU stability questionable; China to democratise eventually with left-green opposition; Russian decline to continue; USA to decline in East but steady growth in West. Stability in the Southern states will continue to erode through Latin corrosion."

Climate change effects to accelerate; water and electricity shortages balanced by emerging technologies. Natural habitat loss to continue in South America, Asia and Africa. Is all fairly obvious."

It all sounded really bad news to me. But what really bothered me was the adults. None of them seemed surprised by these predictions at all. They just nodded and looked worried.

I think it was only then that I began to realise what Lucky was about. Things weren't getting better and we were going to get the whole mess. The adults had no plan. They were just blundering around looking out for themselves hoping everything wouldn't fall apart before they died. The world we were growing up into wasn't a school with a principal and rules. It was random and

**235**

messy. And if nothing changed we would end up with all these problems. It was going to take some pretty amazing people to solve them without more disasters happening.

But Dr Prosperov went on.

"Top down analysis suggests significant individual influence points expected in following areas: internet governance; robotics and artificial intelligence; international legal standardisation, Muslim-Christian reconciliation; energy research; political management of United States, Israel, Iran, Pakistan, and China; and biomedical research. Possible influence points from youth and feminists in Islamic world."

"Is relative simple task to extrapolate from existing trend to determine destinations of children to influence world. Problem is to determine origins. For this using logic and foresight."

"Foresight by VJ Prabhudesai, Mrs Farrow, Lobsang and Tashi produced interesting data. Some profitable, much trivial, some significant.

Children suggested in Central Africa, Arabia, Israel, Eastern US, Amazon basin, Western India, Japan. Some to be politicians, some financiers, and some scientists. Some important traits and even some names suggested. We have hints but not a cohesive picture. However next stage is to engage with other-world colleagues. I will also seek advice on refining amplifier design. I alone will test the amplifier. Am not wanting to repeat Chicago disaster."

To us the fortune *cookies* didn't seem to have achieved much but waste everyone's time. We had learned some useful self-defence in three weeks of daily practice and now that we could use the suits again we were impatient to get started. But Grandpop had a few more things for us to do first.

## CHAPTER FORTY: INTO THE WORLD

It was early September 2007. Officially it was Spring but on Aotea not much changed. It rained, it blew, it was cloudy. The trees were green as they had been all winter. The only differences were a few daffodils, slightly warmer rain, and some early lambs.

We filed into the briefing room and were at once struck that there was a cabbage on one of the chairs. We all wondered what that would be used for.

"Ah jus' hope we ain't gotta eat it. Ah hate cabbage," Ashley said.

"Or feed it to anything," added Scotty.

"Maybe eet's a ball, yeah?" Tarik suggested.

Grandpop came in with his glasses on his nose.

"Well people, you've come a long way." he started. "But all the skydiving, all the diving, all the games. They were just a warmup. Now we start the hard stuff."

We all looked a bit put out. We wanted to get started.

"The hard stuff is dealing with real places and most important of all, new people. Luckily you already know quite a lot about that. But the main problem you will face is being out of place. Who noticed my friend here when they first came in?" he said pointing at the cabbage.

We all put up our hands.

"Well, like it or not, that's you. And you will be most noticeable in places you are most likely to go. Big city in America or Europe during the day? No problem. Just like Auckland. You're a bunch of kids, no-one pays attention. You could probably all be dressed as penguins and nobody would be bothered."

"But what about six kids in hoodies at four in the morning? Ooooh, that's a different story. Then you are out of place," he pointed to the cabbage.

"Cops think kids running around at night are vandals or thieves. People are suspicious of things that are out of place. They think it might be a threat... Even something as harmless as a cabbage."

"Now as I said in Western Europe or the Americas a bunch of kids as racially mixed as you are won't be much of a surprise. But in places like China or India you are obviously different and obviously out of place. You will be noticed and in some places you will be questioned. This isn't my area of expertise so I'm going to pass you on to Mrs Jones when we come to that. What I want to tell you about is being out of place in the environment."

"Let's say you are in the desert. There might be nobody about but you are still out of place. As you move you will disturb the environment and if you are in a place where people listen to their environment, like the desert or a jungle or the arctic you will be as obvious as if you had a big sign over your head saying 'look at me!'"

So for this week I will introduce you to blending into natural environments. Then we will look at blending into night time environments and then Mrs Jones will introduce you to busy environments."

Ashley put her hand up.

"How late are we stayin' up fuh?"

Grandpop smiled.

"You won't be. Globe please Control."

A big globe appeared in the area next to him.

"This is the world right now."

The globe rotated a bit and turned up to show the south and a red dot appeared on Aotea.

"And here we are. And here is the time where we are. Now let's go to New Orleans."

The globe spun and rotated north.

"...where it's midnight...and London..."

The globe span again.

"where it's summer so it's four in the morning...and Ankara..."

The globe moved slightly.

"...where it's six in the morning. Thanks Control."

The globe vanished.

"What this means is we can practically only reach some parts of the world at certain times. Europe and Africa will only be accessible during the week very early in the morning or if we get you up early in the early evening. But it will be dark."

"The Americas will generally be at night; western Asia, early morning; eastern Asia, midday to early afternoon. We should also bear in mind that you will start operations in the northern Fall when, of course, it's starting to get darker and colder. The North is further north than we are south so it's darker for longer and more likely to involve snow."

"So I guess what I'm kind of telling you here is that apart from Asian ops you'll be most likely to be in the dark. Now the obvious problem with your appearing in the dark is the light flare that comes with bending. I've asked Hekator about it but, very long story short, he says it can't be prevented. It's just a

**239**

given."

"This is a problem. Obviously anyone appearing in a burst of bright light will be noticed so we've come to the conclusion the best time to insert you is in bad weather. When it's raining or snowing people don't look around so much and they don't look up so much either. Lightning storms are ideal. Fog is obviously good too."

"That's all fine for about half the world but Asia is a problem. First of all finding somewhere where there isn't *anyone* watching is almost impossible. There are simply too many people. So we may need to find some friends in these parts of the world if we need to go there. We're still working on this."

"But today you are going to a place where there will be no-one around," he looked down at a note in his hand.

"It's called Rub Al Khali or 'The Empty Quarter' and it's in Saudi Arabia. It's 8:12 in the morning and the temperature is a hot thirty nine degrees Celsius. Later it will warm up to reach a paint blistering sixty degrees Cee."

A globe appeared, rotated around and zoomed in on the Arabian peninsular.

"The specific place you are going is the site of a meteorite impact called the Wabar crater."

Everything vanished and was replaced by a 3D view of the bleakest looking place I'd ever seen. It was pale sand as far as the eye could see. There was a dip in the ground in front of us."

"That's it right now. Scientists believe the crater was caused when a meteor hit the earth with the force of a Hiroshima-sized atom bomb some time in the late 1800s[†]. We want you to take these little doohickys..."

He held up a short black rod.

"And press them to the ground in various places around the site. Hekator says they can't go there themselves because of some kind of radiation which is what these things measure."

"As a learning experience for you I want you to try and avoid leaving marks that will make your visit obvious. Don't get too paranoid about this though. The last expedition just left and the previous one was decades before. Literally no-one goes here and the sands in this part of the world shift all the time and cover a lot. Just don't get silly and collapse the edges of the crater by jumping on it. Any questions?"

"How do the thingies work?" asked Scotty.

"No idea. My instructions just say put them against the ground until the light on top starts flashing. When it shows steady green it's finished. When it's steady violet it's ready for use again. Any more questions? No, well you can ask while you're there. Remember this is an easy exercise just to get you used to working on the ground. Don't sweat it."

He looked at us.

"You ready?"

We looked at each other. The answer was yes.

"OK, come grab a thingamybob and then off to the jumpstation. Let's go there!"

The rods were like batons we had used in relay races at school but they fitted in our leg pockets easily enough. We trooped over to the jumpstation and filed down the stairs.

"We thought about dropping you but decided there was no point. You'll arrive on the ground near the crater. There hasn't been anyone there for about six months. Keep an eye out for old tyre tracks. First one to spot them gets a chocolate fish. OK, ready?"

We gave him the thumbs up.

"OK Control," Grandpop called. And then the world folded, lost its colour and drained to a line of whiteness which burst around me and I was standing in a vast world of sand that stretched as far as you could see.

**[+]**

I looked around at the others. We all looked completely out of place in our casual-looking hoodies with our faces covered. It felt weird. The silence was intense. We shuffled into a line looking at the crater.

It was about the size of a playing field. Not big enough for a full scale game of football but still not small either. Around it were dunes that reached out into a haze that danced and shimmered. It was already hot and it was just warming up. There was nothing; not a tree, not a building, not a blade of grass, as far as the eye could see. As for spirits, no soul had been near this place for thousands of years. It was deader than death. Lifeless and against life.

Scotty bent down and picked up some fine pale sand and let it trickle through his fingers. We all watched, fascinated. Then we were all doing it. It somehow made the place seem more real and less like a dream.

The sand was incredibly fine. Nothing like beach sand. More like a powder. It seemed like a handful of something that defied and crushed living things. Seemingly weak but in this place it had swamped anything that might grow or take root.

"It might pay to fan out," Grandpop said quietly in our ears. His voice brought us slowly back from the dream-like feeling of appearing in the middle of the desert miles from anywhere. There was a loud buzzing. Tahira had already got her wings out and she glowed brightly in the sharp desert sun. Then in a cloud of dust she was in the air rising up over the crater. In a moment we had all copied her and we lifted ourselves off the ground until we were about fifty meters over the crater.

"Good thinking Tahira. Now you need to fan out so you aren't all working in the same place," Grandpop told us.

It was fun flying like this. No-one was ever going to spot us here so we just went for it. We zoomed out over the crater like half a dozen oversized bugs and looked around.

"Tyre marks!" called Scotty.

He was on the opposite side from me.

"A couple of vehicles. Maybe three I think."

"Yup, you get the fish Scotty. Good work. OK let's get down there and collect stuff. See who can leave the least marks."

I asked my suit how to avoid leaving marks. It suggested making the soles of my shoes furry. So I did that. I buzzed down lower and landed in a cloud of dust.

We were scattered around the crater site. I applied the rod. It blinked for a while and went green. So I flew somewhere else. After about half an hour of picking over the site Grandpop told us to come home because dinner was due. The intense morning light made it feel funny to think we were going home to dinner, but we came home.

## [+]

To our surprise when we arrived the jumpstation was full of clear liquid. I almost opened my facescreen but my suit stopped me. Sand danced in the oil about us.

"It's to detect and remove contaminants." Grandpop told us. We haven't needed it up til now but as you become operational you will always return to the tank. You can come straight out. No

**243**

point hanging around in it."

We came out and were met by Grandpop who took our rods back. We watched as the jumpstation quickly drained. We noticed the liquid wasn't water. It was almost like a clear oil but all the sand stuck to it. Even so it drained away completely leaving the floor as clean and dry as we were.

We had time for a debrief and Grandpop showed us how we left tracks. He showed us how to walk lightly and choose where to place our feet on soft sand. But he also pointed out how Tarik had reduced his weight to achieve the same result.

It felt funny going to school the next day aware that I had been halfway around the world to a remote desert the evening before and not being able to talk about it. On the bus home we wondered where we would go today.

The answer, after cleaning and homework, was Siberia.

For this briefing Dr Prosperov, Ken and Nergui were waiting for us in the briefing theatre too. Their presence seemed to make Grandpop unusually confused.

"The destination today is another meteor impact site, although this one is better known apparently – though I'd never heard of it," Grandpop told us.

The globe appeared rotated and zoomed in on Eastern Russia. "Tunguska. In 1908 another meteor exploded over the Earth at an estimated height of ten kilometers[†] – I'm getting all this from Wikipedia by the way so you can look it up yourselves if you want to – with the force of ... I can't read my writing ... Well, some big number of hydrogen bombs. The first investigators didn't reach the site until 1913 and took these pictures."

There were a whole lot of black and white pictures of trees all fallen over.

"The mystery at the time was that the trees in the middle that a meteor should have squashed were still standing. This indicated an air explosion and there were a number of weird theories about UFOs blowing up ... though come to think of it, you're going there using alien technology to do a job for some aliens ... so I guess UFOs aren't as weird as I'd normally think. Anyway now they think an explosion occurred because some meteors become unstable on re-entry."

Grandpop took off his glasses.

"This is another job with the rods like yesterday. Dr Prosperov is here because Tunguska is in the state of Krasnoyarsk Krai which is his home town and he just wanted to see the forest ... which is called the Taiga, spelt T...A...I...G...A not the animal way. Ken and Nergui wanted to see it too."

"This is the site as we visited it today."

The screen came up in 3D tracking through a forest in the rain. It was huge. The leaves were just starting to go yellow and brown. It was quite pretty really.

"As you can see it's early autumn in Siberia. It's getting cooler but it's not freezing yet. In fact at midday because of all the rain, the ground is a bit mushy. There is a lot of regrowth and the oldest new trees are over eighty years old."

The view broke out into open ground. The bushes were much lower but in some places still taller than us.

"This is a peat bog. It's very mushy but it's nothing to worry about in itself, other than the fact that it's much more open. Now this site is much bigger than Wabar. To cover the map..." (which appeared) "...you will have to split up. But more importantly this place is not empty. There are certainly animals in this forest. These range from harmless chipmunks and squirrels and the like, up to Siberian Brown bears which are clever and dangerous and not to be messed with."

"But there's one more complication. First this place is a bit of a tourist attraction. Not a lot of people come here – hardly any by most standards – but it's not unknown for choppers to come by. And second it's hunting season for deer in Siberia[†] so there may be hunters. It's not likely you will encounter them in an area this huge, but it is not impossible. Unlike bears, hunters are not out to harm you, but anyone with a gun has to be a potential source of danger. We also don't need stories of flying children in the woods, so be careful about using your wings."

"For that reason you'll work in pairs with one of you placing the instrument and the other keeping watch. Use all the sensors in the suit and all the senses you have to look out. You've got four sites each and you'll bend between then. They're loaded into the maps in your suits. We will also keep watch from here."

"Finally do stay sealed on this trip. It's twelve degrees Celsius at the moment and sunny so it looks nice but the place is alive with biting insects and they will go for your face. Now do any of the adults have any useful tips?"

Dr Prosperov had to say something.

"Please to be aware animals very clever. Not to let down guard. Taiga is gentle now but all animals have survived harsh winter. All stupid or weak ones dead. Is not place to underestimate. But is very beautiful. You are fortunate to see."

Grandpop seemed to have thought of something to say but decided against it.

"OK, decide now who your lookout is on the way to the jumpstation," Grandpop told us.

Tahira wanted to watch, so I ended up putting the short rod

Grandpop handed us in my pocket. Then it was over to the jumpstation and we were there.

[+]

As soon as we arrived we both felt the same shock of arriving in a place far away from the one we had left. Our suits were set to adaptive camouflage so we were almost invisible as the suits blended into the forest.

I ran my hand over the trunk of a white barked tree feeling the rough texture with my hands. I dug my feet into the leaf covered dirt. Just getting dirty seemed to be an important way of connecting with where we were.

We looked around at each other and the place we were in. The quiet was huge. The forest seemed to go on forever. Yet we knew the forest was full of ears. Most safe but some definitely not.

"May as well get started," I said quietly and my voice seemed to be measured by some unseen mind.

I bent down and pulled the rod out of my pocket. The ground was muddy but not squishy. Putting the thing in proved to be more difficult than I expected.

"Stand on it Sam," Grandpop said.

I eventually was able to drive it down and the green light started blinking. I looked around. There were a few birds I didn't recognise flitting about but, other than that, nothing moved. After a while the light stopped blinking and we could move on.

We bent to the next site. This was another clearing. There had been a number of hoofed animals through the place because you could quite easily see their marks and even the odd dropping. While the rod did whatever it was doing I looked around.

Tahira spotted a squirrel about fifty meters away. I'd never seen one before and liked the way it moved with its bushy red tail

247

following along behind. The rod finished and we moved to the next site.

[+]

This was on a hillside under some tall pines. There were a lot of old logs on the ground which I guessed had been knocked down by the explosion almost a hundred years before. The hillside had a fantastic view and after I'd planted the rod I came to join Tahira looking out over the wide, wide valley.

You could see fallen logs among the tall trees for kilometers around. The whole place was just amazingly huge and with the benefit of the suit's vision enhancement we could see for miles. Suddenly Tarik announced, *"There's someone here."*

Our suits helped work out where Tarik and Cam were. There was a river flowing through the valley and they were down in the soft green forest along it's banks. We looked closely in that direction. It was about three kilometers away but we could see brown figures in the river.

*"Bears!"* Tahira said suddenly.

She was right! There was a family of brown bears down there, either fishing or drinking. They were too far away to tell which.

*"Can we go look at the bears*?" asked Cam.

There was a pause. The adults were talking but we didn't know what they were saying.

"OK Cam, as an exercise you two can stalk the bears. But we are watching as well. So here's the drill. You move in turns. One watches out, the other moves. You don't move out of sight of each other. Got that?"

*"Yeah,"* they said.

We wished we got to stalk bears. We watched in their direction for a while. Then I realised the rod would be finished by now. It

**248**

was on the other side of a log between our lookout point and the forest. I walked back along the path I had taken before, and was just about to round the log, when a large brown and tan animal with big teeth suddenly planted its forelegs on the log just three meters in front of me.

I admit I gave a short cry of shock. The animal was gazing at me like someone who had lost his glasses. My camouflage was very good and, although I had frozen in my tracks so it couldn't hear me, it's twitching nose suggested it knew I was there, and was trying to smell me out. It jumped up onto the log showing it was almost as big as me. It was built like a small bear with big claws and was growling in an awful way stalking toward me.

Suddenly there was a shock of sound. The creature leapt off the log and bounded away back into the woods. Tahira was facing me.

"Well done Tahira!" Grandpop boomed in our ears.

"Tahira just scared off a wolverine everyone! Very good work."

I felt like the world's biggest egg. I had a dozen ways to deal with that animal and I'd just frozen. Tahira had saved me when I shouldn't have needed saving. Of course I thanked her anyway but I was really disappointed with myself. I went around the log to pick up the rod.

I went back and joined Tahira. She looked nervous. I felt sick.

"*Sorry Sam. I was meant to look out,*" she thought quietly.

"*I shouldn't have frozen,*" I replied.

"*You were surprised. It was so close to you.*"

That didn't make me feel any better. Nor did the news from the next site that Cam and Tarik had watched the bears unnoticed from twenty meters for five minutes and Scotty and Ashley had found a small herd of deer to watch. I was still feeling dumb when we were finally pulled home.

[+]

Dr Prosperov, Ken and Nergui had gone so we were left with
Grandpop. In the briefing theatre we watched Scotty and Ashley
stalk deer and Tarik and Cam sneak up on the bears. Grandpop
pointed out the biggest problem with moving is getting hooked
into thinking you know where your target is and forgetting there
can always be surprises you didn't expect. Then he *had* to play
Tahira-cam of me face-to-face with a wolverine looking eggier
than my worst nightmare.

"What were you thinking Sam?" he asked gently.

"I ... well ... nothing I was just sorta staring at this big furry thing
with teeth and claws."

"That's the problem with surprises. In combat you find yourself
with a stupid expression on your face..."

He made a face of supreme dumbness. Everyone but me
laughed.

"... while looking down the barrel of an enemy ambush thinking
'where did you come from'. Lucky for me, and you too Sam,
you had support. That's why we work in pairs guys. Sam was in
shock, Tahira covered for him. It was good teamwork. It's what
you are here to learn."

"But, ah, Mr Kahu I did not properly watch," Tahira admitted.

"Don't beat yourself up about it Tahira. Or you Sam. These
training sessions are for you to practice with. If you didn't
make any mistakes you wouldn't learn anything. Normally Sam
meeting a wolverine would very dangerous. But not for you guys.
Even if that Wolverine had jumped Sam it couldn't bite through
the suit and Sam could have shocked it. You weren't in any
real danger, Sam. But you got a good taste of the way surprises

happen. And if you end up in a really dangerous situation knowing that could make all the difference. It's all good."

I felt a bit better after that. Aunty Liz asked me about it at bedtime. It was good to talk to her and she told me just to relax because nobody thought less of me for it. But that night I dreamed that Ax had turned into a Wolverine and was coming after me and I couldn't do anything.

The next day we were sent somewhere rather surprising.

"Believe it or not you are going to Mo-koi-a which is a small town in..."

The big globe moved hardly at all.

"New Zealand! It's just north of Pa-te-a on the south western coast of the North Island. Five months after the Tunguska meteor in July 1908 a fireball appeared in the skies over Tasman sea and a meteorite broke up all over the Mokoia area[+]. The meteor was much smaller than the Tunguska one and arrived intact. Bits of it are in museums all over the world. And here is part of the site today."

The view showed a boring looking paddock. Then it climbed into the air and showed a bunch of paddocks, a few roads on a plateau with a stream in a gully around the north.

"OK, so looks pretty easy, right?" Grandpop smiled.

We nodded and said "yeah."

"Wrong!" he barked sternly.

"The ones that look easy are because you assume too much. Let's say you're in someone's paddock and suddenly a farmer shows up. Lot of houses down there eh? What are you going to do? Vanish in front of him? Zap him ? Explain why you're in his paddock? You see it's tricky. And it's trickier still because this is a small country and you live here. If he gets on the news and describes say a black girl, a white boy, an Asian, two middle eastern kids, and a Maori, people here on Aotea are going to think that sounds real familiar."

There was a pause while Grandpop seemed to be thinking.

"That said it is still pretty easy," he admitted. "The main thing is not to be spotted. That's easiest at night but still leaves the problem of light flare. Farmers are always wary of lights on the properties. It could mean some idiot out with a twenty-two bagging possums or threatening their stock. So this is a good excuse to practise some bend-diving. We could just put you down the bank but what you learn? So what we'll do is drop you one kilometer apart from ten grand. You're to extend your wings and fly a circle to the left checking out the area below with all your senses. If you feel confident about letting the suit do a stall landing let it. If you don't find somewhere to bend to. If your suit is confused it will bend you home without touching down."

"I thought our folks didn't want us doin' stall landings?" Ashley objected.

"Yeah, Hekator said stall landings were for slopes, right?" Tarik added frowning.

"Technically you don't do the stall landing. The suit does. But if you think your parents will give you hell, go for bending. You guys have to make your own calls about what you want to do."

Grandpop was taking a bit of a risk saying that. Patricia Robinson for one would be pretty pissed with him. You could see Ashley thinking about it.

"Can I go last?" she asked.

"Sure but it's you and Scotty. We're doing this in pairs. The pattern we are trying to make is a rectangle."

He tapped the picture of the site in six places. So Tarik and Cam you're here and here. Sam and Tahira here and here. And Ashley and Scotty here and here."

"Make sure no-one can look out on your landing point. With bending there's light flare and stalling you'll need to flap those wings for a few seconds before your final touchdown and the sound may well carry. Best places are in the gullies and depressions. Be very definite about where you are going and keep watching it as you do your fly over. Think about a backup as well. When you hit one grand you must decide. Bend or stall. I recommend you decide earlier but if you haven't decided by one grand you're coming home like it or not."

"OK all clear? Let's have a closer look at your approaches. Come down here and we'll show you an individual simulation based on stalling."

We trooped down to the holostage. The simulations lasted two minutes. First there was a dive angled away from each other, an overshoot and stall. Then a stall turn. The landing was hairy looking and made me nervous. We were meant to come diving down and level out at just ten meters, flying horizontally as we ran out of speed but still doing about a hundred kay getting lower to about two meters before flapping hard and stalling to drop four meters to the ground still running forward at about thirty kay.

"What about telephone or power lines?" Scotty asked looking worried.

"Well, there are some, so you'll have to watch out for them." Grandpop answered.

I was starting to wonder whether stalling was such a great option and I could tell I wasn't the only one. Grandpop seemed a bit surprised by our reaction.

"As I say you make your own call."

He *knew* it was dumb! I decided I was going to bend. The others picked up the same thought and decided they would too.

We filed through to the jumpstation. Then Tarik and Cam were gone. I looked at Tahira. She looked tense. Then we were gone.

**[+]**

There was still a touch of late sun in the sky as we started plummeting from ten thousand feet. The ground below seemed to be cold with a slight fog forming. I took a moment to get used to falling again while extending my wings and started looking around for my target point. It stuck out to me as the suit put a blue dot on it. I spotted a good landing place tucked away in a small gully and marked it in green. As my wings hardened I slowly moved them out to catch the stream of speeding air and in no time I could feel lift beneath them. I deflected air to change the angle of descent and increased my wing span as I began to level out and climb for the first stall. Tahira and me were now five kilometers apart and two kilometers up as we circled around, stalled and dived again. It was a wicked feeling flying like that with the country below you. We dropped three hundred meters in gradual curving dive with our wings in full lift. We were going about sixty kay down and a hundred and twenty forward. I was glad I still knew where my landing point and Tahira were.

"*We're all bending in aren't we?*" Ashley checked.

I was a bit tempted to fly in by the fun I was having but the view in the simulation had put me off the idea of landing on a plain. Scotty was right about power lines and poles. They were too hard to see in the dark at that speed. Too many ways to get taken out for no reason.

"*Well, I sure am,*" Scotty came back.

"*I'm doing it now,*" Tarik answered.

"*Me too,*" said Cam.

I could now see the landing point again about a kilometer ahead and six hundred meters down. I was coming up on it fast. If I was going to fly it I would have to bank around very, very low and I knew I'd never see anything before I hit it. I could tell even the suit didn't like the idea. It was time to go.

"*Bending,*" I said.

And the colour drained and flattened to a white line as usual.

## [+]

I stumbled a bit on landing and fell flat on the grassy bank. It was nice to be on the ground again.

I lay there for a bit retracting my wings and inspecting a big clump of dewy grass in the darkness. Then I unsealed and enjoyed the smell of cold air, dew, and grass.

I looked around. I was down a bank in a gully and at the bottom there was a small creek. I stood up and climbed to the top switching to adaptive camouflage.

"*We all OK?*" Scotty thought.

Everyone was fine.

"OK everyone, good work, this shouldn't take long," Grandpop said.

He seemed quite pleased. I was surprised because I thought he'd be grumpy with us for piking out.

I walked across the field.

"Watch your feet. No funny footprints please!" Grandpop warned.

I'd forgotten about that. I fluffed up my soles to smudge them and walked the 50 meters or so to the target. I knelt, placed the rod and looked around. There were houses all over the place with lights blazing and chimneys smoking. I looked down. My rod had fallen over and I had to start again.

Gradually the others bent home. I was left in the field waiting for the device to finish. But I did know something was happening back home. All the parents were waiting for us. Finally the rod was happy so I picked it up, sealed up and bent home.

**[+]**

I was last to arrive.

*"It was all a setup they wanted to see if we were dumb enough to fly it,"* Ashley warned me telepathically.

I came out of the tank and Aunty Liz gave me a long hug.

"I was so worried you wouldn't be sensible. That you would try to show everyone you were brave. But you've showed us you're brave and sensible and it makes me proud."

Grandpop came over smiling.

"Well done Sam. The parents wanted to be sure you kids weren't going to take silly risks before you went operational. Anyone still flying at two hundred meters would have been brought home. But none of you did. It proved to them they could trust you."

It was a good feeling to know the adults were pleased with us for using our judgement. Of course I was pretty sure Grandpop and Control had gone out of their way to make that simulation scary as hell but they had been right to do so. Better to watch a sim than kill yourself finding out the hard way. I'd lost count of the number of ghosts back home I'd met who had done that.

It was strange being at school the next day knowing that the previous night we'd been skydiving over Mokioa. It made all of us feel far more confident. We felt that people like Marshall were just stupid little boys who'd never done anything and probably never would.

The next night Grandpop had a surprise for us.

"Egypt. Just south of Alexandria to be exact," as the globe zoomed in.

"In 1911 a meteor broke into forty odd pieces above a village called Al-Nakhla⁺. There is a story one of the pieces killed a dog. Today this area looks like this."

The view was early morning. There was a village on a small rise. Our view was across a small lake from an area covered in trees. The view began to circle the settlement passing though orchards and trees and the over fields of low crops. We circled around down tree-lined avenues and viewed more fields more trees and the odd drainage ditch. Already there were obvious signs of early morning traffic and people wandering around.

"This is one of the more densely populated nations in the world so getting you in is tricky. Bend diving is definitely out. The village is tricky enough in itself but the wider area is very heavily populated. People tend to look at the sky in the morning and even with your suits in blend mode they may notice you. So after looking around this place all night we've found six places that should be OK. They are mostly in bushes or behind trees scattered around the place."

"Now our proposal is to do this real fast. We'll put you in, you use full blend, sneak to the nearest point you can place your gizmos. Which should be almost at your feet. Take the reading and bend home. Should be straightforward. If you're spotted and challenged just ignore them. Then run and hide. We can cope with a mystery among the farmers of Al-Nakhla. Questions?"

There were none.

"OK, let's go!"

We went to the jumpstation and sealed up. We were feeling pretty chilled about this whole thing now. We should have known.

The world folded, lost its colour and drained to a line of whiteness which burst around me.

## [+]

I found myself in a clump of bushes by a road. At first I thought there was no-one around. There were no sounds anyway. I turned and made my way to the edge of a field which was full of cucumbers. I was about to place my sensor when someone walked up to me. I looked up. A crowd was gathering across the field. They were forming a ring watching me. Most of them were dressed in Arab clothes or working loincloths. And they were all ghosts.

I placed my sensor carefully in the soil.

"*Lot of presences here,*" Cam telepathed.

"*Tell me about it,*" responded Scotty.

"*Many here,*" Tahira reported.

"*Not very friendly are they?*" said Ashley.

And they weren't. They seemed to be quite irritated by me. They waved their arms, wagged their fingers and pointed. One even succeeded in kicking dirt at me. It wasn't a lot of dirt but it was surprising it could move anything at all. I realised with my facescreen up I must seem rather scary. After all I was a small humanoid figure with no face and amazing camouflage. Perhaps they thought I was attacking their old village.

I unsealed my facescreen. But it turned out that made no difference at all. They just didn't like strangers appearing out of thin air and hiding in the corner of fields. Luckily Hekator's sensor was finished. I sealed up and pocketed the sensor, pushed through the invisible hecklers back into the bushes and bent home.

**[+]**

We all arrived at pretty much the same time.

"*Those ghosts were a pain. Do you think we'll get them every time we go somewhere old?*" Ashley complained through the suit as we trudged to the steps through the swirling oil.

"*Probably,*" Tarik said. "*It's just like Adiyaman.*"

"*and Teheran,*" Tahira added putting Tarik in his place.

"*Many places are old so they have ghosts,*" Cam shrugged.

We came out of the tank to hand over our rods.

"Well that was easy," Grandpop commented.

"Except for the ghosts," Scotty said.

Grandpop looked over his glasses.

"Ghosts?"

I knew Grandpop wasn't much into ghosts – but the others didn't. They all complained long and loud about them.

Grandpop seemed a bit shocked that five kids sent to different places around the village were complaining about ghosts.

"Sam? Did you see ghosts too?" he asked, finally.

I just raised my eyebrows and nodded. I didn't want to set him off.

"Hmmm, I'm going to have to get help on this," he admitted.

We got changed and went upstairs.

"Where did you go today?" Rewa asked at dinner.

"A little village in Egypt. We only stayed five minutes."

"Were there any mummies?"

"No, just cucumbers in a field."

**259**

"What did you do?"

"Put a rod in the ground and took it out again."

"That sounds pretty boring," she complained.

"It was. What's for dessert?"

"Halva, I think."

That was the kind of conversation we often had. I didn't want Rewa to get the idea we had a lot of fun. Nor did we talk about where we went on the bus any more. There was nothing to say. We'd seen a desert, a forest and two fields it was hardly exciting. The next night was Friday and we wondered what the weekend would bring.

## CHAPTER FORTY ONE: TROUBLE

W e've had hot deserts, so now we're off to a cold one," Grandpop began cheerfully.

"December nine 1998 a large bolide – that, apparently, is the word for rocks from space – streaked over the skies above Greenland[†]. It was picked up by the boys at the U.S department of defence who are still on the lookout for Russian missiles and tracked to a spot fifty kilometers north-east of ... now, let me get this right ... Nar-sar-seuq ... airfield in southern Greenland."

"The bolide broke into a bunch of large pieces and was investigated by Danish, German and American scientists. Our job is pretty much the same as it was everywhere else. The main difference being this is an ice plateau rather than sand, farmland or bogs."

"*At least there won't be any ghosts,*" Ashley thought.

"Now strangely enough it isn't all that cold in Greenland at this time of the year during the day. The problem is you won't be there during the day because right now it's very early in the morning. The sun is only just rising and there's a slight breeze. The temperature is minus five."

The view came up. It looked amazing. The sun was yellow and pink and the ice was white and blue. It seemed to stretch forever. In the middle distance there was a dark pattern of gravel on the ice.

"Pretty much nothing lives here. Polar bears stick to the coast because that's where the seals are. There's no grass so the grazing animals don't come, so neither do the predators."

"So from a learning point of view I thought what we should focus on is walking in snow. Snow is a real problem because it's easy to leave tracks in, and no matter how good your camouflage is, a bunch of tracks stick out like dogs' balls ..."

That made the girls smile at each other.

"...and make your route pretty obvious if someone is looking for you. So what I want you to focus on is finding ways of crossing snow and ice without leaving a trail. We'll put you down half a klick from the site together so you can watch and learn from each other. See how stealthy you can be both in terms of trail and in terms of observability. Questions?"

It seemed pretty straight forward. We shrugged and headed for the jumpstation.

"OK, guys when you land spread out a bit so you can tell your trails apart. Off you go."

And we were gone.

## [+]

The air was cool, and the light was yellow, when we arrived on the snowy plain. I had already switched to fluffy feet and full blend and so had everyone else. We looked like a group of small white bears in the white emptiness. That was until we started slipping on the ice. Then we looked like a bunch of skittles. We put our claws out and that made it possible to stand better.

The problem was we were leaving a trail. The claws dug in, and although the fluffy feet swept the surface, you didn't have to be a genius to tell someone had been walking there. We also noticed that some of the snow was becoming wet as the sun quickly climbed in the sky.

We started to experiment with gravity reduction and wings. The wings were too loud. Not that they were really *that* loud, but in a place where there was no noise at all we sounded like a bunch of lawnmowers.

The gravity reduction was better. It allowed us to space our steps better. We landed under maximum gravity reduction so we glowed the most then, and again as we leapt. So we glowed on the ground and changed colour in the air. After watching us for a while Grandpop said we would be less obvious if coloured ourselves pink and green and played brass band music.

"We need skis, yeah?" Tarik suggested.

"We need snowshoes," Ashley corrected him.

"You know Ashley, I think you may be right. Your suits just aren't enough," Grandpop agreed.

"Just fly over to the site and we'll have a think about the kind of other gear you guys may need tomorrow with Lana. I have a feeling there are going to be other situations like this."

It was good just to stop stuffing around and get on with the mission. We popped our wings and buzzed over to the site.

The area was surprisingly large. Stones and gravel were scattered over an area larger than a couple of football fields. We flew into the middle of it.

"Guys Hekator said collect a few rocks if you can as well as placing the sensors. Spread around to the edges," Grandpop told us.

We fanned out around the field. The sun was quite bright now and our facescreens had a denser mesh over them to reduce the glare from the ice. On landing I pocketed a few stones as I got out the rod sensor. Everything seemed quite routine when suddenly Cam pointed at something behind me.

"What's that?" she asked.

I turned to look. It was hard to judge distances in this place but some way off something dull gray glinted in the sun.

It was saucer shaped.

We stared at it for a little while, as it sat there in mid-air not doing anything special. I was just turning to look at my sensor when suddenly it moved at unbelievable speed behind me.

The change in the way the others were looking at it told me everything I didn't want to know. I turned around.

It was hovering silently about fifty meters away. It was a big, gray saucer about the size of a bus. It looked very scary.

"Get out! Get out now!" Control unexpectedly roared at us.

I picked up my sensor at my feet as the others vanished. A brilliant white light flooded down on me, making it impossible to see.

## [+]

I bent immediately and the world folded, but there was a surge of pink light and for almost a second nothing happened. Then slowly the pink light dimmed, drained to a line of whiteness, I fell back, then forward, passed through the realm of presences and then burst into the jumpstation pool.

The others were getting out of the pool. I followed them.

Grandpop was looking wild but we knew it wasn't with us.

"Come through to the briefing room," he called. "Dr Prosperov is coming down I want him to see this. Hekator too."

Ashley looked worried.

"Sir, Mr Kahu. I forgot my sensor. I left it on the ice."

She looked so upset Grandpop gave her a hug.

"Don't worry about that sweetheart. The main thing is you are OK," he looked at me sternly.

"I lost mine too," said Tarik.

"Kids don't worry about equipment. I don't care how rare or important it is to anyone. The only thing that matters is that you guys are OK. I don't mind admitting when I saw that thing I damn near crapped myself. We came a split second away from losing Sam because he *did* pick his sensor up. Control says they nearly jammed you Sam. We just had more grunt. It was too close."

That was what had him riled up. I had wondered what had happened.

We went through to the briefing room. I could still feel the light from the saucer flooding down around me as if I was repeating it in a bad dream.

A view came up in mid-air. It was us flying to our corners of the gravel site. We looked like small white glowing bumblebees. You could see our shadows and the aura of blue light we cast around us reflecting off the stones and ice.

Suddenly Hekator hologrammed in. He was dirty with soot.

"Sorry, I came as soon as I could."

"Watch this."

Just as the view got to the bit where we spotted the saucer, Dr Prosperov came in. He paused looking at the view and moved forward to a chair fascinated by what he was seeing. I turned back just in time to see Scotty vanish, then the view turned to me, crouching down, picking up the sensor. The brilliant light, and then, just as I vanished, a pulse of pink which held for a second and then went out. Then the whole view cut out.

For a moment there was silence.

"I won't put these kids into situations if I don't know how to manage the risks. Now what is that, and what do we do about them?" Grandpop demanded.

Hekator looked worried.

"It's an Administration scout. It was pure bad luck that it was anywhere near the children. What you should do about them is leave as soon as you see one. Don't try to finish anything, don't take any risks, just leave. They can jam bending and they have far more weapons to subdue you than you can imagine. Sam was lucky they didn't realise he was shielded from the white stun light they used on him. Otherwise they'd have caught him and be extracting all the information he has in his brain in no time."

I gulped. I'd assumed I could always escape. That was why I'd stayed calm. We all looked at each other.

"Unfortunately this means the Administration is now aware of six advanced humanoids with an interest in meteors on your planet." Hekator concluded.

"Some of your sensors were left behind when the kids escaped," Grandpop said, noticing Ashley was trying to say something. Ashley sat back, relieved Grandpop was protecting her. But Hekator didn't seem concerned.

"Hmmm. The sensors are nothing special. The technology is old and Svergish. But it may well suggest to the Administration the beings they saw were Sverg. We'll have to think about this."

"Well, it would help it you could provide us with as much intell as you have on these things and what we should do," Grandpop said looking pointedly to Dr Prosperov. "We can't send children to face dangers without every possible effort to protect them."

"We expect nothing less," Hekator agreed. "I'll send a recorded briefing through the portal in the next day or so. But the chances of you encountering a scout again are fairly small. If you did get a rock sample tonight I don't need any more meteorite data."

As it happened I did have a rock. I didn't say anything though because Dr Prosperov was talking.

"Is fortunate training mission not connected to principle mission. Am thinking is good planning to have multiple mission types so as to obscure primary mission if we are encountered by ... other interests."

There was a short pause while we digested that. Nobody was too keen to challenge the boss but we all wanted to know what he meant. Finally Grandpop asked for us.

"What sort of missions Gennady?"

"Remember am raising treasure recovery when negotiating with Scot?" he indicated Scotty, "and information from telecommunications cable and satellite intercepts useful to *all* interests," he added craftily.

"That's illegal ain't it?" Ashley asked.

Dr Prosperov rubbed his chin, tipped his head back and nodded from side to side weighing up the suggestion.

"Yes," he nodded finally. "Yes. Is all completely illegal. Entering country directly illegal, recovering lost treasure illegal, tapping wires illegal, obtaining information about markets in future illegal. Everything not in interest of nation-states illegal. Is illegal immoral? Sometimes yes. Sometimes no. Most of you come from nations where immoral laws exist. Should we obey laws no matter what? Coming from former Soviet Union have difficulty with this concept."

He paused for a moment looking at us like chess opponents.

"Ultimately you must do as you see fit. I cannot *make* you do anything. But what I promise is to tell truth about what you asked to do and why. That is not legal obligation but ethical obligation," then he shrugged. "If you object, then mission cannot proceed."

We all looked at each other. Sounded fair to me. Then Hekator spoke.

"Perhaps then, I should explain what you have been doing with these sensors for us."

We all turned to look at him.

"About one hundred years ago when we came here more often than we can now we became aware that there was some kind of Center settlement programme going on. There were quite a few Center ships arriving. But we also witnessed an ambush on the ship that was destroyed over Russia and we started to realise there was some kind of secret fight going on between the infiltrators who already lived here and some of the new arrivals. Of course we had to vanish fast or we would be blamed for the attack, but it has always intrigued me. Who attacked who, and why? The meteors contain traces of the ships and may give clues as to what destroyed them. We think there is a significant group of infiltrators opposed to the Center based on Earth which may be at the heart of Lucky's claim your planet may indeed be important to the future of the Center. While we don't necessarily support this movement we do want to know about it."

There was a long pause.

"But ... could the flying saucer guys work that out from seeing the kids on the ice? I mean what else would they be doing?" Grandpop asked.

"They might draw that inference, but the Greenland rocks are normal meteors for comparison with the others you already collected. We don't expect them to show any sign of an impact.

Plus they have no idea who they just surprised or where they went. It may just make them a bit sensitive about the other sites but our work there is done."

Hearing all this made us all realise that our involvement with the Fae wasn't fun and games. It was part of a long and deadly history between worlds. It put what we were doing in a bigger picture. It was a bit scary really.

"Look, I have to go," Hekator said. "I will send you that briefing in the next few days, but the main thing is that your operation was not compromised and nobody has been caught or hurt. Maintaining that will require the utmost attention to security and evacuation drills for everyone at Renwick House. If security ever is compromised you will have less than half an hour to gather everyone and get to the evacuation transporter."

And with that he winked out.

We all looked at each other. This was more than we had expected. We all looked a bit nervous.

"What's for dinner?" Scotty asked.

We all laughed. Despite being small and skinny Scotty was always thinking of his stomach.

Hekator sent through some knowledge beads that night. They explained the kind of technology the Galactic Center used.

The first thing we learned was the Galactic Center's symbol is a silver s-shaped lightning bolt. It basically symbolises the power of the Center to strike down lesser worlds. I couldn't help thinking I'd seen it somewhere before.

The scouts were small saucer shaped craft with a crew of two or three and room for as many passengers. The surveyors were tube-shaped craft the size of a bus and had lots of powerful instruments in them for monitoring things on the surface. There were a number of robots of different sizes for different things that could be launched by the scouts or surveyors. Hekator pointed out that our concept of structure was based on rigid forms but that rigid structures were very old engineering. These craft could change shape as well.

They're powered by a dark energy/antimatter vortex. Dark energy accounts for almost all the energy in the Universe[†]. It's not useful in itself but can be used to generate antimatter which turns matter to pure energy on contact. This controlled destruction powers the antigravity generators in the shell which allowed our craft to repel themselves from mass. The craft also have the ability to generate a higher dimensional bubble so they could become inertialess – projected into the ordinary space-time like a kind of 3D hologram. In this state the craft could move at huge speeds in any direction instantly. Without inertia there is no momentum to overcome either for the craft or anything in its way that might produce friction – like air. The craft could just instantly go from still to moving and then reverse without slowing. This was not as advanced as bending. The crew could bend over short distances but nothing like what our suits could do, so we could expect them to want to catch us for the technology.

The main two craft Hekator drew special attention to were a small triangular one which he said were military fighters and a huge triangular one about a kilometer long that was a carrier. They usually meant trouble. They worked for the Service, the Center's military arm. They were seriously dangerous.

He said the local Administration post would be principally concerned with scientific monitoring of events on Earth, and making sure that any extraterrestrial influence was limited by policing Earth's perimeter to prevent unauthorised contact. They would have scouts and survey ships. He said there would almost certainly be infiltrators in important human jobs around the world to gather data and keep an eye on the planet for the Center.

I went to bed and wondered what it was like to visit our world from another. Whether it would seem boring and dull, or strange and wonderful. I thought of the ice, the forests and the deserts I'd been to. I liked to think strange and wonderful but maybe I was biased.

Not surprisingly the UFO scare led to a meeting of the parents the next day (which was a Saturday). We were packed off to go for a stealth test in the bush in the conservation area to the north of Renwick. We also played chasing games and tagged each other with our beams. Tahira and me liked hiding in trees because people always forgot to look up. But Scotty seemed to have an uncanny ability to know when someone was watching him. You had to be quick with him.

We snuck up on animals like wild sheep and pigs. Of course we didn't fly during the day on the island because that could just draw attention to ourselves.

We went home for lunch and found the parents' meeting was over. Apparently they had agreed to our continuing to travel so long as we were clear we had to bend as soon as there was any risk we couldn't handle. And if we didn't Control was to bring us home regardless. Unfortunately it turned out we didn't need to travel at all to find trouble. It found us.

**[+]**

After lunch we bent back out into the bush. Normally the terrible weather would have meant nobody else was out. But on a remote path in the bush near the top of a ridge on the northern side we heard voices. It was wet and windy but under the trees we were sheltered. We all disappeared into the bush and two guys in bush clothes with a gun walked past us less than three meters away. We knew something was up because hunting was totally illegal here in the park.

The one with the rifle was white, older with a green bushshirt, beanie and droopy red moustache. His eyes were bright blue and bloodshot. He looked dangerous. The other guy was younger and Maori. Big and chunky, with short, wet hair and squinty eyes in his fat brown face. He wore a dark nylon top that seemed pretty damp. He looked strong, but nothing like as mean.

There was something a bit sus about the way they were acting so we followed their muddy footprints back to where they had been. It was a natural clearing down a bank by the path as it wound around the hill. We could see the sea below us while we were watching Scotty checking their tracks to try and figure out where they'd been.

Then something told us to watch out. It might have been a bird call or a certain silence. We slid into the bush just in time. The two men had spotted *our* muddy footprints going up the hill and were coming back!

They came into the clearing silently. The Maori guy was in the front. The older white one knelt to check our prints and peered around looking for us. With a motion of the hunting rifle in his right hand he sent the younger guy up the path to look for more signs of us further up. Then he went through a path we hadn't seen behind some nettles. He was there for a while as we all held our breath and lay or crouched where we were.

Then the guy with the gun came back and met up with the

younger guy. They both shook their heads. The older guy laughed quietly.

"Don't worry mate, paranoia's an occupational hazard in this game," he muttered.

He lit himself a cigarette sheltering the match from the rain with his hand. Then he shouldered the gun.

They were about to go when the older guy tossed his dead match and then spotted a fresh footprint off the muddy track leading to where Ashley and Scotty were hiding.

Now they were really edgy-looking. The older guy signalled for the younger one to circle around toward the bush Scotty was hiding under.

"*Do we zap them?*" Tahira thought. She was next to me at the far end of the path behind them.

"*Why don't we just go,*" answered Cam who was halfway around.

"*I want to know what's in that patch over there,*" Ashley thought next to Scotty.

"*So do I,*" said Tarik.

"*It's got to be marijuana,*" I told them.

"*What do we do?*" Ashley asked as the guy holding the rifle in one hand stalked closer.

"*I know! Infrasound him,*" Tarik suggested.

"Bend out!" Cam insisted.

"*Then we have to go home,*" Ashley complained.

"*Better be quick this one is nearly on top of me,*"Scotty warned.

"*I got him,*" Ashley called.

"*I can do the other,*" said Tahira. She seemed excited.

"*Just one! It's too suspicious if they both get it,*" Tarik warned.

"*Spook him,*" I said. "*He's Maori. We're superstitious. We believe in ghosts and fairies.*"

That made us all grin.

"*I can't delay any longer,*" Ashley warned.

The older guy suddenly doubled over and heaved his guts out. It was spectacularly disgusting.

"*Too hard!*" Scotty complained.

"*I want him really sick. He's way too close,*" Ashley came back. "*I'll give him smaller pulses.*"

He was on his hands and knees looking really uncomfortable. Scotty was about four meters away but virtually invisible.

"*I've got the other one,*" Cam said as he passed a few meters from her.

It was nice the way she did it. The Maori dude just seemed to hunch slightly and then slowly look around. He looked completely freaked.

"*Oh no! Ashley, you made him crap himself!*" Scotty complained about the older one.

The Maori dude was bending over his mate.

"Ray are you OK?"

"No."

"You stink pretty disgusting Ray."

"I feel pretty f_____ disgusting."

"Hey, ah I think we should f____ off outa here mate, eh?"

Ray puked again.

"*Ashley!*" Scotty complained.

"*That wasn't me. Maybe his own stink makes him sick,*" Ashley.

"*Give Ray a bit of the spooks too, Ashley,*" I suggested.

"*Can I do that and keep him sick? Oh yeah, I can.*"

"*Gently,*" Cam warned.

"*I am doing it gently,*" Ashley said hotly.

"*Less sick too or he won't notice the spooky sound*," Tahira said.

"*They're noticing Tahira*," Scotty said.

And it was true. They were looking around nervously at the bushes.

"It feels ... bad here Ray ... We gotta go."

"OK, OK, Ricky don't freak out on me. Help me up."

They stood.

"You really do ..."

"Shut the f___ up Ricky! It's probably that f_____ boilup you made me eat. I feel a bit better now."

Then with a sudden move he worked the bolt of the rifle and fired. The bullet hit the tree above Cam.

"Don't do that you crazy f___!" Ricky shouted.

Cam must have reacted instinctively. Ray's face went white and he collapsed unconscious.

"*What are you doing*!?" Tarik yelled silently.

"*Stopping him shooting*!" Cam responded grimly.

"*More fear*," I called.

Ricky was bent over Ray half reaching for the gun. You could see him stop, skin crawling, and look back behind him. He stepped away from his fallen mate looking in Cam's direction with wide, frightened eyes.

"OK, OK, I'm going! I'm going!" he told the tree. And then muttering to himself, "I'm f_____ out of here, man!" as he ran off, squelching down the path.

For a while no-one moved. We stood there listening to the rain and the wind and looking at the man on the ground.

"Well, dat shure was interestin'," said Ashley out loud, and we remembered we could breathe too.

"That was *dumb*!" said Cam. "If that bullet had hit one meter lower I would have been *killed*," she said, pretty pissed off. "Thait's the larst time I loie down to tahke cover. I couldn't do a bloody thing without moving the bush and giving myself away," Scotty said.

"Meeting," said Tarik.

So we moved out from cover looking like walking trees and then unsealed and switched to hoodies and jeans. Scotty went over to the man and took the rifle. He unloaded the magazine then cleared the breech, took out the bullets and pocketed them, then he replaced the magazine and lay it next to the man again. We peeled off the facescreens so we could talk normally. Ashley meanwhile had her fingers on the man's neck.

"What did you do to him, Cam?"

"I zapped him. Is he OK?"

"He's gotta pulse ... it's weak though. Irregular. Maybe he has a bad heart?"

"Hope he doesn't die," Tarik sniffed, as if his main concern would be how inconvenient it would be.

"What am I supposed to do? He shot at me! I didn't even want to stay! I wanted to do like Mike says and go!" Cam complained. She was worried she might have hurt the guy.

"Cam is right," Scotty said. "We didn't need to be here, we could have bent back along the track and then bent back here when they passed us again."

"But we already know how to do dat!" Ashley disagreed. "We loirned somethin' noo from dis!"

"Yeah ... scared man with gun very dangerous. Not much learning Ashley," argued Cam.

"But we did practice with our weapons," Tahira added.

"You were the one who wanted go zap them!" Tarik pointed out.

"You wanted to see what they were doing," Cam said to Tarik.

"It'll be weed," I said.

"Zhou 'av said that already," Tahira told me grumpily.

"My question is why did we have to stay?" Cam asked.

"Well, why did *you* stay? You could have gone," Tarik accused her.

"Because you my friends. I want you all to be safe," she answered.

"Let's see what's back there," said Tarik.

"Watch out! They use booby traps," I warned.

Tahira's wings unfurled. Tarik did the same. In half a minute they were buzzing over the patch.

"Nothing here but plants," Tarik said. "Lots of plants."

The buzzing stopped.

We pushed through the nettles. It wasn't a huge plot. About ten by ten meters. The plants were about a meter tall and densely planted. We gathered together. They were obviously still growing.

"What should we do?" Tarik asked.

"Report it," said Cam.

"Burn it!" laughed Scotty, although it was raining.

"Get one of Mariko's big paper rolls and make a giant dooby!" Ashley laughed.

We laughed about that. But in the end we weren't really interested and came out and gathered around Ray again. Ashley bent close and felt his neck again.

Suddenly he groaned.

"*Do you think we should act like innocent kids who just found him on the trail?*" Ashley said silently to us.

The man's eyelids began to flutter.

"Sir? Sir? You alright?" Ashley asked out loud.

"We should go get some help," Tarik said loudly, thinking it would worry this guy Ray if he thought someone had already left his control.

"Well, go on then," Scotty told him.

So Tarik and Cam ran off down the hill.

Ray opened his eyes. He obviously couldn't see very well.

"What happened?" Ashley asked.

"We heard a shot!" Scotty added.

Ray looked around at us and his blue eyes fell on me. He stared at me frowning for a moment.

"Are you alright, Sir?" Ashley asked again.

Ray tore his eyes off me to look at Ashley.

"Who the f____ are you? Where did you come from?" he asked groggily.

"We live here," Ashley said.

Ray looked at the bush. He checked the path to his crop over Ashley's shoulder but it was hard to tell if we'd been in or not.

"On the island," Scotty explained.

"What 'appened?" Tahira asked.

"Where's Ricky?" he asked sitting up. "Where did that useless c … did you see anyone? A Maori guy?"

We all looked at each other.

"We didn't see anyone," Scotty told him. But I got the feeling he didn't quite believe us.

Ray was feeling better and started to get up.

"My head!"

"What happened Sir?" Ashley persisted.

Ray stared at her thinking.

"He must have clubbed me one," he said half to her, half to himself.

"You av no 'ed wound," Tahira commented from behind him.

"I ... dunno I just collapsed ... He got all nervous and weird. He ran off ... I ... I was sick ... and then I fired ... It's a distress signal, right?" that was an excuse he made up on the spot.

"That's why we came, sir," Scotty said.

"And now he's just buggered off and left me!"

"Maybe he went for help," I suggested.

Ray shot me a look. Again he was looking strangely at me.

"Your name Stephens, kid? You look a helluva lot like someone I know," he asked.

"No," I said and because he was still staring at me added, "Kahu".

Then I realised I shouldn't have even said that. This guy obviously knew my dad.

He sniffed.

"Eugh, That bug went through me real bad," he said.

The smell was pretty terrible but apart from that he seemed to be alright again. He shot a nervous look at the nettles which hid his plantation.

"Tarik and Cam have gone on ahead to get the ranger but they'll be a while. We're a long way in," Scotty said.

Ray obviously didn't want to meet Tama.

"Hey well thanks for uh ... helping but I ... I'd better find out what's happened to my mate. Look, I feel fine. I'm going to head back down the hill and try and catch up with him."

"We're headed out too," Ashley said.

"Yeah, well I've got to go hard. The bugger might nick me car."

And with that he took off. We watched him run.

"Hey guys. What's been happening?" Grandpop asked. Tarik and Cam had obviously reported in.

We all looked at each other nervously. Now we were for it.

**[+]**

But Grandpop wasn't too bad after he'd heard what we'd had to say. He sat us down in the briefing room and made us go over the situation.

"First, and most important, Cam was completely right. Get away. Second Cam was right to zap that guy when he fired. Be decisive. Listen to Cam guys, she's got instincts. But the real worry I have is you were so disorganised. You had no plan. You had no fall back position, no clear story and you were just itching to try out your weapons. Weren't you? Tahira?"

Tahira looked a bit shamefaced, "Yes."

"Ashley?"

Ashley also looked guilty. "Well, ah didn't wanna miss nuthin an go home."

"That's what I mean. You needed a fall back spot and a plan. Instead for no reason you confronted an armed drug dealer. I can't have it guys! Your parents are twitchy as hell about you being in danger and they won't put up with you guys running around like a bunch of headless chooks."

"I told you from the beginning. You are not cleared to fight. Cam ended it cleanly. That said Ashley you didn't panic when an armed man hunting for you with a rifle got close and that is good to know. At least you ambushed them and didn't let them see who they were dealing with."

"But now you know that while you may want to control the situation an enemy is hard to predict and that is what makes them so dangerous when they act suddenly. Now as I've always said the difference between a unit and a bunch of kids playing silly buggers is a plan and teamwork. A plan means thinking about possibilities. In advance! It means having an agreed fall back position. It means communication. It means not shooting first and covering up for it later."

We all felt pretty stink. It wasn't that he was angry with us that stung. It was that he thought we were dumb and useless that hurt.

"You can't afford to be disorganised out there guys. The world you are going into is armed and dangerous. Most people don't deliberately send a group of thirteen-year-olds into it. Most thirteen-year-olds are safe at home. That's why your parents don't want you out there."

"You have to prove you aren't a bunch of kids with fantastic toys but a clued-up operational unit. That means you act like a clued-up operational unit, not a bunch of clowns! And the more you act like a unit the more comfortable your parents will be with letting you do stuff. Don't let yourselves down. OK that's it. Go get changed."

We got up.

"Sam could we have a talk please," he called to me.

He waited until the others were in the changing machines.

"Sam, that guy who recognised your dad in you is a serious threat. I'm going to have to tell Dr Prosperov. "

I felt sick.

"He won't kick us out will he?" I asked.

Grandpop smiled.

"No Sam, you're in the team. He's committed to us. But we may need to plan for what we do if word gets back to Ax. That's all."

I felt so relieved I blabbed away for quarter of an hour before he sent me off to get changed.

The surprises with the drug dealers and the UFO had our

parents nervous. They had been happy with us after the Mokoia mission but as the risks became clearer their worries mounted. Patricia was very grumpy with Ashley about the drug dealers and kept threatening to withdraw her permission. Tensions in Renwick House were building. Muttered conversations in the corridors were starting again and we knew the subject of these conversations was whether we could be kept safe if, and when, we went operational.

Things changed again shortly afterwards when the next set of expected "fortune cookies" arrived. This time they were Fae. They arrived in a blaze of light outside the house that night and told us they had taken over Hekator and Hekati's cave. We had met Fae children, seen the Fae Council, but these two were different again.

Raman was unusual for a Fae because he was a regular human-looking old man. He was dark skinned and looked Indian, with a short white beard and bony body. His skin looked like it was just bored with hanging on him and wanted to go somewhere else. Unlike the younger Fae he wore a soft gray robe wrapped around him, and a black turban with a big blue jewel set in it. He walked carefully with knotted shiny stick with a silver handle. His eyes were dark and gentle with a twinkle and he seemed to smile a lot.

Ishtar was more like a younger Fae. Or I guess she thought she was. She had big, streaked, blond hair and big brown painted eyes with small horns. She was brown (but lighter than Raman), lean, with leathery skin, and millions of wrinkles. Her wings were lovely with white and brown speckled feathers. She wore violet harem pants and sometimes a top over her small wrinkled breasts. She was sharper than Raman but also more lively and insisted on flying around that night. It made everyone nervous she would be seen. But she had insisted that she was a master weaver, and of course no visitors would arrive unexpectedly. Their arrival cooled tensions around the house as people buried their concerns about us under curiosity about the new arrivals. Dr Prosperov went to talk to them and didn't come back before I'd gone to bed. The next day at breakfast he announced we all had appointments to go see them as part of their work. Mine was at two.

Ashley was first to go. She grumbled about 'always being first'. But she came back very happy. She said you sat in a big leaf and things appeared in a big drop of clear liquid. She admitted she'd been so warm and relaxed she'd slept through half of it.

Cam came back at lunch time in a slightly more thoughtful mood. We asked her what they had talked about but she wouldn't say. She would say that they told your fortune but stressed that you could change it if you wanted to.

I got a bit nervous but finally it was time to go up there so I followed the corridor to the base and turned off to the cave. In fact I met them in a smaller cave before the main one. Raman was standing outside leaning on his stick and smiled warmly when he saw me. Unlike Hekator he made no sound when he 'spoke' to me but his 'voice' was deep and strong in my head.

"*Peace and welcome Sam. Are you nervous?*"

It seemed pointless to deny it, so I admitted I was.

"*Don't be. Your path is a long one for your kind. Let us examine it to see if may help us find these others.*"

He ushered me in to a small dark cave. There were three "couches". On the left was a dull blue bush of the kind Hekati and Hekator had in their cave. On the right was a dull red one which was occupied by Ishtar. It also had some pretty red flowers all over it. Ishtar had covered her top which pleased me because I didn't want to gawp at her wrinkly old boobs.

The middle couch was different. It looked like a huge black rubber tree with a lower leaf wrinkled like a wave. I imagined it was like a psychiatrist's couch.

But what really had my attention was a ball of liquid about two meters across hanging above the middle of all three couches from a silky thread. It shone in the low light from a number of luminous plants in the cave.

Raman ushered me to the black leaf. It gave slightly as I climbed on to it. He himself climbed uncomfortably on to his blue couch and settled down quietly while Ishtar spoke to me telepathically.

"*We want to explore your possible futures to see if they help us with the problem of finding these children.*"

"Isn't that like starting at the end?" I asked.

"*Yes, of course it is. But over the millennia we've found most things do. In one human language it's called Satkaryavada,*" she smiled.

I knew at once I was not the first of us to point this out.

"So what do I do?" I asked.

"*Just tell us about your life so far. Tell us about important people and places.*"

So I talked and as I did little pictures from my memory appeared in the bubble and moved around. All the people you would think I would mention appeared. But the surprising thing to me was the way Ax sat in the middle dominating all the others especially Clive.

Raman and Ishtar just listened. I got to this year and the other seven kids, and the adults and Baby Patience appeared as well. I was surprised how big Emma was and how small Mr Wakefield was. Finally I reached the present. They sat still not saying anything. I wasn't sure what to do.

Finally Raman jerked a bit as if he had almost fallen asleep.

"*Sam,*" he began in his deep rolling thoughts that made you feel like you were echoing him.

"*Your great battle will be with your father. The father within,*" he told me.

"*You will travel and grow in more ways than you can now know. Despite the efforts of those here you will commit yourself and there will be great danger. But you are fortunate. Your ancestors, Te Pha-re-te and Papahurihia, watch over you closely, and your shadow in the land of Hine-nui-te-po (Goddess of the dead) is a long one. The closer you are to her realm, the stronger she makes you.*"

He paused.

"*You shall meet a man on a hill by the sea. He is troubled but wise.*"

"*A great new Prophet will find you. This Prophet is part of the greater weaving of which we are all a part. The weaving that binds us together in one common fate.*"

"*You will be the last lone gull in the evening when all seems lost, and in that battle you will summon the rainbow serpent – the great cyclic spirit of all Earth in the coming confrontation.*"

I had no idea what he was talking about as the ideas tolled through me.

"*The Prophet's guide is amusing,*" Ishtar smiled looking at me knowingly.

I said nothing and then realised I was meant to.

"How?"

Ishtar smiled.

"*It is weaving us too,*" she said getting up and looking at Raman. "*Yes, my love ... it is weaving us even now.*"

I had no idea what they meant.

"*You, Sam are one of the children Dr Prosperov's guide seeks. We will make you so, just as you will make them so. We are all part of a great weaving and where it comes from I do not know. There is an even greater power we do not know yet at work here. You are the seam and I think you will see this power when you meet the Prophet. Keep your eyes open. It will be something worth remembering,*" she smiled.

Raman too stood and I realised my time was over. I sort of didn't know whether to thank them or what so I mumbled something and left. I thought about everything that they'd said all along the corridor. When I got back I understood why Ashley and Cam had been so cagey and why I really didn't want to answer the others' questions either. There was too much to think about in what they had said. They had been so right about my dad. He was central to my life and I had grown around him like a Ra-ta tree grows around its host. Ultimately I would have to face him. And yet I also knew I could not be merciless as he had been. Raman and Ishtar stayed for a week until late September. They talked to the adults too. The effect changed people. I noticed Patricia and Ken seemed a lot more relaxed around each other than they had. So too were Mitra and Ali. The focus on us had changed. The adults seemed somehow reassured about us but more concerned about some of the things they had left at home. Dr Prosperov and Dr Morozov spent a lot of time with Raman and Ishtar too apparently. Nobody else found out what went on in those sessions. Some of it was technical but they also seemed to be talking about personal stuff as well.

Dr Prosperov began building a new amplifier. It was based on a sensory deprivation tank which was installed in a new room in the west wing by a group of plumbers. I didn't know what sensory deprivation tanks were but we all got to have a look at it. The tank was like a big black bath with a soundproof black lid. The water was deep, thick and warmish to the touch. Once inside you couldn't see or hear or feel anything. It was meant to make it easier to screen out distractions and focus on your own mind. It seemed a bit scary to me.

The Fae weavers began working on the findings of the other "fortune cookies". Within two weeks they had a list of names and some of the attributes of the people we were meant to be looking for. Then, without fuss they told Dr Prosperov they were off for a holiday around their favourite parts of the Earth and would not be back before they left on the next full moon.

Feeling there was a need to keep everyone behind him Dr Prosperov gave us all a rundown on what the Fae had revealed one night in the lounge.

"Visitors have greatly assisted psychic forecast process. Now is possible to report names and identifying elements of children we are seeking."

"Future US president is Nathan from Washington DC. Mother struggles with alcohol dependence."

"Diana is from Balti, Moldova. She is future specialist in international legal standardisation and extradition. Jeanne is from Democratic Republic of Congo. She is future director of numerous development banks and World Bank. "

"Sarah lives in Haifa, Israel. She is future Israeli Prime Minister. There are eight others who we are not so certain of. Is girl from

Yemen who seems to be most important. There is boy, with no name as yet from Belem on the Amazon river. He is *indigenas* and will be Nobel Prize winning geneticist and biochemist. Others are further from us. Is two from subcontinent. Two from north Asia. Is important to note all children have exceptional intelligence. Some also have psychic abilities. Some also have disabilities and some have yet to face the suffering that will make them change future."

Dr Prosperov paused for a moment.

"Also Fae have made important point. I must warn younger operatives, our task not necessarily to rescue target children from bad things. Merely to ensure survival and motivation. In some cases target children will suffer great pain. Difficult to witness but is vital for motivation to find future global remedy."

"Is also other group of children, not as well identified. Other group forecast to lead outcomes damaging future of planet. At some point interventions may be required to *help* such children. This is to hinder development of negative childhood patterns to reduce greater negative effects later."

"Is bitter irony. We may require help to children destined to cause harm while, by inaction, harm to children destined to cause good."

That sounded twisted. We might have to *help* the baddies so they were less bad in future but abandon the goodies so they would be more good. I couldn't buy into that. But Dr Prosperov wasn't finished yet.

"However first task is positive identification and tracking of target children. Without this step intervention impossible. This requires on site investigation by child operatives. Otherworld visitors have increased precision of forecasts by several orders of magnitude. Combined with advice on forecast technology am now believing is sufficient data for refined forecast engine to guide operations in these locations. Construction of processor next critical step in mission plan."

So Dr Prosperov also began to build a new machine in the same room as his sensory deprivation tank. It had a lot of parts and circuit boards plus several computers as well. He and Dr Morozov and Gursoy spent about two weeks building the device. They even got parts from the Fae through the lighthouse gateway.

By the second week of October the device was ready. Apparently Dr Prosperov spent four hours in it and came out shaking. He summoned Mrs Jones as he still stood dripping and pale faced in his bathrobe by the tank.

"Call meeting of everyone tonight," he told her. "We have run out of time!"

# FACT OR FICTION?

The suggestion of natural dolphin telepathy is made by New Zealand dolphin trainer Frank Robson in his book "Pictures in the Dolphin mind". Mr Robson was a trainer at Marineland in Napier.

The notions of biostructural engineering using insects are entirely my own flight of fancy.

The notion of contact with extra-terrestrials in pre-history was popularised by the Swiss writer Erich Von Daniken. Von Daniken is a convicted fraudster. His work is not science but very popular story-telling. However the concept of angels watching over humans and falling is part of the apochryphal Book of Enoch which dates back to 300BCE. The Book of Enoch is not regarded as Canon by most Jews, Christians or Muslims and even when it was written was accused of being myth-making. The echoes of this story can, however, be found in John Milton's famous poem "Paradise Lost" (1667).

All the meteorite incidents referred to in the story are all factual and the locations accurate. I am not sure of the exact crop growing at Al Nakhlah in August 2007 so I have based this on a scientist's comments from visits in previous years.

The use of sound weapons to induce vomiting and loss of bowel control is fictional. Despite extensive research no evidence of a "brown note" has been found.

# NOTES ON LANGUAGE

Te Rauparaha's haka (war dance/chant) is a motif. This haka was adopted by the New Zealand national rugby team, the All Blacks, and is a tradition before their rugby games.
I have chosen to translate the opening lines of this haka "Ka mate, ka mate, ka ora, ka ora" (often translated "I die, I die, I live, I live") unusually as "Death? Death? Life? Life?"
In Maori "ka" is a tense marker which simply indicates the future (including the future perfect) or the next thing that happens while "mate" pronounced "maté" means death, and "ora" means life. Maori sentences, like many Asian languages, can infer a subject. So Te Rauparaha words literally say "(future tense) death, (future tense) death, (future-tense) life, (future-tense) life". This is because when he composed the haka Te Rauparaha was hiding for his life from enemy warriors who were coming to kill him. I prefer to use the uncertainty of the English question-mark "?" as a proxy for the tense marker "ka" than introduce a subject "I" which isn't in the Maori.

The return of the others is a huge relief to Sam and gives Sue time to find out more about the conflict the Changels are engaged in. As Sam tells Sue how they discovered the full horror of their enemies' plots, he also realises he will soon be forced to confront them again.

**To get your copy visit the website: www.changels.info**